TOO
HARD
TO RESIST

Wherever You Go Series

TOO
HARD
TO RESIST

Wherever You Go Series

ROBIN BIELMAN

Entangled Publishing, LLC
2614 South Timberline Road
Suite 105, PMB 159
Fort Collins, CO 80525
Visit our website at www.entangledpublishing.com.

Embrace is an imprint of Entangled Publishing, LLC.

Edited by Stacy Abrams
Cover design by Mayhem Cover Creations
Cover art from iStock

Manufactured in the United States of America

First Edition April 2018

embrace

To Greg, my favorite person to be next to.

Chapter One

MADISON

I race into the bakery on Washington even though I'm short on time. It took forever to find a parking spot that didn't require a permit, and the thought of being late to my first day on the job stresses me out, but some things are more important than punctuality.

I'm barely inside the door when I come to a screeching halt inches before I bump into the man in front of me. Damn it. With a line this long, so much for a quick grab-and-go. Glancing back down at my phone, I read the group texts from my friends Teague and Harper. *Good luck today! Kick some ass! Meet for dinner later to discuss?* I grin at their supportive words. I'd be lost without these two girls. I send a text back. *Can't tonight. I've got a date. Rain check! xoxo*

I tuck my phone back in my purse, then close my eyes for a quick wish. Please let tonight's date be better than last week's. One more creep and I may never go out again. Which, come to think of it, might not be a bad thing. I could stay home, read, and spend time with book boyfriends. They never let me down.

My leg starts to bounce as I take a look around the trendy café. The sprawling, sophisticated eatery is all stainless steel, glass, and pastries. The smell of coffee and fresh-baked bread fills the space. I can't wait to sink my teeth into a chocolate croissant, or for this line to move faster. When my eyes come back to rest on the guy in front of me, he's taken a step forward and I'm able to better appreciate the view. From the back, he's definitely hot. A light-blue dress shirt stretches across broad shoulders that taper down to a trim waist. The shirt is tucked into black dress pants and holy moly, his ass is tight and round and the most attractive rear end I've ever stood this close to. His legs are long, making him well over six feet. In my heels I'm five eight, and I only reach the tops of his shoulders.

"Je serai en contact."

At the sound of his voice, I raise my head. He's talking to someone on his cell. His accent is deep, rich, masculine ear candy. I maybe swoon a little. The sleeve of his shirt is rolled up to reveal a strong forearm and a thick silver watch on his wrist. His black hair curls at the back of his neck, just inside his shirt collar. It's untidy, sexy, and seems out of character for a man dressed so impeccably. He's probably so busy with whatever work he does that he hasn't had time for a haircut.

He inches forward. I inch forward. Maybe closer than what is acceptable for maintaining personal space, but it's hard not to. He smells good, too, and I wouldn't mind hearing more of that accent. It's not eavesdropping if I can't understand what he's saying.

"Merci pour votre temps," he says next.

The extent of my French is *merci beaucoup, au revoir,* and the line from the song "Lady Marmalade," *voulez-vous coucher avec moi ce soir*. Oh! And croissant. That's French, right?

He ends his call and slides the phone into the front pocket of his pants. We're almost to the front of the line now, so I pull my attention to what's inside the glass display case. I spy two chocolate croissants on a round decorative plate. Perfect. I'm never going to get rid of the ten pounds I've gained these past few months by continuing to indulge my carb cravings, but whatever. I'm hungry.

"I love your handbag."

I turn to the woman behind me dressed in workout gear and holding a toddler in her arms. "Thank you." I love my handmade black suede bag with three stitched organza roses. It goes perfectly with my black pencil skirt and bell sleeve pale-pink sweater. The temp agency told me casual dress would be fine for the office I'm headed to this morning, but I want to make a strong first impression.

"It's been so long since I've dressed up," the woman says.

"How old is he?" I smile at her adorable little boy. He's wearing T. rex pajamas and holding a sippy cup under his chin.

"He was two last week. I've also got a four, six, and eight-year-old."

"Wow." I don't know what else to say, except to maybe recommend birth control. I glance over my shoulder. Mr. Tight Buns is placing his order, so I move up. And wait a second. He's taking the last two chocolate croissants? I should tell him that's no way to maintain his "Buns of Steel" and to please leave them for me.

Ha! I would never say something like that out loud.

"Today it's just this little guy and me," the woman says affectionately.

I quickly wish her a good day before focusing back on the croissant thief. *Ask him to compromise, toss out a "Hey, think you could leave one of those for me?"* But he doesn't stop there. Without a word, the girl behind the counter loads up a box filled with the remaining plain croissants, too.

That's taking it too far, buddy. Yes, the café is probably baking more as I stand here, but I need to hurry or be late to my first day at ZipMeds. This is my sixth temp job in as many months, and I'm crossing my fingers this one sticks. I desperately need a steady paycheck. Like yesterday. If I don't save enough money to move out of my parents' house soon, I'm going to go insane.

Okay, Madison. Speak up. I'm not concerned about myself so much as the woman outside waiting on me. "Excuse me?" I say.

He's about to turn when a tall, stunning woman with enough cleavage to distract the Pope bounces up to the register and snags his attention. He immediately forgets about me—the jerk—and while I know this man is a complete stranger and I shouldn't take his slight personally, I do, because once again I'm reminded of my cheating ex-fiancé. I may have left Henry at the altar, but he left me with a damaged soul.

Stunning Woman's big, bright smile blocks out the image of my ex, and I imagine the guy in front of me smiles back. Heck, everyone around us is suddenly smiling at her.

She giggles at something he whispers to her—right before she orders a coffee! I hate people who cut in line. I'm about to tap the guy on the shoulder to negotiate pastries (and remind him there is a line of people who did not cheat—I mean cut) when the little boy behind me lets out a bloodcurdling cry. I twist around to make sure everything is okay when I'm sprayed with chocolate milk as he pulls the lid off his cup and swings his little arms.

"Oh my God! I'm so sorry," his mom says.

I look down at my sweater dripping in chocolate milk and let out a deep breath. "It's okay." Absolutely nothing is going my way lately. I twist back around in search of napkins.

"Good morning! What can I get you?" the chipper girl behind the counter asks, oblivious to my predicament. Probably because her eyes are glued to the ass walking off with all the croissants. "Miss?" Oh, right. I need to drag my eyes away, too, and place my order.

"Two cinnamon buns, please," I say without thought. Then feel myself blush. *Buns.*

"For here or to go?"

"To go, please. And could you put them in separate bags?"

"Sure." While she grabs the buns, I snag some napkins. They don't help the blotchy disaster that is my sweater. If only *my* boobs were on display to garner a distraction. I sigh. Would it be weird if I grabbed a newspaper and clutched it to my chest all day? I *could* probably get away with a legal-size notepad. The thought makes me feel better.

I pay for my runner-up pastries and say goodbye to the mom and her son. Outside, it's a chilly February L.A. morning. Clouds hide the blue sky, and if I don't hurry to my destination, the Pacific Coast air will turn my soft curls into crazy frizzy ones.

"Ma'am?" I kneel down to the homeless woman sitting hunched over against the side of the building, a threadbare gray blanket in her lap and a big black garbage bag beside her. She'd asked me for money when I walked by on my way to ZipMeds. I gave her a five and asked if she was hungry. She requested a chocolate croissant. "They ran out of croissants, so I got you something else."

She lifts her head and I'm so stunned I almost fall backward. She's finishing a chocolate croissant. Mr. Tight Buns gave her one! I take back my jerk comment.

"Thank you," she says, her voice rough like sandpaper. She gives me a thin-lipped smile and wraps dirty fingers around the small brown to-go bag.

My heart goes out to her. "You're welcome."

With less than five minutes to spare before I'm officially late, I scarf down my cinnamon bun as I hurry toward the next block. Turning right, a sleek, modern building comes into view. ZipMeds.

I open the front glass door with no idea what to expect. The previous places I've worked have all been in run-of-the-mill office buildings. At each job, one thing or another happened to prevent me from gaining permanent employment. *For the best*, I've tried to tell myself. The job I'm meant to have is still out there.

Going by looks alone, I hope ZipMeds is that job. The warehouse-like interior is amazing with polished cement flooring, a towering ceiling, beautiful large-framed landscape photographs, couches, and, get this, a two-story, grass-covered hill. Stairs lead to an open-air second floor. My heels *click-clack* on the way to the reception desk. A pretty brunette around my age sits behind the sophisticated wood counter. She watches me approach with friendly eyes.

"Good morning. I'm Madison Hastings, the temp hired for the finance department."

"Madison! Hi. Welcome to ZipMeds."

"Thank you."

"Okay, quit being more chipper than me, Auggie," a thirtysomething woman says, striding up to the desk. I didn't hear her approach because she's wearing cute white athletic shoes with her cute black cotton pants and collared long-sleeve T-shirt. "You already have a job. Don't add reception goals to your list of achievements," she says with obvious affection, and I immediately like both these women.

"Sorry, boss." Auggie puts her hand over her mouth and mock whispers, "She knows everything that goes on around here, so if you need anything, she's the person to ask."

"Hi. I'm Hazel." Hazel scoots Auggie out of her chair in

order to look down at a planner on her desk. "It's nice to meet you, Madison. Thanks for coming. You'll be working as the assistant to our finance manager." She and Auggie exchange wary glances. *Uh-oh.*

"I'll show her around and get her situated," Auggie offers. She's also dressed in stylish athletic shoes with sporty pants and a fitted shirt. But while Hazel is Nordstrom-chic, Auggie is more Urban Outfitter-trendy with her rainbow-thread friendship bracelet with beads that say DONT WORRY, followed by a bumblebee and a smiley face. Peeking out of the collar of her shirt is a colorful tattoo that looks like part of a butterfly.

I guess I should have taken the temp agency's advice on dress attire. "Is there a restroom I can use first?" I'm hoping a little soap and water helps my sweater situation.

"Of course. Come on."

"That's not real grass, is it?" I ask, nodding toward the indoor hill.

"No. It's eco-friendly, UltraLush artificial. Every Friday we do a picnic and team-building activities or rolling contests. If you're…"

"If I'm dressed appropriately?" I tease.

Auggie chuckles, then looks around as if making sure we're alone. "I was going to say if you're still here. Lately, our finance manager can't seem to keep an assistant for longer than three days."

I reach up to twirl a piece of hair behind my neck. I appreciate her honesty but really don't need to know that. The terrible insecurity of failing once again and being stuck living at home forever crowds my chest. I love my parents, but I can't take much more of their smothering. It's time I made something of myself on my own. "Is he awful?"

Auggie pulls me into the bathroom and locks the steel door. "Madison. I like you. I liked you the minute you walked in the door dressed for success with a big stain on your sweater."

I scrunch up my nose in embarrassment. "I was hoping it wasn't that noticeable."

She turns on the water faucet with one hand while grabbing some paper towels with the other.

"We'll fix it." She proceeds to soap up a towel and dab at my sweater, completely comfortable with her actions and me. I stop playing with my hair. "So, here's the thing. Our FM is demanding, meticulous, a little intense, and super busy. He needs an assistant who doesn't require directions every ten minutes and who understands numbers. You were an accounting major, right?"

"How did you know that?" I ask incredulously.

"We were at Loyola together. I remember seeing you in class."

I study her more closely. "Sorry. I don't—"

She waves away my apology. "I flew way under the radar back then. I'm Abigail August. Everyone calls me Auggie."

"It's nice to meet you."

"There," she says with a proud smile, standing taller and tossing the paper towels into the trash, "it's not perfect, but better."

"Much better. Thank you. Do you work in the finance department, too?"

"I'm the assistant to the CEO, so I pretty much have my fingers in all the departments. Come on, I better give you a quick tour and get you to your desk before the meeting ends."

"Meeting?" I fall in step beside her. The sound of my heels echoes, and I'm tempted to take them off so as not to draw attention to myself. Instead, I do my best to step lightly.

"Monday morning exec meeting."

"Got it." Yesterday, I did a quick Google search of ZipMeds. The company builds drones that transport lifesaving drugs and medical supplies to countries where poor roads and poverty-stricken healthcare infrastructure make it difficult to reach patients. The start-up is only in its sophomore year and its worthwhile and important focus is admirable. I cross my fingers in silent hope I can outlast the previous temp.

Auggie shows me the kitchen, a gorgeous space with stainless steel appliances, a chalkboard wall, and an oversize weathered hardwood table with white wooden chairs, and a break room with a Ping Pong table, foosball table, bunk beds, and bookshelves.

"Most of our brilliant technology team is in the building next door, and here we do everything else," she says, taking me upstairs. The second floor is also open and airy, with side-by-side workstations. I count seven people typing on laptops. Auggie gives them a wave before she leads me down a wide hallway. A glass wall takes up the right side, cubicles occupy the left. The first office we come to is a conference room, where it looks like the exec meeting is taking place. Several people sit in swivel chairs around a large metal table. The room is stark, but with floor-to-ceiling windows that offer a view of the ocean in the distance, nothing else is needed.

We've almost passed the room when my gaze catches on broad shoulders in a light-blue shirt, black hair curling at his nape. No freaking way. The box of croissants sits on the table. My pulse quickens, a mixture of excitement and nervousness over the thought of seeing the bakery shop guy.

"This is you," Auggie says, stopping at a cubicle. "I'm two down, so if you need anything, don't hesitate to ask."

The space is modern with clean lines. There's a computer, printer, and bookshelf. On the desk sits a temporary parking permit. At the very least I'll be back tomorrow.

"There's one more stop on our tour." Auggie motions for me to follow her farther down the hall, pointing out her colorful workspace as we pass. She opens a door to a stairwell. About a dozen steps later, we open another door and walk outside onto a rooftop garden.

"This is amazing."

"Right?" Auggie says. "We've got permission to fly our drones out here. The flight pattern is specific, but it goes all the way to the beach."

"That's so cool." I notice a fancy tent set up on the other side of the rooftop. There's a freestanding swing between two large tree planters, too.

"If you ever need a few minutes by yourself to decompress, feel free to pop up here."

"I will. Thanks." I appreciate that her tone suggests I'm here for the long haul. Now to prove to my new boss I'm indispensable—because I like it here. It already feels way more comfortable than my previous temporary assignments.

Auggie's phone is ringing when we get back downstairs. "I need to grab that. You good?"

I nod. "Oh, wait..." I'm too late. She's picked up the call and settled in at her desk. I forgot to ask what the finance manager's name is.

Sitting down in my cubicle, I swivel my chair to check out his office. The door is shut, but gray curtains are drawn open, giving me an easy view through the glass. Which means he'll have an easy view of me, too, unless I press myself against my workspace so I'm hidden behind the slight partition.

There's a large glass desk, two upholstered chairs, a side table, and several brown moving boxes stacked in the corner. A remote-control car is parked in the middle of the room. The toy seems out of character, given Auggie's description of the man.

Voices puncture the silence, startling me into action. I put my purse away (with the parking permit) and turn on the computer. A man in dark dress pants and a beige sweater walks past. "Auggie?" he says.

I don't hear her reply because I'm stuck on the backside of the man opening the finance manager's door. I've got a couple of names for him, but "Boss" is not one of them. Until now. Which means I cannot freaking look at his ass ever again. I raise my eyes just as he must sense my presence because he turns around.

"Madison?"

Holy shit, I can't believe I didn't recognize Elliot Sax. He's one of my oldest friends' best friends, and our paths have crossed for years. I've always considered him extremely attractive, but I can think of several other guys I feel the same way about. So the fact that he's my new boss at a company I really want to work for is no big deal.

Right?

Chapter Two

ELLIOT

"Hi," Madison says like her presence in my office is not something so far out of left field I wonder if she's got a doppelgänger. But then she slowly rises to her feet, wide blue eyes clueing me in to her shock as well. "Good morning."

"Good morning. You're here to...?"

"Assist you?" Her voice wobbles, and I wonder what she's heard about me while I was in our Monday morning meeting. I'm well aware I have a reputation as a hardnose.

"Give me a minute?"

"Sure."

It's rude, stepping away from her like this, but I need to think, and I can't do that while looking at her pretty face. I walk into my office and head straight to my chair, turning it so I look out the window, the view of Venice Beach in the distance. Madison Hastings is my new temporary assistant. *Fuck!* I have no idea if that's a good thing or a bad thing, and I pride myself on knowing exactly what things are.

When I started this job three months ago, it came with an assistant. Jaclyn aced everything I threw at her, then her husband got a transfer and they moved back east. For the past several weeks, temp after temp has shown up with expectations that far outweigh their intelligence and staying power. Male and female alike, they want a paycheck they don't have to work for. Don't even get me started on the idiocy that accompanies their entitlement.

Along with producing financial reports and developing company strategy, I've been hired to raise money. A shit ton of it. From venture capitalists and others willing to invest in a company doing a hell of a lot of good in third world countries. The added pressure of showing profits larger than my boss's last start-up (and now run by his hateful ex-wife) doubles my stress. If I don't perform to expectations, I'm out. There's a long line of guys willing to take my place, and more than anything, I want to stay right where I am. The financial potential is staggering. The feel-good factor worth the long hours and no social life. My five-year plan is well on its way to becoming a reality.

I can't have incompetent assistants fucking anything up. If a simple haircut appointment is too hard to handle, then no way in hell am I trusting them with anything finance related.

With my patience wearing thin, I've fired the last few temps before they even lasted a week. I'd rather have no assistance than incompetency, but our CEO, James, insists I have help, so he continues to send temporary employees my way until I've got time for a proper interview process.

Which brings me to Madison. We're friends. Not close friends, by any means, but she's like a sister to my best friend and roommate, Mateo, so over the years we've seen each other at social events. I'd say I don't know much about her, but now that I'm thinking about it, I probably know a few things others don't.

I know she cried for hours on her wedding day. She left her asshole fiancé at the altar and Mateo brought her to our house to hide out. Her parents picked her up later that night.

I know she's a vegetarian, because at a barbecue last summer, she brought some extra tofu burgers for anyone who wanted to try them. (I didn't.)

And I know she's a C-cup because I accidentally groped her the night a group of us went out to celebrate the job my other best friend and roommate, Levi, had just gotten in Australia. We'd all been drinking, and I had nowhere else to put my hand when asked to pose for a picture. As soon as I realized where my palm was I pulled it away, but two seconds is all it takes for my grip to decipher a woman's breast size. I quickly apologized, only to find Madison smile sweetly and tell me she hadn't even noticed my transgression. That was three-and-a-half months ago, and I haven't seen her since.

In theory, it doesn't matter that I know these things. It also doesn't matter that she's a close friend to one of mine. One degree of separation makes this a friend-of-a-friend situation, but it sucks enough firing someone I don't know.

Jesus. I'm already thinking about letting her go. I drag my fingers across my mouth. I have no idea what Madison is capable of, but she can't be any worse than the girl last week. If it doesn't work out and we see each other with our mutual friends, it might be awkward, but this *is* a "temp job." So in reality, I'm not firing bad personnel. I'm simply telling them their services are no longer required.

I spin my chair around. Madison is talking on the telephone. With her free hand, she's twisting a strand of blond hair around her finger. Her back is straight. Her expression is serious. I watch as a smile gradually blooms across her face while her shoulders relax. She slowly unravels her hair, her fingertips slipping delicately down the front of her sweater until her arm drops fully. Gone is the nervous woman whose voice wavered at "hello." In her place is a beautiful, poised woman I've never seen before.

Our eyes meet through the glass. Even from this far away, I'm hit with vibrant blue and, I quickly realize, more intelligence than I've given her credit for. She says something to the person on the other line, her generous, pale-pink lips moving swiftly.

She breaks our connection first, turning toward her desk. A split second later my phone rings. Glancing at the display, I see it's her extension. I pick up the receiver. "Yes?"

"Mr. Sax, Mr. Young is calling for you."

Point to Miss Hastings. It took my last assistant five dropped calls before she figured out how to transfer them. "Thank you."

"You're welcome."

Right before I say hello to "Mr. Young," she meets my steady gaze again. I've looked into many girls' eyes, and something tells me Madison is different. I blink away the foolish thought. "Hey, Drake."

"Morning. Please tell me Madison is hot."

Our CFO, the man I report directly to, can say that, since he's six hundred miles away in our San Francisco office. The guy is a few years older than my twenty-four, smart as hell, and has a reputation as a womanizer. Hooking up at work in this office, however—even flirting with someone in a blatant way—is grounds for immediate dismissal. This isn't my rule, but our CEO's, for a very good reason.

"Depends on if you think Kate Hudson is hot." Drake is messing with me, so I'll mess back. Although, a quick glance in my new assistant's direction confirms the description isn't too far off the mark.

He doesn't hesitate to tell me how he feels about that before we talk about work. When through, I press the numbers to Madison's extension. She studies the phone for a moment before picking it up.

"Hello?"

"It's me. Can you please come into my office?"

"Sure."

She carries herself with a feminine grace I've never noticed before—most likely because I've never watched her move without the distraction of our friends. "Please close the door."

Before she fully sits in the seat across from me, she says, "If this is a problem, I can get the temp agency to send someone else."

"Why would this be a problem?"

"Because we're friend...ly."

"Would you prefer to work for someone you don't know?"

She takes a moment to consider my question. *"Maybe?"*

I rest my elbows on the desk. "I get it. That's why I needed a minute. But if you're game to give it a try, I am, too. It's not like we see each other that often, and people who work together can be friends outside the office."

"True."

"It's also nice to know you're a normal person. I've had a couple of assistants who were borderline psychopaths."

"I'm super normal," she says cheerily. "Mostly." Her face glows with amusement I'm not sure is directed at herself or me. Either way, it's intriguing.

We stare at one another longer than necessary. I'm unable to help myself. I'm alone with her after years of passing by each other and I want to see what's there. I find a freckle on her cheek—the only blemish on her otherwise smooth, flawless skin. Her nose is straight and a little pointy at the bottom. Long, dark eyelashes make her eyes pop.

"All right. So, let's get started," I say, breaking our silent connection. Fuck, I hope I'm not making a mistake. I live and breathe this job, and nothing matters more to me right now.

She lets out a breath, relieved, I think, that we've come to this agreement. "I'd like that."

"I typically start each morning with an agenda for what I want to accomplish by the end of the day…"

The time passes quickly. Madison takes instruction well and isn't afraid to ask questions or speak up. She's organized, proficient at handling documents on the shared computer drive, and most importantly, understands time zones. A major plus, given I spend a lot of my time on the phone with investors across the globe.

Around one o'clock, I'm behind on drafting a presentation for a meeting later this week, so Madison offers to pick up lunch for us. "I had no idea you didn't have a job," I say before taking a bite of my turkey on whole wheat.

"What did you think I did?" Her Caesar salad with shrimp and enough croutons for three more salads is perched on the other side of my desk. I can see through the glass desktop that her legs are crossed at the ankles. Her black heels are tied with a thick bow. They're girlish, but hot as hell.

"I don't know. Teacher maybe?" Why I thought that is a mystery. She does have a gentle way about her, so maybe that's it.

She picks up a piece of shrimp with her fork. "I graduated with a major in accounting and a minor in management science."

"Really?"

"That shocks you?"

I lean back in my chair. "Kind of. You don't seem like a numbers girl."

"What do I seem like?"

"A teacher."

She laughs. "I'll take that as a compliment."

"Good. I meant it as one."

Spots of pink dot her cheeks. Her attention darts to the

floor. "My favorite teacher in high school taught accounting. She made a point of telling the girls in class it was important to understand finances and to not be intimidated by math. She made it fun, too, so in college I decided to stick with it."

"Are you a CPA?"

"No. I got engaged right after graduation and wedding planning took precedence over anything job related. Plus..."

I raise my eyebrows.

She doesn't answer right away so I fill in the silence. "Your douchebag ex didn't want you to work." I met the guy briefly and got the impression he liked to be in total control, including keeping Madison on a very short leash.

"Right. And looking back, I'm really mad at myself for letting him get his way on everything."

"Not everything."

She looks at me in confusion.

"He didn't get to marry you."

Her face softens, pinning me to my chair with appreciation. It's been a long time since I've felt gratitude from a girl over something other than a screaming orgasm.

"What about you?" she asks.

"What about me?"

"Do you have a girlfriend?"

This is why hiring a friend is a bad idea. Madison's been here all of five hours and we're already getting personal. I do realize it goes both ways. I started it, after all, but I make a mental note to keep quiet about our private lives moving forward. "No."

"I didn't think so," she says, like there's something wrong with me. If I wanted a girlfriend, I'd have one.

"Why didn't you think so?"

She shrugs. "You don't seem the type."

"Really?" I ignore the uncomfortable stab to my gut. I've never been the right "type." My parent-pleasing, perfect older brother is the Stanford grad with PhD after his name and a smart, loving wife. My can-do-no-wrong younger sister is the recent Yale grad with a medical research job and brand-new fiancé. I'm the UCLA grad who left his consulting job to work for a start-up, and according to his parents has always dated the wrong kind of girl.

"Why am I not the type?" I add.

"I didn't mean to offend you."

The apology in her tone pisses me off. I didn't think I'd given away my unease. "You didn't. I'm just curious."

"I don't know."

"Yeah, you do. Come on, tell me."

She runs her fork through her salad. "You seem like you have a short attention span."

I nearly choke on my sandwich. She can't be serious. I'm so focused, I can recall everything discussed in this morning's meeting down to the last word. "Now I'm offended."

Her jaw drops. "You…" She uncrosses her legs, sits up taller. "You pressed me for why."

"I also just spent the past five hours trying to impress you with my business skills."

Lines crease her forehead. "You wanted to impress me?"

I'm more surprised than she is. Trust me. *What the hell, Elliot?* I always say what's on my mind, though, so I guess I did. "Yes."

"You did."

Awareness sparks between us, deeper than the compliment, but it's nothing I can't handle. I can be attracted to Madison and not act on it. Hell, I was attracted to the woman in the café this morning and didn't act on it. This weird chemistry is just two acquaintances learning more about each other and appreciating it.

"And I didn't mean at work. I can see how you've gotten so far so fast. I meant outside the office."

"Oh, okay. Thanks."

At the sound of the phone ringing on her desk, she jumps to her feet. "I should get that." She grabs her lunch to take with her.

I watch her retreat. The black pencil skirt does nice things to her ass. Her hair falls in soft waves past her shoulders. Before she sits, she glances over her shoulder. Catching my eyes on her chases her gaze away.

As the day progresses, it seems I'm not the only one happy with Madison's presence. James stops to talk with her more than once. Auggie likes to perch herself atop her desk to whisper things back and forth. My new assistant is friendly, smart, dynamic even.

When five o'clock rolls around and she says goodbye, one thing is glaringly clear. Madison is by far the best assistant I've had, which means no more noticing anything about her that isn't business related.

Chapter Three

Dating sucks.

I can't believe I rushed home after work to fix my hair in a sexy up-do and change into jeans and a cute off-the-shoulder top for *this*.

"…I'm not gonna lie. Women think it's hot that I've won so many competitions. After the Tough Mudder, one chick wanted to do it in the mud." My date's eyes dip to my chest. "If she had a rack like yours, I might have been tempted. Most athletic girls have small tits."

Meaning I'm not athletic?

I'm not. But it isn't because of my breast size.

And yes, his crass remark about my boobs is bothersome, but it's the third time he's mentioned them. I'm over it.

"The 10K I ran last weekend, I took first in my age group without even trying. In college I…"

I tune him out. Is it illegal to stab someone with a fork if he's so full of himself he needs to be deflated? He's talked nonstop about his "impressive successes," pausing only long enough to take bites of his fillet. At least the food is good in the trendy Beverly Hills restaurant he chose to meet at. I finish off my delicious panko-crusted salmon and sautéed spinach. I've had plenty of time to enjoy it since Sir Brags-A-Lot is monopolizing the conversation.

"Has anyone ever told you, you have the most beautiful blue eyes?"

I'm about to say thanks, when I realize he's not speaking to me.

Our waitress bats her eyelashes. "No one as handsome as you." She flirts back.

Hello? Am I invisible? Does no one but me know this is a date? And news flash: he already knows he's handsome, no need to fuel his overinflated ego any further. He won baby beauty pageants. I know this because he's told me about every single one of his trophies. He didn't say so, but I'm guessing his mom has turned his bedroom into a shrine.

"Would you like another drink, Allison?" he asks.

For a second I have no idea who he's talking to. It can't be me.

"Allison?"

Or it can. "My name is Madison."

"Shit. That's right. Allison was my date last night." A smarmy smile tilts the corners of his mouth.

Suddenly, I have a horrible taste in the back of my throat. His expression tells me more than I want to know. Does he have dates lined up every night of the week in hopes of getting laid with a different girl each time?

It's not cheating, but it is disgusting, and whenever I meet a slimeball, I'm reminded of Henry.

Henry, who is engaged again—a mere eight months after our failed wedding day. Does *she* know he's a lying, cheating bastard? Probably not. For the first few years we were together, I didn't. Then I caught him with one of my sorority sisters. He apologized, told me he loved me. Said it was a mistake that would never happen again. His promise meant nothing if I was to believe the rumors that continued, so I chose to believe in him. Us.

He was my first love. The only guy I've ever slept with. He was my everything.

Until I finally—*finally*—realized I wasn't his. I shocked everyone when on our wedding day I ran down (or is that up) the aisle, out the hotel front door, and straight into a cab. No one could believe prim-and-proper Madison Hastings was capable of such a horrible thing. Yes, that's right. I was the bad person. Not the unfaithful groom.

"Just some water, please. And the check?" I say to the waitress, hoping she hurries. I'm ready to pay my half and rush out of here. I've learned my lesson, though, I'm ashamed to admit it took a while. I ignored my gut for a long time because I didn't want to be alone. Deep down, I knew Henry was cheating—there were obvious signs. But he'd always say something sweet or bring me flowers to chase away my hurt. He loved me. I know he did. He just didn't love monogamy. It's that reasoning that has helped me start dating. Not all guys are cheaters. But if I have doubts for even a split second, it's over. I'll never neglect myself again.

Watch out for the Dick Sticks, Harper told me when I started dating for the first time in seven years. Meaning guys who only want to stick their dicks in as many holes as possible.

Not to be confused with delfies. I've gotten two of those. At the very least, a guy with balls big enough to send a selfie of his dick should *have* a big dick.

"I love that you're anxious to get out of here, babe. I am, too." He pushes his plate to the side to lean his elbows on the table. "Dessert at my place or yours?"

"I'm not—"

"Because what I'm serving is finger-licking good."

I throw up in my mouth.

"I've also got this for you." He hands me a tiny clear bag with some kind of large pill inside it. Holy smokes. Please don't let me be on a date with a drug dealer.

"What is this?"

"It's an intimacy capsule." He licks his lips. *Gross.* "I had a feeling this would be your first time."

"First time for what?"

"Coming with candy-scented sparkles."

I am so uncomfortable right now it's not even funny. This guy is a sex lunatic! I'm obviously using the wrong messaging technique on my dating app. "You want me to put this capsule inside my…"

"I do, babe. It dissolves inside you and when we have sex, glitter dust goes everywhere. It's like you're a fucking princess."

I burst out laughing. Is this guy for real? I didn't think I could sit across from anyone worse than the jerk last week, but boy was I wrong. "I'm not going anywhere with you to have sex."

He lifts his eyebrows. "Rather get it on here? No problem. You walk to the bathroom first, and I'll follow."

I'm completely dumbstruck. He can't be this dense. "You're misunderstanding me. I'm not interested. Thanks for dinner, but—"

"Here you go." The waitress puts the check down on our table.

"Thanks, gorgeous. Hey, what time are you off tonight?"

What the ever-loving hell? I turn him down, so he immediately asks another girl out right in front of me? This King of Jerks takes offensive behavior to a whole new level.

"Nine."

He checks his iPhone sitting on the table. "That's fifteen

minutes." He looks at me. "You don't mind, do you?"

I shrug because words completely and utterly fail me. I think about giving our waitress a warning, but nope. She's as bad as he is when it comes to good manners. Never in a million years would I flirt with a guy on a date with another girl.

"Great." He reaches into his pants pocket while our waitress saunters off. With a frown, he pats his other pocket. "I must have left my wallet in the car. I'll be right back."

I'm tempted to tell him not to worry about it and pay for both of us. But then I remember the budget I've put myself on so I can move into my own apartment. My mom and dad mean well, but they're making decisions for me, treating me with kid gloves because of my failed wedding. I'm beyond eager to put distance between us. In order to do that, I need to watch what I spend. And spending even a penny on the guy across from me makes me sick to my stomach.

"Okay."

He steps away, then turns around. "Can I have that back?"

Since I have no plans to *ever* add glitter to my vagina, I put the wrapped capsule in his hand. He walks away without another word or backward glance. A minute passes. Then two. A busboy comes by and clears our dishes. The waitress flits around her other tables, seemingly over the exchange with my date.

Five minutes pass.

I get a sinking feeling. He's not coming back. The douchebag skipped out on me. "Asshole," I say under my breath.

"Excuse me?" a woman says to my right.

I turn my head to the table where three expensively dressed women around my mom's age have been eating dinner. I noticed them when I sat down earlier because they were laughing and having a great time.

"Yes?"

"I'm sorry, but we couldn't help but overhear you and your date. He didn't really leave you with the bill, did he?"

"Looks like."

"Can we join you? We have sons about his age and well…" Without waiting for an answer, the Mom Squad surrounds me.

"If this is an intervention, you're a little late," I say with a smile.

"I cannot believe the things he said to you," the same woman says, her voice both sweet and surprised.

"Me, either."

"So not all your dates talk like that?"

"Well…"

The woman holds up her hand. "Wait." She and the other two women introduce themselves. I do, too. They've been friends since their sons met in elementary school, and even though the boys don't keep in touch anymore, the moms have maintained their close friendship and get together every few months to catch up.

Boys. Their sons are all twenty-five, a year older than me.

I tell them about a few of my dating catastrophes, and how hard it's been to meet a nice, normal guy. When it slips out I left my fiancé at the altar because he cheated on me, they do what all kind, warmhearted moms should: order us a round of shots.

"I sincerely hope Liam treats his dates with the manners I taught him."

"I'll throttle Jesse if he's disrespectful to the girls he takes out."

"If I found out Brooks offered a glitter capsule to a girl, I'd be mortified."

"Your son's name is Brooks?" I ask. "That's a nice name."

Brooks's mom smiles at me before turning her attention to her friends. "I have an idea."

"She's our idea woman," Jesse's mom says.

"Let's hire Madison to date our sons."

I put my water glass down and choke out a "what?"

"Here's what I'm thinking," she says, keeping her focus on her girlfriends. "We've raised our sons to be good, upstanding young men, but we have no idea how they act when we're not around. What if Madison goes out with each of them and reports back to us how the date went? Were they polite? Did they say please and thank you? Pull out her chair? Speak respectfully? I'm mortified by what I heard tonight and have this burning desire to know my son isn't like that."

"That's a brilliant idea," Liam's mom says. "I need to know, too."

"I second the brilliance," Jesse's mom says.

The three women look at me with a mix of hope and excitement.

"You want to pay me to go out with your sons," I say, even though no clarification is really necessary. This is the weirdest night I've ever had.

"Yes," they say in unison.

"I'm pretty sure that makes me a—"

"Oh God. You're right," Brooks's mom says. "This came out all wrong." She gives my arm a quick squeeze. "What I'm trying to say is you seem like an intelligent, kind, sweet young woman and we want your help. You'd be like a PI, investigating our sons' dating behaviors and sharing what you find out. You absolutely do not need to engage in any physical interaction with them."

"Unless you want to," Jesse's mom says. "*What?* Madison could hit it off with one of our boys. You never know."

You never know. Those three words have me seriously considering this crazy plan. I want to meet someone special and maybe it's Brooks or Liam or Jesse.

Or Elliot.

Whoa. Where did that insane idea come from? Yes, I saw a whole new side to him today. And no, I'm not talking about his ass. Not *only* talking about it. I kind of can't stop picturing it. Anyway, no matter how attractive or smart he is, he's my boss and I really liked working with him today.

That over the years I've noticed Elliot before today does not mean anything. With his olive-toned skin, wavy black hair, sparkling, know-it-all blue eyes, and full bottom lip, every girl notices him.

"Isn't this kind of deceitful?" I ask, focusing back on the current discussion.

"Let's call it sneaky," Jesse's mom says. "We don't want you to mislead our sons. Just go on a date, get to know them, and report back."

"What if they find out?"

"They won't." Brooks's mom pulls a small notepad out of her Gucci purse. "We'll correspond via email." She writes down her email address, then passes the pad to her friends like this is a done deal. "But we should pay you in cash so there's no paper trail."

I smile. This is ridiculous, but kind of fun. I've led a sheltered, boring life and the past eight months since my breakup have been especially dull and stifling with my parents, so some undercover dating sounds exciting. So unlike me. It may even call for three new outfits.

"How much do you want to pay me?" New clothes aren't in my current budget. And honestly, I'm not comfortable with being paid to go on a date, but if I keep it in the same perspective as these nice ladies, then I'm doing a public service, right?

Brooks's mom writes something down on her cocktail napkin, then slides it to me. She's really enjoying this clandestine dating operation.

$500

"Oh no, that's—"

"Each," she interrupts.

Each? Holy crap. I was about to tell her that was too much for all three.

"Madison," she says sincerely, "this truly is a favor to us, nothing else. And you should not feel bad about it in any way. This is a job we curious and well-meaning moms have hired you for, so please don't look so scandalized."

I close my dropped jaw. Fifteen hundred helps me reach my move-out goal sooner rather than later.

My phone pings inside my small purse. The unique sound is my dating app telling me I have a message.

The chime reminds me of one very important factor we've forgotten about. "That is very generous of you, but I just realized something. How am I going to connect with your sons?"

"She's right," Liam's mom says.

"Aren't all you young people on dating sites?" This from Jesse's mom.

"I'm on one, yes, but what if your sons aren't?"

"Can you check?"

Why not? We've come this far. "Sure." I grab my phone and open the app. "What are your last names?"

One by one we discover that all three guys are on the site with me. It seems fate has brought me to these ladies. "There's still one more issue. There's no guarantee they'll want to go out with me."

"Message them, or do whatever you do to make contact, and let us know. We'll go from there. Sound good?"

Three dates. And one of them could turn out to be just the guy I'm looking for. "Yes."

I slip the piece of paper with their email addresses into

my purse.

"Love that handbag," Brooks's mom says as she picks up the check my date left me with.

"Thank you, and I can get that."

"No woman on a date should pay for dinner. Make sure to let us know if our boys pick up the check or not."

"Okay, thanks again." My phone, still in my hand, chimes with a text. I glance down. It's from Elliot. *You like chocolate croissants?*

I smile. "Excuse me a minute?"

My new employers nod.

I do, I text back.

Three tiny dots immediately dance on my screen at the same time unfamiliar quivers bounce around inside my stomach. *Can I lure you into the office a little early tomorrow if I have one waiting for you?*

My smile grows. *You can.*

Excellent.

You're not still at the office, are you?

Leaving now.

That is a seriously long day. He's got to be exhausted. *I hear you have a new assistant who can help make sure you don't work crazy hours.*

I can't scare her off too soon.

She doesn't scare easily.

Good to know. Good night, Madison.

Good night, Elliot.

I look up to find the Mom Squad halfway across the restaurant on their way out. Before I stand to follow, I reread my exchange with Elliot. It's more friendly than boss-y and I feel myself blush. He's got me twisted up, feeling differently toward him than I'm used to, and depending on how things go, there's the potential for a long-term relationship. *Working* relationship, I remind myself. Not anything more.

Chapter Four

Fuck.

"I double-checked the numbers twice," Madison says, her voice small. "I don't understand how the error happened." She twists a strand of hair at her shoulder around her finger and fidgets in the chair on the other side of my desk.

"I'm sure you did, but I can't afford mistakes like this." Thankfully, I read through the report before presenting it to James. It's habit, a quick once-over that's saved my ass more than once.

"I'll redo it right now." She stands and takes backward steps. I suspect her ruddy complexion is due to embarrassment. She's soaked up everything I've said to her this past week, writing things down, studying previous reports, but maybe I've piled too much, too soon, on her. The problem is I was slammed with a couple of new work orders two days after she started, and I needed the help.

"My meeting is in"—I glance at my watch—"thirty

minutes. You've got twenty."

She nods before escaping to her desk like she can't get out of my office fast enough. It's not like I've never made an error, but if Madison wants to make it in the world of finance, she's got to learn to be meticulous and, at this point in her career, triple-check her work.

Which at this juncture, I don't have time for. *Shit.* I pick up the phone and hit her extension.

"Hello?"

"On second thought, I've got this. Reschedule my conference call to tomorrow and then get back to work on the profitability spreadsheet. I need that before you leave today. I'd also like an update on the market research I asked you to do, with a full evaluation by Wednesday, please."

"O-okay. I'm so—"

"No apology necessary. Questions?"

"I don't think so."

"Great. Thanks." I hang up and get to work. Ten minutes in, I've got the report corrected. She'd transposed a couple of numbers, a common error I'll forgive this time. That done, I resume work on the special project James asked me to get to him as soon as possible. It's taking more time and energy than I'd anticipated.

The CEO of ZipMeds expects his team to work as hard as he does, challenging our expertise while also making time to get a feel for where people stand.

I glance up from my computer to look in Madison's direction. I should check in with her rather than bark orders.

My phone rings as I stand. It's our tech manager, Tony, asking if I've signed off on the budget adjustment he requested. I have, I tell him, and pick it up off my desk to have Madison deliver it. James is old school when it comes to certain documents and likes paper as well as digital copies.

"Can you—" Madison jumps at the sound of my voice.

"Sorry, I didn't mean to startle you. Can you run this next door to Tony, please?"

"Sure."

I hand off the doc and rather than go back to my office, let my curiosity get the better of me. I sit down in her chair. She's got Excel open on her monitor. A mechanical pencil and notebook filled with notes rests beside the keyboard. In the corner of her desk is a girlish tray with matching binder clips, sticky notes, a stapler, and scissors. The small cubicle smells like *her*. A cock-teasing mix of strawberries and cream.

Don't even think about it. It's no less than the tenth time I've mentally reprimanded my dick for twitching at the scent of Madison. I jump to my feet. James's smell does nothing for me, so I head to his office a little early for our meeting.

Ninety minutes later I return to my office to find Madison telling two delivery guys where to place my new bookshelf. It's a good thing I've caught them because they're putting the piece on the wrong wall.

"Thanks for bringing that up, but it's supposed to go over there." I nod toward the opposite wall.

The guys pause to look at my assistant. She's got a pencil tucked behind her ear, a sweet juxtaposition to the beige power skirt, white blouse, and black stilettos. She fills the room with her presence so it's no surprise these dudes' attention zeroes in on her.

"You said you wanted it on the east wall," Madison says, eyes on me.

"That's right."

She points toward the bookshelf. "That's the east wall."

"No, that's the west."

"It's east," she reaffirms without an ounce of hesitation.

"Should I get out my compass?" I half tease. I'm a little irritated she's arguing with me.

"If you have one, yes." She crosses her arms and stands

her ground. Is it possible I've mixed up my east and west?

"Want to bet?" *What the hell, Elliot?* I can't believe that just came out of my mouth. I don't make bets at work. This is my brain acting on friendship rather than workship.

She lifts her chin. "Okay."

"A dollar says I'm right." The minuscule wager isn't because I think I'm wrong. It's because of the heat flaring at the back of my neck telling me this is inappropriate at work.

"You're on," she says around a small, confident smile.

"She's right," one of the deliverymen says, pulling my attention. He's got his phone palm up in his hand, so we can see the screen and compass on display. It's pointing at the bookcase and the letter *E*.

Fuck me.

"Sign here," the other deliveryman says, handing a clipboard to Madison.

"Sure thing."

I step around her to my desk and pull a dollar bill out of my wallet.

"Thank you!" she calls after the men, triumph in her voice.

"Here you go."

She accepts the bill as she sits across from me. "Thanks." Then turning her head to contemplate the bookshelf she says, "It looks good there."

It's then that I realize despite my confusion over east and west, the piece of furniture is not against the wall I wanted. I think I just got played—thankfully so—because she's right. It looks perfect where it is.

"You knew it would look best on that wall no matter what, didn't you?" I ask.

"Maybe."

"You're proving to be indispensable, Miss Hastings." I hold her pretty blue gaze for a moment before reminding myself I don't belong there and drag my attention to the boxes in the corner. "When you get a chance, I need you to unpack those for me and fill the shelves bottom to top, please. I've got a meeting with an investor from Vision Capital here tomorrow at eleven, right? So before then would be great. How's the spreadsheet coming?"

"I'll have it for you by the end of the day."

"Good. Thanks. Next up, I'd also like you to do some research on clinics in Indonesia and Rwanda." She pulls the pencil from behind her ear, snags a notepad off my desk, and starts writing. "I need to know how many people are served monthly and annually, ages, male or female, and any other pertinent information that can help me put together a cost analysis on starting a national program to deliver vaccines and blood on demand. I've been working on it from a technology standpoint, but we need the whole picture. I'll help with it, too."

She refers to her notes to repeat what I said, something none of my previous assistants did.

"Right," I tell her before she tears the paper out of the notebook and turns to go. I watch her walk back to her desk, the sway of her hips just as teasing as her sweet scent.

I cool my engines by calling Drake to fill him in on the discussion with James.

The afternoon flies by after that, darkness falling outside my window before I know it. I sit back in my chair and rub my tired eyes. Through the glass wall I see Madison reading something on her computer monitor. A second later, a familiar dark-haired guy stops at her desk—my roommate and best friend, Mateo.

"Hey, bro," I say, coming to stand beside him. He's been to the office once before, right after I started working here. "Did I forget we have plans tonight?"

"Hey. No, you didn't forget. I'm here for Madison."

"Oh?" I look to my assistant for the reason why, not that I'm owed an explanation. The two of them go back to diapers and can get together whenever they want.

"I took my car in for service this morning, and Mateo drove me to work. He's taking me to pick it up and then we're grabbing dinner."

"I need to make sure her new boss is treating her right."

"Let me know what you find out," I say, unbothered. We're always poking at each other. Then to Madison, "You done with that spreadsheet?"

"Saving it now." Her fingers move swiftly over the keyboard as she saves and then shuts down the computer. "I just need to use the bathroom really quick. Be right back." She hurries down the hallway, her heels *pitter-pattering* on the polished floor.

"Did you just check out her ass?" Mateo says.

I jerk my concentration back to him. "*What?* No," I lie.

"I think you did."

"You think wrong."

"Elliot, don't even think about going there."

"I'm not." I stride back into my office. The hallway is not the place to talk about my assistant. I sit at my desk. Mateo slouches in a chair across from me, picking up the remote control for the toy sports car parked under the side table. He turns it on. The miniature car is badass and allows me to have some fun on days when work gets overly stressful.

"You know why I'm telling you this," Mateo says, his eyes on the car as he drives it around my office.

"Because I work with her? You know how seriously I take my job, so it pisses me off that you would even think that."

"You're almost too focused on work, which means you have zero time for a relationship, and Madison is—"

"I know what Madison is, and you don't have to worry." She's wholesome. Caring. Intelligent. Not my typical date as of late.

"She's not the kind of girl you sleep with and never call again."

"Seriously, you can drop the big brother routine. I'm not going to sully her or attempt any kind of relationship beyond what we've already established." I can handle myself around Madison. That she has me on edge doesn't mean I won't be able to keep my word to my best friend. A guy doesn't throw a wrench into ten years of friendship because of a girl.

"All right. But it would really suck if something happened between you two and it ended badly. You're my best friend and she's like family, and I don't want to have to choose between you, so keep it in your pants."

"You'll be happy to know there's a nonfraternization rule here."

He grins. "Perfect."

"What's perfect?" Madison asks, stepping into my office.

Mateo stops playing with the high-end toy and stands. "Your timing. Ready to go? I'm starving."

"I'm ready. Elliot, do you want to join us for dinner?"

Her question is a pleasant surprise that I would absolutely take her up on if I didn't feel this weird tug toward her. "Thanks, but I've got a few things I want to finish before I leave." The first of which is to turn off my brain to her appeal.

"Okay. See you tomorrow."

I nod in goodbye and end up spending three more hours at my desk before I head out, grab some food, then fall into bed, thankfully too exhausted to dream.

• • •

"Good morning."

I look up from getting situated at my desk to see Madison standing in the doorway. It's a good morning now. She's been an even bigger asset her second week on the job, taking everything I toss at her in stride. "Morning."

"How did the presentation go?"

"Great. You should come with me the next time."

"Really?"

"Yeah, if you're interested." I force myself to keep my eyes on hers when what I really want is to run them up and down her body. The office is casual, but I always wear business clothes because it's what I do, a comfortable habit from the two years I worked in corporate finance before landing here. When I meet with investors, I enjoy a suit and tie.

Madison seems to have the same mentality, dressing in skirts and heels. Today is different, though, since the team typically eats lunch as a group on the hill on Fridays. She's wearing a soft pink sweater with painted-on jeans. The look is wholesome, like her, until you get to the footwear. Black stilettos with leopard heels.

"I'm interested," she says, smiling.

Me, too.

"Pencil yourself in for the Callahan meeting." I turn my focus to my computer screen to find a dozen new emails during the two hours I was gone. I wish it were a hundred. I need something to keep my mind off my assistant.

"I will. Thanks." She spins around and is at her desk for all of two seconds when Auggie scoops her up. "Time for lunch," Auggie says loud enough for the entire floor to hear.

I'm not in the mood to be around everyone, but James will chew my ass out if I don't attend. He's big on weekly collaborative tasks to keep communication open and comfortable among his entire team.

I shrug out of my coat and ditch my tie before heading downstairs. As I step into the kitchen for my gourmet-boxed lunch, the first person my gaze lands on is Madison. She and Auggie have their heads close together, whispering, as they grab their food ahead of me.

Lunch in hand, I join James near the top of the hill. We talk business—the guy is brilliant and has taken on a mentor role, one I'm grateful for—before he tells me about his weekend plans with his three-year-old daughter. He shares custody with his ex, the one good thing in a costly and hostile divorce. Before they married, he and his ex were platonic business partners. Their working relationship turned into romance and marriage, until things personally unraveled between them. She got their company, a rival start-up doing similar drone work, and he got enough working capital to start a new one. He's still not over the collapse of their relationship. Hence the reason for his firm rule on workplace dating. He knows firsthand what a shit storm it can lead to, and he doesn't want anything disrupting the harmony he's created at ZipMeds.

"All right, everyone," Hazel calls out from the middle of the artificial grass. "This week's team building is Blind Drawing. It's a two-person activity that focuses on interpretation and communication. Auggie is walking around with some names. Please divvy up and then sit back-to-back."

As luck would have it—or not—I draw Madison's name and make my way over to her. She looks up at me with her big blue eyes. "I'm stuck with you?"

"Is that any way to speak to your boss?" I deadpan.

"You're right." She slips off her heels and lines them up beside her before turning to give me her back. "I'm stuck with you, sir?" she tosses over her shoulder.

Her playful mouth is dangerous, so I ignore it. If we weren't friends, she'd probably speak to me in a completely different manner.

I sit behind her, leaving space between our backs. I haven't touched her, not so much as a brush of the arms, since that night at the bar a few months ago.

"I'm sorry," she whispers, perhaps noting my stiffness. "That wasn't appropriate."

Damn right, it wasn't. Not with my boss sitting only a few feet away.

"I don't know why I said it," she continues. "It won't happen again."

"Thanks," I say appreciatively.

"All right," Hazel calls out to the group. "One of you is receiving a pen and paper while the other is getting a picture."

I'm handed a picture of a lake with a dock. On the dock is a toy sailboat on its side.

"Thank you," Madison says. She's obviously received the paper and pen.

"Here's how this works. The person with the picture describes the photo to their partner without actually saying what it is. So if the image is a dog in a doghouse, don't say 'draw a doghouse with a dog inside it.' You also can't use synonyms. Those of you with pen and paper will draw what you think the picture depicts based on your partner's description. You've got ten minutes. Go."

Madison shifts so our backs touch. I don't know if it's because she's uncomfortable sitting with her legs crossed in her lap and needs support, or if it's because she thinks the contact will help with our task, but the connection triggers an unwelcome current of awareness down my spine.

"Ready," she says to me.

The only thing I'm creative with is money, so I've no clue how to describe what I'm looking at. I'm reminded of the art camp my mom sent my siblings and me to for one summer when we were young. My brother and sister came home with perfect charcoal drawings of a dinosaur, a UFO in outer space, flowers in a vase, a brown bear in the forest, and a sailboat. Five frame-worthy pieces of art for each day of camp. I came home with my fellow campers' snack money in my pockets. Instead of drawing, I walked around and bet on who would finish first and who would be awarded Camper of the Day.

"Elliot?"

Madison's soft voice punctures my recollection.

"A body," I say off the top of my head. What a lame description, but a lake *is* a body of water.

"You want me to draw a body?" she asks.

"Yes. I'm looking at something smooth. Calming."

"Okay. What else?"

"There's a"—how do I describe a dock without saying dock?—"place to sit."

"Got it." She starts to draw. I know this because I feel the vibrations.

I give her a few minutes before adding "There's also something small…it floats."

"Smaller than the place to sit?"

"Yes, much. The wind helps it move."

She's quiet while she works. I look around and notice the other teams are finished. Hazel walks by us. "One minute."

"Okay," Madison answers, right before I hear Hazel catch her breath.

Our office manager leans back into my periphery to check out the picture of the dock in my hands. I lift my head to find her looking at me like I've got two noses or something. What does she want from me? These exercises are annoying as shit sometimes. If I want to communicate with Madison, I talk to her in plain English, no interpretation required.

"Time," Hazel says.

I spin around to see what Madison's drawn. Holy shit. It's amazing. And nothing at all like the photo in my hands. "I suck at descriptions, and you should be an artist because that is unbelievable."

Madison looks from her drawing to the photograph, then

her eyes meet mine. "We definitely aren't in sync."

"No."

"Although I interpreted the sailboat right."

"Minor miracle."

She chuckles. "I see now what you meant by 'body' but 'place to sit' for a dock is pretty funny."

"Agreed. I don't know what I was thinking." I slip the paper from her fingers to get a closer look at this masterpiece. "I do know you're in the wrong profession." The picture— or sketch is probably a better term for it—is on caliber with professional artists. Madison's "body" is a nude male form, his backside to the viewer. He's straddling a chair. On his right shoulder blade is a tattoo of a sailboat. "This is incredible."

She blushes. "Thanks. I've loved to draw since I was little."

"You didn't want to make a career out of it?"

"No. It's just something I do for fun."

Word spreads about her drawing, which leads to teasing about my descriptive skills. The entire team is communicating now—at my expense. It doesn't bother me. I'm competitive as hell, but where I failed, my partner more than made up for in raw talent. It's interesting. In the three months I've worked here, this is the first time I feel like I truly belong with the whole group.

People disperse until I'm standing with Madison and Auggie. Auggie is holding the picture in her hands, staring at it like if she tries hard enough the guy might come to life. "Broad shoulders, round, tight ass, and in need of a haircut," she says. "Is this anyone we know?"

Madison plucks the paper out of Auggie's hands. "No."

"Shame," Auggie says.

"How could it be someone I know when I drew it from Elliot's description?"

"The subconscious works in mysterious ways, my friend."

She looks past us, up the hill. "James is motioning for me. Gotta go."

I glance at my watch.

"Your call is in ten minutes," Madison says, before I've even registered the time.

"Thanks for keeping me on schedule, Miss Hastings."

"You're welcome, Mr. Sax."

"Have time to sit in and take notes?" The call is with an investor back east who's really making me work for it. I get being thorough, but he's trying my patience and after today's phone call, I may have to move on.

"Definitely." She grabs her heels to walk up the hill to the second floor. They dangle from her hand until we reach the concrete flooring. Stopping to slip her feet back into them, she teeters. I give her my elbow for balance.

Long, delicate fingers grip my biceps. She smiles up at me.

And my look-but-don't-touch rule bites the dust.

Chapter Five

Madison

"They're pimping you out!" Harper says around her cocktail straw.

I choke down my Diet Coke.

"It's a fucking brilliant idea, though."

"That's not what they're doing," I say, looking around the restaurant to be sure no one can hear us. We're in a large booth at Donahue's sharing appetizers for dinner.

"It kind of is." Teague puts her hand on my arm. "But there's a better way of saying it."

Over the past year these two girls have become my closest friends. I met Teague while planning my wedding. She worked—still does work—with Gabrielle Gallagher, the biggest wedding planner in Beverly Hills, and my godmother. Harper and Teague have been best friends since college. After my wedding disaster, they stepped up and helped me keep it together when my other so-called friends didn't.

"And what would that be, sweet potato fry?" Harper asks,

putting a sweet potato fry in her mouth. Harper is brazen, smart, and beautiful inside and out. She recently started her own foundation to raise awareness for swim safety. Teague is sweet, smart, and just as beautiful. She thrives on happily-ever-afters and plans honeymoons for couples.

"I don't know. Date for hire? Did you know you could hire a maid of honor or bridesmaids if you need them? Isn't that crazy?"

"Way crazier than what our girl, Madison, is up to," Harper says.

I could definitely be a hired MOH. If my job with ZipMeds doesn't work out, maybe I'll look into it. I've planned a wedding, so I know what goes into it. I know what I appreciated and didn't from my bridesmaids. I also think it's probably easier than the dating job I've gotten myself into, considering I'm fairly certain the three dates I've got lined up are with very experienced guys if their flirtatious messages are any indication. Although, I guess that's the point of dating apps. Flirt online first. Meet in person second.

Ugh. "Maybe I should cancel." I cut into a crab cake, one of my favorite foods.

"No way. You are not chickening out." Harper points her fork at me. "I'm sorry for what I said. You're doing a cool thing for some curious—and caring—moms. If you didn't know my brothers, I'd hire you to date them. I'd kill to know what they're like when they take a girl out."

I cover my face with my hands. "No way is this turning into anything more."

"Never say never," Harper says.

"The moms could refer you," Teague adds.

"No. No. No," I say with a shake of my head. "I do not want a reputation for something like this. What if *my* mother found out?" Beverly Hills can be a small town. Panic rises in my chest. "She'd be mortified."

Harper *pffts*. "You're going on one date with these guys, not fucking them."

"True." Teague nods in quick agreement. "And they could be really nice. Have you got the first one lined up?"

"Yes, for next Thursday." It took me forever to tell these girls what I'd gotten myself into, and there was no way I was moving forward without talking to them first. I'm planning to spread the dates out, one per week. I think it cheapens the date otherwise. Cheapens me. It's ridiculous, I know, but Henry gutted me with his behavior, and until I start dating one person exclusively, that's the way it is. I met Henry when I was sixteen and he's the only boyfriend I've ever had, so dating isn't exactly something I'm good at, or even like, to be honest. I thought I'd be married by now.

"Maddy," Harper says, her tone softening. "Maybe one of them will sweep you off your feet."

"Maybe."

"Or at the very least, be the guy to dust off your vagina," she adds, a lot more perky.

"Shut up." My cheeks heat at the thought of getting naked with someone. I've been with one person, and hearing Harper and Teague talk, what Henry did with me was very ho-hum. *Because he was getting his freak on with other girls.* What would it be like to have mind-blowing sex?

"Harper?" Teague puts down her chicken wing, her gaze going over my shoulder. "Did you tell the guys we were here?"

"No." Harper looks past me, too, her eyes lighting up because she's no doubt locked in on her guy.

I give a brief turn of my head. "The guys" are Teague's boyfriend, Mateo, Harper's boyfriend, Levi, and the guys' best friend and roommate...Elliot. Otherwise known as my boss. I wiggle in my seat. This is the first time I've seen Elliot in a social setting since I started working with him. I'd invited him to dinner the other night with me and Matty out of good manners and been both relieved and disappointed he hadn't joined us. "I thought they were going to a Lakers game tonight," I say.

"I guess they changed their minds." Harper's eyes find mine. "You said it's been good working with Elliot, and it's inevitable that you'll see him outside the office, but if you don't feel like—"

"It's fine." And what I actually said was it's been *great* working with him.

"Hi, beautiful," Levi says to Harper. "This is a nice surprise." He gives her a kiss hello.

"Hi, Knox." Mateo says, using his nickname for Teague before he plants a kiss on her. Then being the good pal he is, he says, "Hey, Mad," and gives me a kiss on the cheek. He and Levi get comfortable in the booth, and then it's Elliot's turn to greet us.

"Hi," I say, trying to act like he doesn't affect me when in reality my heart is running a race.

"Hey," he says, taking a seat next to me. I've been this close to him before, but tonight it's too close for some reason.

I take a slow, deep breath. This is silly. He's my boss and my friend and there is no reason for this weird reaction to him.

"Looks like we arrived just in time," Mateo says. "Did you order *every* appetizer on the menu?" He picks up a celery stick from the plate of wings.

"We did," Teague says. "We're celebrating Madison's new jobs."

"Jobs, plural?" Elliot questions.

"Teague," I warn. The last thing I want is to talk about my dating life with the guys here.

Mateo drills me with a look of concern. He's taken on a big brother role since my breakup with Henry, and his overprotectiveness is sweet but unnecessary. "What's going on, Mad?"

"Nothing," I say, hating the way that one word tastes on my tongue. I've never been a liar, but this is private.

Elliot turns his head to look at me. The attention is like a magnet, and I'm helpless to keep my focus straight ahead, damn him. "Are you working another job, too?"

Is lying to my boss outside the office grounds for dismissal? Because the past two weeks have been the best I've had in a very long time, and I don't want to lose my job. I never imagined clicking with Elliot like we have. We've totally meshed, falling into a professional groove I haven't had with anyone else. Like we've been working together for months, not weeks. Working with him is interesting, challenging, fun even. And ZipMeds is a worthwhile, fascinating, friendly workplace. I don't want to give it up.

"It's temporary," I say, hoping that satisfies his curiosity.

"So is ours." His words cut through me even though they're the truth. Does he think I need the reminder? Does he even give one iota about my future? Obviously these past weeks haven't meant as much to him as they have to me.

"It's a dating thing." The second the words are out of my mouth, I wish I could take them back. I said them to…hurt him? See if that bothered him? Show him I have a life outside of ZipMeds and whatever strange vibe we've experienced at work means nothing to me? *Temporary* is fine by me.

A familiar spark of awareness flashes in his eyes, but it disappears so fast, I might have imagined it. "Do tell."

I look to Teague and Harper for help. Damn it. I have no idea how to proceed. I care what Elliot thinks of me. I care about what everyone at the table thinks of me.

"May I?" Harper asks.

"I guess so."

"Madison is working undercover as a dating specialist. She dates guys and then reports back to their moms on their behavior."

"Three guys. I'm only dating three guys."

"At the same time?" Mateo asks, shocked.

"No. Of course not," I say. "Three weeks. Three dates. Then that temporary job ends." I'll continue with my other temporary job until Elliot tells me otherwise.

"Unless you make a love connection," Teague offers optimistically. "You're amazing, Maddy, and one of these guys could fall for you."

"Back up," Mateo says. "You're going on a date to report back to their *moms*? Why?"

"Hey, guys," our waitress, Kym, says, stopping at our booth. "Can I get you something to drink?"

The boys order beers on tap, then Harper launches into the quick and dirty version of my dating disaster from the other night.

"Jesus," Levi says. "That guy should be banned from coming within a hundred feet of the opposite sex."

"I want to hunt him down and shove a few capsules down his throat," Mateo says.

Elliot stays quiet.

"So these moms want to make sure their sons aren't like that," I say, speaking up because it's time I own this conversation. These are my friends. I should be able to tell them stuff, even if it makes me uncomfortable.

"I didn't know your dates were going so badly," Mateo says.

"They haven't all been that terrible."

Teague and Harper frown at me.

"Okay, so maybe they have, but I hate admitting that because then I feel like there's something wrong with me."

"There's nothing wrong with you," Elliot says adamantly.

I freeze, both pleased and unsettled by his response. Everyone else at the table looks at him like they're wondering the same thing as me: was that a rote reply to make me feel okay or something more? Mateo shoots him an especially odd kind of scrutinizing look.

"What? I've worked with her for a couple of weeks, I know she's not the problem."

Okay then. Good to know I'm not a thorn in his side.

"That's right," Levi says. "Madison, you probably deserve a medal for putting up with him."

"And a raise," Harper adds. She knows how hard I'm saving so I can move out of my parents' house.

"It's been ten work days," Elliot counters.

"And who was the last assistant to go that long?" Levi asks with a knowing smile. These guys are the closest of friends and have been for a decade, so I imagine Elliot's complained about work now and then.

"Can I talk to you for a second?" Elliot says to me. "Alone."

"Uh, sure."

"You better be nice to her," Harper says as we scoot out of the booth.

"When am I ever not nice?" To prove his point, he helps me to my feet. It's not calculated, it's natural. Then he puts his hand on my lower back to guide me around the busy restaurant. Heat burns through the sweater I wore to work today.

We land at the end of the bar, a dimly lit corner with one available stool. He motions for me to sit. "Can I buy you a drink?" he asks.

Since my nerves are doing jumping jacks in my stomach, yes he can. "Okay."

He waves the bartender over. The guy behind the counter is attractive and greets Elliot like he knows him. I order a tequila sunrise. Elliot orders a beer. He'd yet to receive his drink at the table.

"This is weird," he says.

I let out the breath I was saving for later, happy I'm not the only one who is restless. "It is."

"It shouldn't be." He leans his elbows on the bar. Like me, he's still in his work clothes. His shirtsleeves are rolled up. His collar is loose. He smells really good, a mix of man and some kind of cologne. His hair is finger-combed sexy, and I wonder if it's as soft as it looks. "I don't want it to be."

"Me, either."

He shifts, rests his side against the counter. Electric-blue eyes fringed with dark lashes hold me in place. "So let's not let it. We work great together, and I don't want to do anything to jeopardize that."

"Agreed. So, maybe when we're not at work, we just forget we work together?"

"I can do that. What's harder is forgetting we're friends, too, while at work."

I swallow. The way he's looking at me...I think the attraction I feel isn't one-sided. My heart starts to pound.

"I like you," he says.

And my heart pounds double-time. "I like you, too." But even if he weren't my boss...he's a million miles out of my comfort zone. I'd never be enough for someone like him. Someone far more experienced than I am—in love and life. I've heard enough stories from Mateo, and I've seen him with enough different girls over the years to know Elliot Sax is a playboy and isn't interested in anything serious.

"Sometime this week, though—I take that back—I know exactly when. On Wednesday morning when you presented me with a month-long agenda divided into three sections that included strategy, growth, and investor management—we became a team."

A huge smile splits my face in two.

"And correct me if I'm wrong, but I think you're happy

at ZipMeds."

"I am. Very."

"So friends it is, with the caveat that I am your boss, and there's a line there we have to be careful of."

"Right," I say, realizing he likes me, but he doesn't *like* me. Which is for the best.

"I have no idea what you get paid, but I'll look into it."

"That's not—"

"I also want to make your position permanent."

"You don't have—" I stop myself. "What did you say?" Before the grin taking over my face gets too big again, I need to hear that one more time.

"Here you go." In my periphery, the bartender puts our drinks down. Without taking his eyes off mine, Elliot picks up our glasses. He hands me mine.

"Congratulations, Madison."

"You want to hire me full-time?"

"If that's what you want."

"Yes, it's what I want."

"Then we have ourselves a deal." He clinks his glass to mine, then takes a big gulp of his beer.

I watch his lips move, his throat work. It's sexy and—I dart my gaze everywhere else but at his face while I take a sip from my tiny straw. One sip turns into two, turns into three. I'm just going to drink the whole yummy thing. When I lift my eyes to his, I find them lasered in on my mouth. My breasts grow suddenly heavy. I ache between my thighs. It's like he can command my body to respond just to his regard. This is bad.

But feels so good.

"Elliot?"

We both turn. A beautiful woman a little older than us smiles at him. "I thought that was you."

"Michaela. Hi. How are you?"

"I'm good. You? I miss you at Goldman. My trips out here aren't the same."

They smile at each other. It's small, almost unnoticeable, but that makes it worse because it means they share a secret, and I'm guessing it's a sex secret. Whatever I was feeling a minute ago comes to a screeching halt. Sitting here is now painful.

"I'm great." He blinks as if just remembering I'm a mere foot away. "This is Madison. Madison, this is Michaela. She's in HR for the firm I used to work for. She's based in New York, but makes her way out here a few times a year."

"Nice to meet you," I say.

Michaela looks back and forth between Elliot and me before settling her big brown eyes on Elliot. "You, too."

"Madison and I work together."

"Oh?" she says with a raise of her perfectly sculpted eyebrows. She's dressed like she stepped out of the pages of Beautiful Corporate Woman, not that that's a real publication. But if it were, she'd be on the cover. "You don't mind if I steal him away, then, do you?"

I wait for Elliot to tell her "no" since she's looking directly at him when she asks the question, but he doesn't say anything.

He doesn't even spare me a glance. I guess our celebration is over.

It's stupid to feel disappointed, but I do. Elliot doesn't owe me a thing, but once again I come in second place. I slide off the stool. "Not at all," I say. "In fact, you can take my seat."

"Madison," Elliot says to my back.

With all the sounds in the restaurant, I pretend I don't hear him and keep walking.

Chapter Six

ELLIOT

Closing a deal and getting funding is almost as good as sex. My blood pumps faster, endorphins kick in like I ran a mile under seven minutes, confidence steamrolls through my muscles. I'm fucking great at this job. And today is an especially good day because I've just been guaranteed five million dollars, bringing the company's total capital raised to forty million dollars to date.

I look up from my desk as Madison walks into view and sits down at her desk. I've never been happier to have glass walls than I am since she started working here. Today's heels are red strappy pumps with silver studs. A form-fitting, off-white skirt and red blouse with a slit in each long sleeve finishes the outfit. Her hair is in a bun on top of her head, leaving the long column of her neck open to my daydreams. Not that I let my mind go there for long.

I felt like shit the other night letting Michaela barge in on us at the bar, but watching Madison wrap those incredible lips of hers around her cocktail straw was too much. My lips tingled in response. My mouth had never fucking done that before, and I was relieved when Michaela showed up. If she hadn't, I couldn't promise I wouldn't have kissed my assistant. With the way Madison had been looking at me, I'm pretty confident she would have let me.

"*Merci, je vous parlerai la semaine prochaine,*" I say when Jean-Luc comes back on the phone line to say goodbye. I'll talk to him next week.

Madison's eye catches mine as I remove my earbuds. I wave her into my office. This deserves a celebration. "Did you need something?" she asks, peeking her head around the door I'd left closed.

Yeah, you could say that physically keeping the door closed helps with those daydreams, too. Our third week together is proving more difficult for me to keep my thoughts from straying into dangerous territory. For the past few days I've questioned my sanity in hiring her full-time, but the bottom line is she's excellent at her job. And she needs a solid paycheck. Unbeknownst to her, Mateo and I talked about her after her first day working here. He told me she's desperate to move out of her parents' house and be on her own. Make something of herself without parental input. I understand that, so if I can help her get there, I will.

I'm a grown-ass adult, and I can keep this attraction I can't shake platonic. That I didn't sleep with Michaela last Friday night because I couldn't get a certain blonde assistant out of my head doesn't mean anything.

"Have a seat," I tell Madison.

"You closed the deal," she says around a smile.

I smile back. "I closed the deal."

"*Toutes nos félicitations!* I knew you would." At my happily stunned expression she adds, "I Googled how to say congratulations."

This girl. I want to close the curtains in my office, lock the door, and fuck her on top of my desk as thanks. But I won't.

"Did I pronounce it right?" she asks when I've yet to say anything. My goddamn tongue is stuck.

"You did. Thanks."

"*What?* You're looking at me funnier than normal." She squirms in her chair.

I walk around my desk until I'm beside her and lean back against the glass top with my legs crossed at the ankles. My hands grip the smooth edge. I've got to hold onto something or I may reach for her. "You're great is all. Do you go the extra mile for everyone?"

She gazes up at me. "No. Not everyone."

Good answer. Although I'm not sure I believe her. She's the kind of person who would give the shirt off her back.

There's an image I'd like to see firsthand.

"And hold up. What do you mean 'funnier than normal'? Are you implying I'm funny looking all the time?"

Her lips twitch. "You said it, not me."

"It takes one to know one."

She laughs.

I know. I sound like a five-year-old. I've apparently maxed out my brain cells for the day.

"You sound like a five-year-old," she says.

"Seriously? You need to stop doing that."

"What am I doing?" Big, expectant pools of fathomless blue challenge me. In her left eye, there's a ring of green I've never noticed before.

"Thinking what I'm thinking."

"I don't do that."

"You do, sometimes."

"Okay. Think something right now." She fixes me with a look to placate me.

It's a good thing she doesn't want to buy into this, because once again, I'm thinking about fucking her on my desk. I can't seem to stop myself. I want to bend her over, lift her skirt, and sink into her. Untie her bun and thread my fingers through her hair before I fist the strands and turn her head in order to bring that ripe mouth of hers to mine. I want to suck her tongue into my mouth while I pound—

She draws in a breath, breaks eye contact.

I push off the desk and return to my chair before she notices the bulge in my pants. I'm not positive what just happened, but the air is thick with more than simple air molecules.

Fuck. This seesaw of propriety I'm on has got to stop. No girl is worth losing my job over. And I don't want to lose her as an assistant. I comb my fingers through my hair, remembering I still need a haircut.

Madison's chest rises and falls. She's got spectacular—*stop!*

"We need to do something about this," I say, discreetly adjusting my pants.

"Agreed."

For a second we almost share a smile because, hello? We're on the same fucking wavelength. What I'm feeling isn't one-sided and I'd bet money it hasn't been for a while. When she signed her new-hire paperwork on Monday, though, included in the packet was a right to terminate agreement and at the top of the sheet is fraternizing with coworkers.

"Liking each other is proving a little problematic," she adds.

"Exactly. And you're too valuable to me as an assistant." I flick a pen between my fingers. "We're attracted to each other. That's healthy. Normal even. But we need to stay focused on keeping things strictly professional."

"We need a strategy," she offers.

See why this girl is so great? She's speaking my language. "Exactly." If we simply say we can handle this, it's only going to get worse. But a plan of attack gives our minds something else to do.

She brings her hand to the side of her neck. "I have an idea. It's a little inane, but I think it could work. A friend of mine once had to...it's a long story, but I think the same principles could work here."

"Let's hear it."

"Whenever we have"—pink colors her cheekbones— "non-work-related thoughts about each other, we write a not-so-nice note instead so that the person on the receiving end wants nothing to do with the other person."

I scratch my chin. "*That's* the plan?"

"It'll work. You'll see." She stands up. "I'll go first to give you an example." With that she walks out of my office.

Five minutes later, she silently drops a nondescript white envelope on my desk then tiptoes away like she's hoping I didn't see her. My eyes are glued to her backside as she leaves so the stealthy part of her delivery fails. *Dude, the note. Focus on the note.*

I open the envelope. Inside it is a neatly folded piece of paper and a tiny white piece of candy...a breath mint.

Mr. Sax,

You have terrible breath. It's like something crawled into your mouth and died. You may want to see a dental professional. At the very least, purchase mouthwash.

Sincerely,
Miss Hastings

She's joking, right? I blow a breath onto the palm of

my hand, but I can't tell if my breath is bad or not. No one has ever called me out on halitosis before, so this is bullshit. Good bullshit because I'm kind of pissed at her right now. I brush my teeth every morning and every night without fail. Floss, too. I notice she's very busy at her desk, paying me no attention.

Nicely played, Miss Hastings. Round one is yours.

I pop the mint into my mouth, just in case.

Since I'm a scorecard kind of guy, I reach across my desk for my planner. My scorekeeping goes back to middle school when I made a bet with Levi about who could run the mile faster. He won, and ever since we've tossed bets back and forth. Being the competitive person I am, I've kept track of every bet we've made. It bugs the shit out of him, which makes it even more fun. Flipping my planner open to the plain sheets of paper in back, I start a scoresheet for Madison and me. The leather-bound book, a gift from my sister, has quotes at the top of all the pages, and I laugh as I read the one on this page: **"Just because you consider yourself a genius doesn't mean you are smart." —Mark W. Boyer**.

Things are about to get a lot more interesting.

• • •

The next day James and I, along with our CTO and Executive VP, spend the morning and most of the afternoon in the conference room going over financial reports, forecasts, and the possibility of expanding into Indonesia and Rwanda. James isn't thrilled I haven't finished the project he asked for, but I've only got so many hours to get shit done. Drake videoconferences in from San Francisco, congratulating me first and foremost on the five-million-dollar investment I secured yesterday. When we're through, I'm anxious to catch Madison up before she heads home. The two of us need to put all our energy into completing the expansion project.

I find her in my office. Bending over. So, naturally my dick perks up. *Down, dick.* (The truth is, it doesn't matter what part of her I look at. I'm constantly telling my cock to behave.) She picks up the folder she dropped and straightens. She's wearing a beige sweater dress today, the soft cotton conforming to her curvy body like a well-worn glove. Not too tight, but close-fitting. The hem falls to the tops of her knees. Knee-length, high-heeled brown leather boots finish the outfit.

"Hey," she says over her shoulder, snapping me out of my gawking. She puts the file on my desk and turns.

"Hey. Have a seat." I sit on my side of the desk and fill her in on my meeting. We've got our work cut out for us in the coming months. She listens attentively, asks intelligent questions, and shows zero worry about the challenges ahead. The expectations on me continue to be high, but with the way she looks at me—with confidence, trust, respect—I feel like I've got this with my eyes closed and my hands tied behind my back. "We *must* get the Indo-Rwanda report to James sooner rather than later."

"I forgot to tell you! I've got a friend who works for Mercy Corps and she's based in Indonesia. I'm working with her to get the numbers we need, for there at least."

"That's fantastic." If I ever doubted Madison's value, I don't now.

We've just finished talking when Auggie pokes her head inside the office. "Sorry to interrupt, but I'm heading out and wanted to catch you before I go."

"No worries. What's up?" I ask.

"The company retreat is scheduled for the weekend of March twenty-third. Mark your calendars, please. Details will follow."

"Will do. Thanks."

"Oh, and, Madison. Have fun tonight." Auggie smiles at my assistant, then waves goodbye.

"Thanks," Madison says before turning back to me. "If that's everything, I'm going to head out, too."

"What's tonight?" I ask before I think better of it. I've done a good job of not getting too friendly with her this week, but all of a sudden I wonder if tonight is her "other job." I overheard her say something to Auggie about a date, which doesn't bother me. She can have a date every night of the week if she wants. But now that I know about the assholes she's been out with, my protective instinct kicks in. We're friends, she and I, and what kind of friend would I be if I wasn't concerned for her well-being?

"I have a date."

"With one of the guys—"

"Yes," she's quick to say. "But no one else knows the background behind these dates, so if you could please keep that to yourself, I'd appreciate it."

"Of course."

"Thanks. So, if that's—"

"Where is he taking you?" I'm aware this is none of my business, but I have the urge to know where she'll be tonight, just in case.

"We're meeting at Wild Beast."

I'm glad she's *meeting* him there. A girl should never have a guy she doesn't know pick her up at home. "It's good. I've been there." As far as cocktail lounges go, it's one of the best.

"Can I ask you a question?" she says quietly.

I lean forward on my desk. Her soft voice and tone are saying, *Can I ask you a confidential question?* "Sure." I'm ready to spout off whatever dating advice she needs, even though it ties my stomach in knots.

"Is the company retreat mandatory?"

It takes a second for her question to register. I'm an idiot.

She's keeping things professional, and I'm the irresponsible boss hoping to what? Get a better picture inside her head?

I sit back in my chair. I have no idea if it's mandatory. "Do you have a conflict that weekend?"

She scrunches up her nose. "Kind of?"

"Get out of it," I say, leaving no room for argument. I'm stern for two reasons. The first is her expression and uncertainty indicates a mere possibility of a conflict, meaning it's not something important. It might even be something she wants to renege on and now I've helped her out. The second reason is I want her there.

With me.

And the rest of the team, of course.

"All right." She stands. "I'll see you tomorrow."

"Have a good night."

"You, too."

A few minutes later, my cell rings. It's my friend Phoebe. She wants to know if I want to grab a drink. She and I dated briefly in college, but realized we were better off as friends. Occasionally that includes benefits if one of us has an itch that needs to be scratched. When she suggests Wild Beast, it's like being struck by lightning. What are the chances? The coincidence has to mean something, though, right? Fate or some weird universe thing, so I agree.

When she and I walk into the place, I tell myself it's because I want to be sure Madison has backup if her date turns out to be a prick. That I'm hungry and have a craving for some Baja street food, which is excellent here, is another good reason.

The lounge is fairly small and as the hostess leads us across the tiled floor to a round green table, I spot Madison immediately. We walk past her and her date to be seated two tables over. I pull out a chair for Phoebe, then sit across from her in the upholstered bench seat that lines the entire wall.

This spot gives me a better view of Madison.

"Thanks," Phoebe says, getting comfortable.

I'm not sure I deserve any thanks tonight, since I think being with her is to camouflage the somewhat stalker circumstances I realize I'm in, but we'll enjoy a meal together and catch up.

Phoebe fills me in on law school and we order drinks. Madison hasn't noticed me, which is good. What's not good is her attention is glued to her date. The guy looks decent enough. He says something to make her laugh.

"Do you know them?" Phoebe asks, following my line of sight.

So much for being subtle. "Yes. Madison is my…a friend." We're outside of work so I see no reason to elaborate.

"Should we say hello?"

"You want to?"

"Do *you* want to?"

Fuck, if I know. I glance back over to her table and *Bam*. Our eyes meet. She looks away before I have a chance to read them. She says something to her date, then stands and walks toward the restrooms.

Our waitress delivers our drinks. "Excuse me a minute?" I say to Phoebe. She nods.

I find Madison standing outside the restroom, and by the fire lit in her blue eyes, she's no doubt waiting for me. "What are you doing here?" she demands. Her annoyance is kind of hot.

"Well?" she insists, putting her hands on her hips.

It takes effort not to crack a smile. I wonder if she'll tap her foot at me next. "I'm here to eat."

"Really?" The "no-shit-Sherlock" is implied.

"Plus, they have the best craft beers."

She narrows her eyes. "You knew I was coming here."

"True. But it wasn't my idea. My friend, Phoebe, actually

suggested it."

"She did?" Madison visibly relaxes.

"Yes."

"Oh, okay. I thought maybe you were here to spy on me. That Mateo put you up to it because he's worried I can't take care of myself. I can. I'm getting really good at it, actually."

"I promise I haven't spoken to Mateo. Did you tell him you were going to be here?"

"Yes. He's asked me to text him where I'm at on dates now. He's worse than my brother. It's sweet, but it's not like I'm on top of a mountain or the middle of a lake. I always go to very public and popular places."

"That's smart."

"I know," she says, her patience wearing thin. Several beats of silence pass. "Well, have fun on your date." Without giving me a chance to respond, she strides off.

I follow behind, almost bumping into someone's chair because my eyes are on the sweet curves of her backside. I imagine what it would be like if I were the guy sitting across from her, sharing a meal and making her laugh. We'd stay until closing, the conversation never lagging, then I'd walk her to her car, kiss her like she's never been kissed before, and ask her out on a second date. Because a girl like Madison deserves to be romanced.

Instead, I return to Phoebe and we fall back into easy discussions about current events and mutual friends while I notice Madison's date is on his cell. He's been talking on it since I sat back down.

Look at me, Madison. Look. At. Me. Her gaze flits to mine. She's not thrilled with the guy.

"Mind if I do say hello?" I nod my head to the side, indicating Madison. She might not want my interference, but at the moment, I don't care.

Chapter Seven

MADISON

Cell phone to his ear, Liam keeps looking at me with apologetic eyes while he talks one of his employees through a wiring problem on a house. Liam is a contractor and this is his first big project, so he doesn't want it screwed up. I get that, being I don't want to screw up my job, either, and I sincerely hope I haven't. I wasn't exactly polite to Elliot in the hallway.

But talk about shock. I thought I was daydreaming about him again when our eyes met and the total disrespect that meant for Liam had me jerking my gaze away, only to realize Elliot was indeed sitting a few feet away. How am I supposed to concentrate when he's a huge distraction I don't need? I'm nervous enough with Liam. I keep thinking he's going to blurt out, "I know my mom hired you to go on this date so thanks for nothing, bitch." My mind can be very annoying sometimes.

"Here you go," the waitress says, dropping off our food. I'm grateful I have something to do. It's taking Wonder

Woman strength not to glance at Elliot and his pretty companion. Is she someone he's seeing? Is it a first date like mine? Not that it matters. He's free to do whatever he wants with whomever he wants.

Liam holds up his pointer finger to indicate one more minute. I nod in understanding, but really, I'm...not upset exactly, but not happy, either. The date started off so well; why did he have to get a phone call? He complimented my appearance, listened to me talk rather than monopolize the conversation, and made me laugh. He seems like a good guy.

I slip an ocean trout street taco onto my plate while I look around the lounge. The feel is old Hollywood with dark woods, red leather upholstery, and white tile floor. By accident, my gaze slips to Elliot. Again. Okay, not by accident. I swear he's been mentally calling my name or something. He blinks at me, so I blink back. It's the second time we've done this. I have no idea what the blinks mean and quickly look away.

But two seconds later, at the exact same time Liam finishes his phone call, Elliot is standing at our table. "Madison? Hey. How are you?"

He's pretending he just noticed me? I want to punch his smile right off his face. "Hi. I'm good. You?"

"I'm great." He looks from me to Liam. "Hey, I'm Elliot." He puts his hand out.

"Liam. Nice to meet you." They shake. "Do I know you from somewhere?"

"I don't think so," Elliot says before turning his attention back to me. "God, it's been forever. You look amazing."

Against my will, my cheeks heat. "Thank you."

The three of us look at one another in uncomfortable silence. "Well, it was nice to see you," I say. *Now move along and stop this ridiculous game.*

He threads his fingers through his silky, dark hair. "Yeah, wow, it's just been so long and who knows when I'll see you again."

Tomorrow. You'll see me at work tomorrow. I stare up at him, wondering if this is some kind of attempt to rescue me. I'd appreciate the assist if I needed it, but I don't. I put my elbow on the table and try to casually wave him off.

His eyes flit to my hand. "So, I'll call you some time to catch up. I'll just go back to my table now and leave you two alone. Have a good night."

"You, too," I say.

"Ex-boyfriend?" Liam asks as soon as Elliot steps away.

"Oh no. Nothing like that." I leave it there. I don't want to talk about Elliot. It's bad enough I think about him all the time.

Liam glances over at Elliot sitting too close for my comfort. "He looks familiar. What's his last name?"

"Sax."

Recognition dawns on Liam's face. "I knew I knew the guy. Not personally. I've seen him in pictures. He dated my sister a couple years ago."

"Oh?" I'm dying to know more, but at the same time, I'm trying to leave Elliot out of the conversation this evening.

"He was a real jerk. Broke her heart. Back then I wanted to bash his face in." He picks up a taco. "You're friends with him?" He asks this like he's disgusted. Like by knowing Elliot it somehow makes me less of a person.

I don't like his judgy tone. What does it matter who I'm friendly with? "I am."

"That's a shame."

"Why is that a shame?"

"I couldn't date someone who's friends with that asshole."

I bristle at his description. "He's not."

"An asshole? You sure? What kind of guy leaves his date alone to hit up another girl?"

"He wasn't hitting me up."

"Right. He just butted his nose into *our* date."

Okay, so maybe Elliot's behavior wasn't the best tonight, but that doesn't automatically make him an asshole. I take another bite of my food and think back to last Friday night when he blew me off for *Michaela*. The sting of his rejection blooms fresh in the pit of my stomach. Doubt creeps into my impression of him. I know him at work. I don't *really* know him socially.

Unfortunately, Liam and I can't find our way back to our carefree, easygoing beginning. It's just as well. There weren't any sparks, and I've gotten what I need as far as a report for his mom. His manners are respectable.

He pays for our meal, then we walk out of the restaurant together. The air is cold, the ground wet. I breathe in the smell of rain. Liam valet parked while I found a spot around the corner. He doesn't offer to walk me to my car, but that's okay. There are plenty of people around. Hollywood on a Thursday night is always busy, even on a winter night.

"Madison."

I startle and drop my keys inches from my car.

"Sorry," Elliot says. "I didn't mean to scare you."

"What is wrong with you?" I say, spinning around.

Elliot picks up my keys with a sheepish look on his handsome face. I pluck them out of his hand. "Apparently stalker tendencies I didn't know I had."

It's difficult not to smile. He's cute when he's regretful. I'm also secretly flattered. "Now that you know, stop it."

"After you're safely in your car, you got it. I'll never interrupt one of your dates again."

"Thank you." A group of people walks by, laughing and talking. The area is well lit under streetlamps, but evening shadows offer Elliot and me a bit of privacy.

"How did it go?" he asks. "I've got to say a guy who doesn't walk a girl to her car is pretty lame."

"Where's your date?" I retaliate. I'm not usually so combative, but with Elliot I feel like I can let go a little. Say what's on my mind without him thinking less of me or finding fault with my words.

"She's still inside." He tilts his head in the direction of the restaurant.

"What kind of guy does *that*?" Now I sound accusatory. I have no idea what has gotten into me.

"You answer my question first." He smirks. Why is he smirking?

I cross my arms over my chest. "It was fine."

"Just fine?"

"It would have been a lot better if you hadn't shown up."

He shows off all his perfect white teeth "I know I'm better looking, but the guy seemed all right."

"You're impossible."

"You're beautiful and the guy's an idiot."

I've blushed more these past few weeks than I have in my entire life. He isn't supposed to say things like that. "Elliot."

"What? I'm just speaking as a friend." His gaze dips to my mouth, making my lips tingle. "As far as Phoebe goes, she's inside because a couple friends of hers showed up and she wanted to stay to hang out with them. I've got to be in the office early so figured I'd call it a night."

"And check on me."

"A happy coincidence."

We both know it's more than that, but it's safer not to think that way. We can't complicate our working relationship any more than it already is. "I should go." I motion over my shoulder with my keys.

"I am sorry if my interference did more harm than good."

"Why would it be good?"

He waves away my question. "It doesn't matter."

Frustrated that he always seems to want to direct our

conversations, I spill what's been sitting in the back of my mind. "You know how Liam asked if he knew you from somewhere? He remembered where. You dated his sister. You never met in person, but I guess he saw pictures of you with her."

His thick brows furrow. "What's his last name?"

"Jacobson. His sister's name was—"

"Lisbeth," he says, like the word hurts to say. Huh?

"Liam called you a couple of very unfriendly names and said you broke her heart."

Elliot's strong jaw clenches. "And you believed him?" Without warning, giant raindrops spill down from the sky.

"Why wouldn't I?" I ask.

The rain falls harder. "Get in the car." Elliot hurries to open my door, jogs around the hood to open the passenger door, and climbs inside.

His dark-blue shirt clings to his shoulders and chest. He runs his hands down his pant legs. You know the saying *clothes shouldn't wear a man. The man should wear the clothes*? This applies to Elliot. He's always impeccably dressed, his slacks and dress shirts fitting him in a classy, sexy way.

I lean back against my seat. He takes up all the space in the small confines of my car, and unfamiliar urges, like climbing onto his lap and rubbing against him, fill my head.

"So, Claire is one of the moms who hired you to spy on her son," he says, completely toneless.

I turn my head toward him. He's watching the rain slide down the windshield. "You dated Lisbeth long enough to meet her mom?"

"We were together for about nine months, and I didn't break her heart, she broke mine."

"What?"

"She cheated on me with her high school boyfriend. I think they're still together."

Rain *pitter-patters* on the rooftop, the loud taps gaining frequency. I don't know what to say. I can't believe Elliot knows what it feels like to be cheated on. My skin prickles with sympathy and shared understanding. Lisbeth is a rotten, horrible person.

He shrugs.

"Why did Liam say what he said then?"

"Because she told everyone I broke up with her so she wouldn't have to admit the truth. Claire thinks she has perfect children and no way was Lisbeth going to change her mom's perception. Our close friends knew the truth, but everyone else made me the asshole who dumped her."

I wonder if he loved her and if they'd still be a couple today if she hadn't cheated on him. "I'm sorry that happened to you."

He rolls his head to the side to look at me. "I'm over it. What about you?"

"What about me?"

"Are you over it?"

I drop my gaze. "I think our situations are very different." I dated Henry for seven years. I was loyal to a fault. Trusted him when I shouldn't have. Believed in him when he lied right to my face. Loved him when I should have known better. I'm not sure I'll trust someone fully ever again. But if that's the case, then I'll never be over it. A familiar knot anchors itself in the back of my throat. I will never be that gullible again.

Elliot lifts my chin, his touch gentle. "You're right, and I shouldn't have asked. Let's strike it from the record."

"The record?" A tiny smile plays at the corner of my mouth.

He concentrates his attention there, on my lips, and once again they feel like I've eaten something hot and spicy. I can't help but stare back at how beautifully his top lip lines up against his fuller lower lip. I bet he kisses like an expert—takes charge, doesn't hold back, and leaves a woman completely satisfied.

"You don't know this about me yet, but along with my incredible good looks and charming personality, I have a photographic memory."

"Really? There's room inside that cocky head of yours?"

"It's a little crowded sometimes, but nothing I can't handle." He trails a finger over my shoulder and down my arm to my elbow. It's electrifying, even through the soft cotton of my sweater dress. I shiver.

What would happen if I kissed him? Just once. Just inside this car with the rain shrouding us in secrecy. No one knows the two of us are together right now. He's teaching me so much at work, maybe he could teach me what it feels like to have my mouth possessed. Henry never kissed me like he was starving for a taste.

Handle me, I want to say. Then we can strike that from the record, too.

Instead I whisper, "The rain has stopped," because deep in my core I'm still the respectable girl who knows right from wrong and never takes a risk.

"I should walk to my car then."

"You should."

"Off the record," he says, something dark and hungry in his eyes. "If things were different, I'd fuck you in the back seat of this car so good you'd still feel it tomorrow."

My jaw drops at the same time I throb between my legs and my nipples tighten.

"Good night, Madison." He hops out of the car without waiting for me to respond. I watch him through the droplets trickling down the windows, my body more turned on than it's ever been before. I can't believe he said that to me. Worse, I like his dirty mouth and my body's response to his announcement. I close my eyes and imagine him lifting my dress, tearing my panties off, and thrusting inside me. The sound of a car honking breaks the spell. *Thank you, Hollywood traffic.* Thoughts like that are dangerous and foolish.

• • •

The next morning the first thing I do when I get to the office is write him another note.

Mr. Sax,

You really should consider hiring a personal shopper if you want to maintain a professional image. The pants and shirts you wear are basic and ill fitting. Compared to other businessmen I've worked for, I'd call them cheap. Just a suggestion, since it seems image is important to you.

Sincerely,
Miss Hastings

For the rest of the day, he barely spares me a glance.

"Even before I met you I was far from indifferent to you."
— Oscar Wilde

Sax/Hastings
Workplace Strategy
Scorecard

Sax – 0
Hastings – 2

Chapter Eight

ELLIOT

Fucking Monday. And I don't mean that in a put-my-dick-to-good-use way. Arguably the worst day of the week, today I can't seem to get my act together at all. It took me thirty minutes to get dressed this morning. Thirty damn minutes. I never deliberate that long on my attire. I pick a pair of pants and a dress shirt and I'm done. My clothes are expensive, well-made pieces from top designers. Cheap and ill fitting, my ass. Madison's full of bullshit again. Nevertheless, I barely spoke to her on Friday.

Not entirely because of her well-done strategy to piss me off. I never should have said what I said to her in her car Thursday night. I took a friend moment and turned it into something else. Something selfish because I couldn't keep my thoughts to myself. All my hesitations—*she's a sweet girl, don't corrupt her, she deserves more, Mateo will beat the shit out of me*—flew out the window when her feminine scent and unassuming sexiness surrounded me inside the car. So I kept to myself the next day like a dog with his tail between his legs. Which is something I have never done before. She didn't seem to mind, and of course did the right thing with her note. Which only fueled my disgust with myself. She's a fantastic assistant and I don't want to jeopardize that.

This isn't the first time trouble has tempted me. I made a habit of it throughout my childhood. Acting out was the best way to get attention from my parents. It got worse in high school, when home runs and perfect grades were overlooked because of something my brother or sister did better. Let's just say my sleepover at the police station is something my parents will never forget.

I'm not sure who I'm competing against in the case of Madison, though. Thursday night it was obviously Liam, but here at work? Sure, I've noticed some of the guys checking her out, but coworkers are off-limits, so I need to chill.

And get laid. It's been a few months, which is probably the reason I'm thinking with my dick so much.

I look up from the mess of papers on my desk, unable to focus. Madison is currently working on some cash flow spreadsheets I asked her to proofread. She looks really pretty today in a simple burgundy cotton dress and a tan long, slouchy cardigan. Her pointy-toe pumps are classic stiletto. Her hair falls in loose waves down her back. As usual, we discussed the day's agenda earlier, and her smiles and good nature should have set me at ease. Not turned me on.

Fuck.

It's time to call up some self-control and concentrate on the most important thing in my life: this job. To do it well, I need a kick-ass assistant and now that I've got one, no blowing it by lusting after her. Her connection in Indonesia is proving invaluable, and James is thrilled with our preliminary research. I couldn't do this special project without her, and I imagine it won't be the last time my financial skills alone won't be enough.

I put my head back down and get to work.

"Hey." James strides into my office a few minutes later, offering a welcome distraction. "I need a favor."

"You got it." Whatever it is, I'm happy to help.

"I've got a flight to Seattle in two hours for a dinner meeting and I need you to go in my place. The preschool just called. Riley's got a hundred and two fever so I'm going to go pick her up and take her home. Work the rest of the day from there."

"No problem. I hope she feels better."

"Thanks. Auggie will email you all the details." He turns to go. "Oh, and take Madison with you."

I'm about to ask why Madison needs to accompany me, but James is already halfway out the door. "Thanks again. I appreciate it," he says.

A new email pings on my computer. It's from Auggie and she's cc'd Madison. Dinner is with one of our largest shareholders, Joaquin Santos. James is diligent about keeping our investors informed, traveling often to meet with them face-to-face because that's the kind of man he is. Two plane tickets have been transferred to Madison and me, and we leave for the airport in fifteen. Our return flight is for ten o'clock tonight.

I clean up my desk, then grab the extra sports coat I leave in the office for emergencies like this. As I do so, Auggie is talking to Madison and I can't help but overhear. "He's young and gorgeous," Auggie says. "I asked James if I could still go, but he said no. Be sure to ask Joaquin how he thinks the Mariners are going to do this season. He'll love you for the rest of dinner after that. He's single, too, so you never know…" She trails off like our investor is potential boyfriend material. I think not.

"*Ahem.*" I clear my throat.

Auggie spins around. "Hi. Here you go." She hands me our itinerary. "There's a shuttle waiting for you downstairs. Mr. Santos is expecting you both at his rooftop restaurant at five. I've got a car picking you up at the airport to take you there and then back to the airport after dinner, so you're all set. Have a good trip."

"Thanks, Auggie." She nods and returns to her desk. "You ready?" I ask Madison.

She looks a little shell-shocked, so I add, "Things sometimes happen quickly around here. Is it okay for you to be gone until late tonight?"

"Yes." She picks up her purse and a notebook. "I'm good."

"You sure?"

"Uh-huh." She's not, but I'm not sure why that is.

With typical L.A. traffic, we get to LAX with barely a minute to spare before we're boarding our first-class flight. I offer Madison the window or aisle seat. She takes the window and looks out at the rain. It's been coming down for days and the forecast calls for more of the same.

"You're unusually quiet," I say.

She slumps back against her seat. "I know. It's because I'm a little worried."

"About the meeting?"

"No, it's not that." She tilts her head to the side to make eye contact for the first time since we left the office. "I'm not the best flyer. I'm not afraid, I just have really bad motion sickness and with the weather the way it is, I hope we don't hit a lot of turbulence."

I wave my hand to catch the flight attendant's attention and ask if there's any medication on board to help Madison. There isn't, but the attendant brings her some crackers and an extra airsickness bag.

She covers her face with her hands. "This is so embarrassing."

Hardly. I take her hand and lace our fingers together. Her skin is soft, delicate, in stark contrast to my much larger palm. "No. Embarrassing is when you push open a glass door but it's a pull-open, so you slam your forehead against the glass, which leaves a big red mark, and you have an important meeting in five minutes."

"Oh no. That really happened to you?"

"No. I'm sharing for a friend," I tease.

She swats me in the chest with her free hand. "Jerk."

"Worth it to see you smile." I'm pretty sure I'd do a lot of humiliating things to see her pretty mouth turn up in the corners.

The plane gives a slight jolt as it backs away from the terminal. She squeezes my hand, then slips it free. "Thanks."

I watch her gather her sweater closer to her chest and shut her eyes, a sort of Zen-like quality coming over her. I've got no problem with any kind of motion sickness, but I'm guessing she's concentrating on not getting sick.

"I feel you staring," she says.

It's hard not to. She's achingly appealing even when not feeling her best. "Sorry, but there's nothing else interesting to look at."

"Elliot."

"Okay. Okay." I grab the airline magazine to read. Once we're in the air, the plane at cruising altitude, I venture to start a conversation. Whenever my family traveled, my siblings and I would play true or false to kill the time. We'd take turns looking stuff up on our mom's phone or in the flight magazine if flying, and keep score, and I remember all the useless stuff we talked about. "True or false. When hippos are angry, their sweat turns red."

"False," she answers, barely moving a muscle.

"Correct. Hippos don't sweat. They secrete a natural substance that turns red-orange. True or False? Pteronophobia is a fear of birds."

She cracks a smile. "Is this the kind of travel game you played as a kid or something?"

"Yes. You have a better one?"

"No. And I like this one." Her eyes are still closed, but I can see her thinking. "I'm going to say true based on my limited knowledge of pterodactyls and how scary they were."

"Minus one point for Miss Hastings. It's a fear of being tickled by feathers."

Her lashes flutter until I'm hit with brilliant blue. "That cannot be true. Feathers feel good when they tickle your skin."

And now I want to run a feather over her skin to see her reaction. "Cross my heart." I make an *X* over my chest with my finger. "Another ridiculous fear is cherophobia."

"Fear of those very scary angels known as cherubs?"

I laugh. "Nice try, but that one is a fear of happiness."

"*What?* People are afraid of happiness?" She scoots up to sit taller. "That is completely fatuous."

"Tossing out the big words, huh? I like it."

"Figured I should keep up with your phobias."

"The only difference is I know what fatuous means." I lean closer so I can whisper in her ear. "It means absurd, and I agree with you."

She wiggles her shoulder and tilts her head like my breath tickled her neck. I love that I have that effect on her. "Your head is full of all this useless knowledge, too, huh?"

I ignore the slight because not many people besides my roommates poke fun at me and I like that she feels comfortable enough to do it. I tap the side of my forehead. "Can't stop the photographic memory. I listen to a lot of NPR when I'm in the car, too. Where does your extra knowledge come from?"

"*Jeopardy!*" She purses her lips together like she wishes she could slip the word back inside her mouth.

"Is there something wrong with that?" I ask, amused.

"Yeeesss," she laments. "How many twenty-four-year-olds do you know who watch that show? I'll tell you how many. One. Me. Because I live with my parents, and they watch it every night and insist I sit with them, too, so I do, and I learn things, but how boring and awkward is my life that I'm more familiar with a silver-haired, TV-show host than guys my age." She lets out a breath that is adorable after that long-winded explanation.

"You haven't watched it every night the past few weeks. I know for a fact your boss kept you late at work several times."

"Yeah, he can be very demanding sometimes."

"You have no idea." My mind immediately dives to the gutter. The things I'd demand from her in the bedroom… minimum two orgasms at a time.

"Anyway," she says, darting her eyes to the industrial-carpeted floor, "tell me about the investor we're meeting and what you'd like me to do."

We talk business for the next hour, moving beyond dinner tonight to the coming weeks. Madison has a thirst for knowledge and preparedness that rivals my own. Since we've started working together I've seen a side to her I had no idea was there. I'm not sure she knew it was, either, her ex having relegated her to planning their wedding and nothing more. Now that she has the opportunity to explore this part of her personality, the last thing I want is to stifle it. She could very well be in my shoes in a couple of years.

"Crap," she says, gripping the arms of her seat when a patch of turbulence tosses the plane around. She closes her eyes. Fine lines crease her forehead in concentration. The unstable air doesn't let up and when we start our descent, Madison turns a few shades paler than normal.

"What can I do?"

"Nothing."

A swallow works its way down her throat. The plane dips.

Whatever color was left in her cheeks wanes. She quickly grabs the airsick bag and leans forward with her face in it. I gather her hair and hold it behind her neck. It's softer than I imagined. Smells heavenly, too, like strawberries and mint. She cuts me a brief, appreciative side-glance.

The pilot comes on the loudspeaker to let us know things will be bumpy and to keep our seat belts securely fastened. Apparently we've flown into a larger storm than the one we left behind. When the plane sinks, then bobs back up, Madison loses the battle.

I secure her hair with one hand and rub her back with the other. She vomits a few times before sealing the bag and sitting up. The flight attendant brings her a warm cloth to wipe her mouth, in exchange for the bag. "Thank you," Madison says. I can tell by the sound of her voice she still doesn't feel well.

My assumption is confirmed when she grabs the other airsick bag to keep under her chin. "Just in case," she says to me as she hands the flight attendant the used towel. I lift the armrest between us and wrap my arm around her shoulders. She readily leans closer until her head is resting on my chest.

"Sorry," she whispers.

"You have nothing to be sorry for."

"I'm just gonna stay right here if that's okay."

"It's more than okay." She fits under my arm more comfortably than is wise, but I can mentally run through accounts and market analysis to keep my mind off the fit of her soft, warm body against my harder one.

After the wheels touch down and the plane slows, she lifts away from me. "I am so glad that's over," she says.

"Feeling better?" Her complexion is still sallow even though her mood is brighter.

"I'm a little nauseated, but once we're off the plane and I grab a Sprite, I'll be fine. I'd also like to stop and buy a toothbrush and toothpaste."

"We can do that."

She looks at me with genuine gratitude. "Thanks for not being grossed out and holding me. It helped."

"Why do I get the feeling that makes me unique?"

"Because it does." She angles herself against the window, her attention outside. "It's raining pretty hard."

Her change in topic makes me think there is no limit to her ex's offenses. I watch over her shoulder as we taxi to our gate. Once the plane comes to a complete stop, we unclick our seat belts.

"You're different than I thought you'd be," Madison says softly as we stand to disembark. She passes me to exit single file.

I'm not sure what that says about how she used to think of me, but it doesn't matter. We've formed a nice partnership, and I plan to nurture it rather than take advantage of it. A good assistant—and good friend—is hard to find so I'm hanging on to this one.

We get to the restaurant right on time, with Madison feeling much better. She giggles when her stomach growls loud enough for the both of us to hear.

"Elliot, it's good to meet you," Joaquin says when we reach his table. His handshake is firm but considerably friendly for a man who garners quite a bit of unwanted attention in the local media. Last year he was voted Seattle's Most Eligible Bachelor or something like that.

"Likewise. This is my assistant, Madison Hastings."

"It's a pleasure," he says, taking her hand.

"Thank you. Nice to meet you."

The three of us sit to views of the city. I imagine on a clear evening I'd be able to see for miles. Before we jump into business, Joaquin tells us about Seattle since it's the first time Madison and I have been. When she brings up the Mariners, he talks for a good fifteen minutes about his favorite team. Luckily, I know a thing or two about baseball and we end up betting on who will make it to the World Series. (My vote is the Dodgers.) The meeting continues to go well despite my annoyance that Joaquin can't take his eyes off Madison. He's not being creepy or forward, just appreciating *his* view. That she doesn't seem fazed by the attention is immensely satisfying.

We end the meal on a positive note, Joaquin happy for the personal touch and extending an invitation for us to return for a Mariners game sometime this season.

The wind is howling and it's pouring rain when we get inside the Town Car taking us back to the airport. Madison doesn't say anything, but I can feel her anxiety building over the flight home. I check my phone for the weather. It's pretty much Storm America on the entire west coast. Damn it. I start to slip my phone back into my pocket when I get an update from the airline. Due to unsafe weather conditions, our flight has been canceled. This is excellent news. I think.

"They just canceled our flight."

"Really?"

I show her the alert on my phone. I'm not sure what to make of her silence, but I can't worry about it. I do a fast search for hotels near the airport. If our flight was canceled, that means others are, too, and instead of my main priority being get Madison through our flight home, it's get Madison a warm bed to sleep in tonight.

"What are you doing?" she asks.

"Getting us a hotel." I use my points to make us a reservation for a two-bedroom suite, then let our driver know the change in destination. I'm acting on instinct here. Something Mateo has told me is a good idea when in doubt. The guy is a genius, especially when it comes to relationships. Before he got together with Teague, he worked for the number one radio station in L.A. as the Dating Guy. He gave advice to millions of listeners, so I take his suggestions as gospel.

I could have gotten two separate hotel rooms, but I don't want to let Madison out of my sight. Call me domineering, but I feel responsible for her while we're out of town, and I'm inclined to make this decision. It's foolish. Trust me, I know. This is the wrong move for a hundred reasons.

But it's the right move for one: my sanity.

Or maybe it's insanity. That's probably more accurate.

"You're awfully quiet over there," I say to Madison's profile, her focus out the window as I shoot off an email to Auggie asking her to reschedule our flight when she gets to work in the morning.

"I'm feeling a little queasy."

Shit. She's sick over the idea of staying overnight with me. My ego takes a big hit at that. Am I really that hard for her to be around?

"I'm not great in back seats," she adds.

And my confidence tops the meter again. She's feeling carsick. Not Elliot sick. The ride to dinner was a lot smoother, the rain and traffic lighter. "Hey, Bud," I say to our driver, whose name really is Bud, "we almost there?"

"Five minutes away," he says.

"Hear that, Mads, only a few more minutes."

She nods and adjusts the air conditioning vent. "Could I please get a little air back here?" She closes her eyes when cold air hits her face.

As soon as Bud pulls up to the hotel entrance, I jump out of the car and then open Madison's door. She lets out a breath of relief. With my hand on the small of her back, we walk to the registration desk to check-in. "Hi, the last name is Sax."

"You didn't get me my own room?" Madison whispers in my ear when she hears we've got a suite.

"I did. It's a two bedroom."

She lets out another breath, this one of resignation. We

look each other in the eyes. "We're in friend mode now," I say quietly. The more I get to know her at work, the more I want to be friends with her away from the office, too. She's… interesting and keeps me engaged. Besides Mateo and Levi, I don't have a lot of close personal friends and Madison is nice to be around.

"Okay."

I flash her a grin that says *we've got this*.

I'm not gonna lie. The elevator ride up to our floor is ripe with *Fifty Shades* tension (what? I saw the trailer on TV), and okay, some not-so-friend-like scenarios play in my mind, but after our meeting with Joaquin, I realized once again we're a great team. After only a few weeks, we've learned to have each other's backs. When I faltered on some financial information Joaquin asked about, Madison picked the ball up and made a fucking touchdown, reciting the correct numbers from the cash flow reports she'd proofread this morning.

So, I'm not going to risk the professional magic that is E&M. I'll just jack off in the shower. It won't take long knowing she's right in the next room.

We both practically jump out of the elevator when the doors slide open. I've got to say, Madison *is* handling this like a trouper. She hasn't once complained about our situation or having no change of clothes or other overnight necessities. She's one up on me with a toothbrush and toothpaste, but that's hardly reason for comfort.

I push open the door to our suite and allow her entrance first. We flip on lights and check out the common areas. It's weird not having any luggage to take into a bedroom, so we both stand there, looking at each other with uncertainty. "How are you feeling?" I ask. "I can grab you a Sprite from the vending machine, or order something from room service."

"I'm much better, but I wouldn't mind something from room service." She plops down on the couch, grabs the leather-bound menu on the coffee table, and uses her free hand to slide off her heels.

I sit across from her and slip off my sports coat, grateful the doubt from a minute ago is gone.

"Weirdly, I'm kind of hungry for something sweet," she says, flipping through pages.

I bet you taste sweet.

Did I not give myself a mental talking to just five minutes ago? Jesus.

She could taste like the best cheesecake ever and you are not getting a taste, buddy. She's in the friends-and-coworkers zone and that zone is banned from your pleasure.

"Will you share a piece of cheesecake with me?"

She's killing me. "That's like asking a bear if he'll share some honey."

She looks up from the menu. "Cheesecake it is then. Coffee sound good, too?" She leans over to pick up the telephone on the side table.

"Sure." At this point, I'll be up all night trying not to think about her, so I may as well relax with some caffeine.

"It should be here in fifteen minutes," she says, hanging up the phone and getting to her feet. I notice her toes are painted red. "Do you want to pick a bedroom? I need to use the bathroom."

"Your choice."

"Okay." She dangles her shoes from her fingers and tucks her purse against her side. "I'll be back out in a few."

I busy myself on my phone, checking sports scores and CNN. When Madison returns she's wearing one of the hotel's plush white robes. The material falls below her knees, so I have no idea if she's wearing anything underneath it.

Which means I'm left to wonder.

And fantasize about eating cheesecake off her stomach.

Think she'd let me?

Chapter Nine

MADISON

Elliot's eyes rake over my body like I'm wearing lingerie, not a thick robe that hides almost every inch of my skin. When he looks at me like that, it's extremely hard to pretend being near him is easy. I'm not sure he realizes the effect he has on me, or even if his focus makes me special. Maybe I'm one of a hundred girls dressed like this he'd find attractive.

The last time I wore this kind of fluffy robe I was with Henry. We'd flown to New York for a friends' wedding. I pictured it being a romantic weekend getaway, but he barely noticed me. A couple of hours before the ceremony, I'd showered, shaved my legs, put strawberry-scented lotion on, and sauntered out of the bathroom ready to drop the thick terry cover-up to the floor and show him the tiny landing strip my hairdresser had convinced me to get, only to find him so engrossed in his phone he didn't spare me a glance or flirty word. I'd stood there for five solid minutes. No joke.

So the appreciation in Elliot's piercing blue eyes is nice.

It's what I was hoping for when I decided to change out of my work clothes. My skirt was tight and my blouse reminded me of throwing up on the airplane, and with nothing else to change into, I wanted to get comfortable. Do I wish I was bold enough to drop the robe and see what Elliot would do next? Yes. But our working relationship prohibits any kind of physical intimacy.

Look, but don't touch, our motto.

And by look, I don't mean his tight butt or athlete's shoulders or cheekbones that make my legs feel useless. Because those attributes are serious grounds for throwing caution aside and welcoming trouble.

I've never been in that kind of trouble. Sexy will-I-regret-it-in-the-morning-my-body-is-on-fire-and-only-you-can-put-it-out-trouble. Actually, the fire part happened the other night in my car, but let's not go there.

I flop down on the couch across from him, prepared to ignore all his good qualities. That he's also charming, caring, and well mannered is a real pain in the butt. He held my hair for me while I threw up, for gosh sakes. Then folded an arm around me. And it helped. With the side of my head pressed to his chest, I concentrated on the beat of his heart instead of the churning in my stomach. If I were asked to send a report to his mom, he'd get an A-plus.

He drops his phone next to him like it's hot. "Are you naked under there?"

Oh my God. That's the first thing he says to me? A mini-flame springs up in my belly. And a little voice in the back of my mind says, *pick trouble*. "No. I have my bra and panties on, not that it's any concern of yours."

"I'm a guy. Undergarments always interest me. Do they match?"

"Wouldn't you like to know," I flirt back.

He wields a slow, self-assured smile that is dazzling. "I

think—no, I know—they do."

The air around me heats up by a million degrees. His attention is like two laser beams, and so help me, I want to cool down by taking the robe off and showing him what's underneath.

"How do you know that?"

"Being the good friend that I am, I can tell by the way you dress that you're not a mismatched underwear kind of girl." He's sitting slightly slouched with his arms stretched wide over the back of the couch, his legs spread, the top two buttons of his shirt undone. The casual pose might be the sexiest thing I've ever seen.

"So?" he prompts when I fail to answer right away. "Should we bet that I'm right?"

"I'm not betting with you on this."

"There's my answer." His expression is smug. And sexy, damn him.

"I *may* like to match underneath my clothes." I absolutely do. I'm kind of anal about it, in fact. With my new self-imposed budget, I've found lots of cute sets shopping at discount clothing stores.

He smiles, proud of himself. "You should probably give me a peek to confirm."

"I should, huh? You know, just because we're in a hotel room in another state from where we work, we're still technically on a business trip."

"I'd argue we're off the clock."

"I suppose that's true." I'm being coy on purpose now, enjoying the sexual tension between us. I've never felt anticipation like this before.

"And I'm making it my *personal* business to put my mind at rest."

"What does that mean?"

"It means I *need* to know what color they are, Mads."

I like that he's the first person to call me Mads. I'm Maddy or Mad or Madison Michelle when my mom feels like using my middle name. "I can just tell you."

"Not the same."

"True, but…" If we do this, things won't be the same between us. Reality trespasses on the fantasy of Elliot and me. Come tomorrow, we're back at work.

"But what?"

"What are we doing, Elliot?"

"I don't know. Not what we originally agreed on. But we're not on the clock tonight and my curiosity is killing me."

His interest is flattering and exciting, but if we're not completely certain…I notice a pad of paper and pen next to the telephone on the side table. I reach over to pick them up.

"What are you doing?" he asks.

"Writing you a note."

"Oh no you don't." He snakes the paper and pen right out of my hands, then falls back onto the couch. "You're two up on me already. It's my turn." He scrawls something down, rips the sheet off the pad, and slaps it down on the coffee table for me to read.

Miss Hastings,

I suspect the heart of a risk-taker beats underneath your whip-smart attitude. But in the competitive world of financial management, you also need to be fearless. Perhaps we should discuss your qualifications for this field and brainstorm other job possibilities.

Sincerely,
Mr. Sax

I read the note a second a time. The goal is to make me

angry, and it does. *I'm fearless. I left my douchedog fiancé at the altar, didn't I?* But the flip side this time is Elliot is hoping to make me mad enough to show him my lingerie. Which means our strategy in this situation is a no-win. Well, I guess Elliot would win. Mr. Smarty-pants.

You would, too. I knew I'd get a reaction from him if I came out in just the robe, but there's no going back if things escalate between us. Am I truly ready for that?

"Hmm...I did think about going to design school for a while. And I've made a few of my handbags. Maybe I should start my own line of lingerie. I could call it Madison's *Secret*."

Elliot holds his face in his hand, his palm covering his mouth. He rubs his fingers over his lips, then drops his arm. "Fine. Just tell me then."

I raise my eyebrows. It's hard not to chuckle at his cute disappointment.

"Clearly, I need to work on my note-writing skills."

There's a knock on the door. *Room service.*

Elliot doesn't wait for me to answer him. He stands and goes to receive our food (I only look at his ass for two seconds. Maybe five. But that's it, I swear.) He tips the server, carries the tray back, and puts it down on the coffee table. Rather than sitting where he was, he situates himself next to me, his thigh brushing mine.

A shudder moves through me. I'm pretty sure he notices, because he gives me a look that says *I feel you and want to feel underneath your robe, too.* Or maybe that's my overactive imagination talking. I've never been starved for sex before, but I'm pretty sure that's what's happening here. For the millionth time, though, I remind myself of how much I love my job, and that means getting involved with Elliot *would* be a mistake.

He pours us each a cup of coffee, adding a little cream to his and remembering that I like cream and sugar in mine. "So design, but not art," he says.

I'm glad for the safer topic, even if a little disappointed our flirting is over. "They kind of go hand in hand."

"I guess." He passes me the plate of cheesecake. "You could still do it."

I cut into the creamy dessert goodness. "Are you trying to get rid of me?"

"How about for a week? You quit. I do unspeakable things to your body for seven days. Then you have a change of heart and return. And being the gracious boss that I am, I take you back."

I choke down a bite of cheesecake. The flirt is back. "Are you insane? That is the worst idea in the history of ideas." My nipples think otherwise, ready to punch holes through my bra, but I ignore them.

"Figured it was worth a shot."

"You keep teasing me, but we both know you won't really break the rules." I offer him the cheesecake so he can have a bite.

He puts the plate down on the coffee table instead. Then he dips a finger into the cream cheese, coating his long forefinger from tip to knuckle. He moves so fast after that, I don't have time to resist. Not that I would have. With one arm around my middle, he lifts me onto his lap until I'm straddling him.

I gasp or squeak or make some such surprised sound. My robe gapes open. Not a lot, but enough to reveal a hint of cleavage. His eyes dart there before bouncing back to my face. I'd be lying if I said I didn't like exactly where I was.

"I've broken a lot of rules," he says, his voice deep, authoritative. "Not so much anymore, but if there's something I really want, something that's too hard to resist, a rule isn't going to stop me." He puts the pad of his cheesecake finger at the base of my throat. "Mind?"

I shake my head "no," too stunned to say anything. Plus, in all honesty, I don't want to ruin this moment of sheer electricity.

Slowly, so, so slowly, he skims his finger down the center of my chest. I feel the sticky dessert on my skin like it's radioactive. "I've done some things I'm not proud of. Things I would have done differently. Yet, I wouldn't undo any of them." His finger stops at the top of the valley between my breasts. The robe is almost open enough to expose the lace of my pale-blue bra.

Don't stop! Keep going. Touch me there. I pull my shoulders back, only a fraction, because this might feel right between friends, but it's also wrong between coworkers.

He lifts his finger, brings it to my mouth. I part my lips. It's involuntary. Necessary. Like breathing. Am I still breathing?

"Something tells me breaking a rule with you, though…" He slips his finger inside my mouth and I instinctively suck.

The hand he has on my waist tightens. He lets out a tiny sound—a groan he's helpless to hold back, I think. "Jesus," he mutters between clenched teeth. "Suck it harder."

I wrap my hand around his wrist so I can control the suction. I lick and suck, enjoying the way his eyes sparkle as they watch me do something I've never done before.

When his finger is clean, he withdraws it. "Can I taste now?"

"Yes," I whisper. I want his mouth on me so badly, I'll worry about the consequences later.

He bends his head and licks the cream cheese off my neck.

Great balls of fire, his tongue is on me. It's thrilling. My body is pulsing like crazy.

"Mmm. Sweet. Delicious. So damn good." He presses those words against my flesh, imprinting them on me. I'll remember this moment for as long as I live. His tiny declaration is what I need right now. A reminder that *I am* those things. It's not just the dessert.

He kisses down my chest, each brush of his lips igniting a thousand tingles. I don't want these sensations to end. His leisurely pace is killing me in the best possible way. I wiggle in his lap, then freeze. He's hard, his erection like a steel pipe.

Suddenly this is all very real and dangerous in more ways than one. It's not just about us working together. It's about me. I like Elliot. And I'm not the kind of girl to fool around with a guy and then pretend it never happened, or pretend it didn't mean something. He may be experienced at this sort of thing, but I'm not.

"Breaking a rule with me is a bad idea," I say, circling back to what he never finished saying.

He licks the last bit of cheesecake and then lifts his head. "No doubt, light blue."

My pounding heart skitters to a halt. My shoulders sag. "You did all this to see what color my bra was?"

"I had to do something."

"You are such a jerk!" I scramble off his lap, gripping the collar of my robe so it stays tightly closed.

He shrugs like it's no big deal. "It's not like you didn't enjoy yourself."

I seethe. "I seriously want to punch you right now. That doesn't make it okay. You used me, Elliot."

He has the decency to blanche at that. "I—"

"I don't care." I pick up the cheesecake and my coffee. "I don't want to be around you anymore. Good night." I storm off into my room, shut and lock the door. I can't believe what a total ass he was out there. Guys suck.

I settle onto the king-size bed, fluffing a pillow behind my back. I wish I were home, in my own bed, far away from Elliot. I wish I'd never set foot in ZipMeds.

I wish he'd never talked to me.

Looked at me.

Touched me.

Only none of that is really true. My feelings are hurt, but I'll recover. One thing I've learned from my life so far is I always recover.

And guys suck. That bears repeating.

I'm especially mad at Elliot because on top of being the jerkiest jerk, he has now ruined cheesecake for me. I put the plate down on the bedside table. I will never be able to eat it again without thinking about him. His lips. His tongue. The zings of pleasure that spiraled through me while his mouth connected with my skin.

I sink down, kicking the covers so I can crawl underneath them. I tend to lose my head when I'm with him, but that stops right now. He's my boss, and I've learned a lot from him these past weeks. I plan to learn more. I don't want to rely on anyone for anything, and keeping my job, learning from it, is a big step in the right direction. It's terrible how good-looking Elliot is, but he's also wicked smart and willing to teach me rather than simply ordering me around. So, from here on out, that's where I'll focus. What happened between us tonight is forgotten.

I take that back. I won't forget it. He showed me a side of him I don't like very much. I'll remember the way my heart stopped when his motives were revealed. I've seen him ruthless in business. I should have realized he could be cruel outside of work, too. This shouldn't have been newfound knowledge.

To my credit, there's the unfair look of him. His friendliness. Humor. Concern. I can't forget the way he treated me on the airplane.

Elliot Sax is like a crash course in business and relationships with the opposite sex, and as I try to fall asleep, I puzzle over which will impact me more.

Chapter Ten

ELLIOT

I'm an ass.

I get up from the couch to pace around the suite. Watching Madison stalk away just about killed me, but it's for her own good. I lied about touching her just to see the color of her lingerie. I lied because it was too much. I lied because no way in hell would I have been able to stop if I'd kept going, and Madison deserves more than a quick fuck on a hotel couch. That's how gone I was for her. Ready to bang her and worry about the aftermath later.

Worry about her feelings later.

This is uncharted territory for me. Yes, I've screwed a coworker before, but not anyone I work directly with on a daily basis. Not anyone who wasn't equally experienced and in it for nothing but a quick release. And definitely not when it's against office policy.

Damn, she tasted good. Felt good. Smelled good. She is everything good. An innocent in a new land of work and travel, while I'm anything but.

I press a few fingers to my sternum. Further complicating matters is a rare tugging in my chest. I didn't fucking give my heart permission to get involved.

Too late, asshat. You care about her.

And therein lies my reason for hurting her. We've agreed how important our jobs are and that means even in friend mode, we have to play on opposite sides of the sandbox. I can't park my shovel anywhere near her bucket.

I still owe her an apology for being a dick, though.

"Madison?" I say against her closed bedroom door. When I get no answer, I knock lightly. "Mads?"

She's either asleep or ignoring me. I contemplate trying the handle, then take a step back. It doesn't matter what she is, I shouldn't disturb her. Instead I go back to the couch, pick up my cell, and text Mateo and Levi where I'm at.

They both respond in less than a minute.

Mateo: *Thanks for the update. Don't get any ideas.*

Levi: *Thanks for letting us know. And what ideas? Why don't I know about these ideas?*

I contemplate sending the middle finger emoji, but take too long and Levi texts again.

Levi: *Wait. Are these ideas about Madison? Dude.*

Mateo: *Caught him checking out her ass.*

Levi: *Bad idea, man. She's the best thing to happen to you at work.*

Mateo: *Yep.*

Levi: *Harper will kick your ass if you do something stupid.*

Mateo: *She'll have to get behind me. He knows this, though.*

The texts are popping up one right after the other, so I see no reason to break up their little conversation. The fuckers are probably sitting next to each other at home.

Levi: *What happened to that HR girl? Leave a deposit with her again.*

Mateo: *Good idea. In the meantime, Dick meet Jack.*

Levi: *Twice if necessary.*

Jesus. My best friends are telling me to jack off.

Me: *You done?*

Mateo/Levi: *Yes.*

Me: *Next time I'm not checking in.*

Mateo: *Touchy.*

Me: *Annoyed. I'm going to sleep now.*

Levi: *By sleep you mean…*

Mateo: *Alone, right?*

Me: *Good to know I've got your support, assholes.*

Mateo: *More than you know, asshole.*

Levi: *Brothers from other mothers, asshole.*

That's the truth. We've been best friends for more than a decade, and I know they've got my back. Just like I've always had theirs. I look out the floor-to-ceiling window. Rain pelts the glass, the storm showing no signs of calling it a night.

Me: *How's the weather there?*

Mateo: *Big-ass storm here, too.*

Levi: *It's supposed to let up tomorrow.*

Me: *Okay. Talk then.*

Mateo: *Remember two-foot berth, dude.*

Me: *What happens in Seattle, stays in Seattle.*

I press the home button and toss the phone onto the other couch. I've gotten enough warning, thank you very much. I also have no plans to tell him that two feet is bullshit and I'm no saint. If Madison walked out of her room right now and wanted me, I don't think I could refuse her.

Would my conscience make it difficult to look James in the face afterward? No doubt, yes. With that thought in mind, I drop to the side of the couch and bang out some push-ups. I need to do something to relieve the tension in my muscles, and pushing myself until they burn with exhaustion is about the only way I'm going to get any sleep tonight.

I've counted to forty when I sense Madison's eyes on me. I turn my head and find her standing in the doorway of her room.

"Don't let me stop you," she says.

I do another ten. I could keep showing off, but I'd rather not waste any more time when I could be talking to her. I'm winded when I get to my feet, my muscles tired and my breathing shallow. "Hey."

"Hey."

"I'm sorry for being a jerk."

She lifts a brow as if to say, *for what exactly?*

I deserve that. I acted like a dick on several counts. "I'm sorry for taking advantage of our situation and forgetting myself. I should have left you alone, and I'm really sorry if I hurt your feelings." I've never been more sincere in my life.

"Apology accepted. I'm sorry if I—"

"You don't owe me any apologies, Mads. This is on me. I didn't act like a gentleman, and it won't happen again." I walk to the small kitchen to grab a bottle of water. "Would you like a water?" I ask, pulling one out of the fridge. "There's juice bottles and sports drinks, too."

"Water would be great. Thanks." She takes a seat on the couch.

I do the smart thing and sit across from her.

She twists off the cap and takes a long sip. I watch her throat work, mesmerized by the tiny flex of her smooth skin. I lick my lips, remembering the taste of her and wanting another so badly I ache. "Want to watch a movie?" she asks. "I'm not tired enough to fall asleep."

"Sure." I scramble for the television remote before I let my thoughts get too carried away. Unfortunately the TV is behind me, which means I need to get my ass up and park it next to hers in order to watch anything.

"Elliot."

"Yeah?" I sit as far away from her as I can.

"I don't want things to be weird again."

I settle down and look at her. "I don't, either. Truth, though?"

"Yes, please."

"Weird isn't necessarily a bad thing. It will remind us to keep some distance."

"Okay."

Ten minutes into a romcom she wanted to watch—she hates anything scary or violent—weird disappears and we couldn't sit any closer if we tried. She's snuggled against my side, our feet are on the coffee table, and we're laughing at the same jokes. It's comfortable.

Dangerous.

"In a world full of temporary things, you are a perpetual feeling."
—Sanober Khan

Sax/Hastings
Workplace Strategy
Scorecard

Sax – -1 (need to up my game)
Hastings – 2

Chapter Eleven

MADISON

When I say I don't like scary things, I mean I really, really don't like them. Even those Troll dolls with the neon-colored hair freak me out. Don't even get me started on clowns. (Sorry, clowns. I know you get a bad rap.) Ghost stories? No thank you. And I've never been within a few hundred feet of a haunted house. I'm also terrible with blood. I am not your go-to person if you need bandaging up. My brother tortured me when we were younger by hiding creepy pictures in my homework and playing scary soundtracks from horror movies when we were home alone. He said he kept doing those things to toughen me up. I said he was the meanest brother on the planet.

I'm having similar negative thoughts about my date tonight. When Jesse asked me to meet him at an arcade bar in Hollywood, I thought it sounded like a fun way to spend a Friday night. Right off the bat, he scored points for originality.

He met me outside the nondescript building and led

me inside to a darkly lit blend of childhood fun and adult intoxication. It was different than what I'd pictured, so I was a little nervous. "Let's hit the bar first," he said.

To get to the bar, we walked through a huge selection of games and drunken people. That didn't bother me. What took me by unwelcome surprise were the carnival-like toys peeking out of every nook and cranny. My childhood nightmares came flooding back. Sweat broke out on the back of my neck. I swear the clown doll next to *Ms. Pac-Man* stared at me the entire way across the room. "Jesse?" I said, my voice strained with obvious misery.

He didn't stop. He kept right on walking to the bar like he didn't hear me. Which very well might have been the case with the noise from the various games and '80s background music playing through hidden speakers. "What would you like to drink?" he asked when we reached the blue-lit bar.

"I'm sorry, but do you think we could grab a drink somewhere else?"

"Why?" he asked like I was talking crazy.

Because I'm freaking out. "I feel a little claustrophobic in here."

"Really? This place is over two thousand square feet."

And that brings me to right now. It shouldn't matter how big the building is if I'm uncomfortable. The bartender, a pretty brunette, smiles at him. "Hey, LuLu," he says. "I'll have my usual, and Madison will have…" He lifts an eyebrow at me. It's an impatient arch, not a considerate one. He doesn't understand how much this place gives me the creeps.

If I weren't being paid for this date, I'd turn around and walk out the door. But I owe it to Jesse's mom to stick this out if I can. "Diet Coke, please."

Jesse makes a disappointed face. I smile at him. No way am I taking even a sip of alcohol in this place. I need all my wits about me in order to keep one eye on the creepy decorations to be sure they don't come to life. He motions to a barstool so I sit while he leans against his, his feet on the floor.

"You don't like to drink?"

"I do. Just not feeling it tonight."

He gives me an indifferent shrug. "So you're in finance? That sounds like a fun job," he says full of sarcasm.

"And you're a game designer, so I imagine you have loads of fun."

"Every single day." He looks me up and down a little more closely, his eyes lingering on my chest longer than good manners dictate. I had time to go home and change clothes after work. It finally stopped raining today, but it's chilly, so I have on jeans, a V-neck sweater, and ankle boots. "I design characters for the company I work for. Female assassins primarily."

That he's artistic has me intrigued. "Do you sketch them by hand or are they computer generated?"

"Both."

The bartender delivers our drinks. Jesse's is a dark beer. My Diet Coke has a cherry in it. LuLu winks at me like I'm twelve. Jesse pays for both, then stands and says, "Come on. Let's play."

Classic pinball machines are lined up against one wall. Each has a cup holder for endless alcohol-fueled sessions, I assume. Several people playing the games are using slurred words to express their excitement.

On another wall are video machines like *Mortal Kombat*, *X-Men*, *Donkey Kong*, and *Galaga*. Gameplay seems to be taken more seriously here because the players are quieter. Focused. I've never been a big fan of arcades, mostly because I'm not the best player, but on a few family vacations my brother and I spent some fun hours in the hotel game room.

Jesse leads me to a table version of *Pac-Man* and we sit

across from each other. I'm sure to be ten times worse than normal because my concentration is on keeping my focus off the nightmarish stuffed—oh crap. There's another clown.

I close my eyes for a moment. When I open them, I stare at the video screen. Jesse slips some quarters into the game. He starts first, oblivious to me, my dilemma, and pretty much everything else around us. He's completely engrossed in the game, to the extent that he continues to the next level, and the one after that, and the one after that, before I get a turn. My Pac-Man is gobbled up in less than ten seconds.

"Wow, you suck at this," Jesse says, his tone hard to decipher.

You suck at first dates. "Gee thanks."

"You say that like I'm wrong."

Is he for real right now? "Are you this complimentary to all the girls you meet?"

He leans back in his chair. "What are you saying?"

"I'm saying if you don't have something nice to say, don't say anything at all." Apparently Jesse used up all his friendly words in our messages to each other.

"Here's something"—he leans onto his elbows, blocking the blinking colors of the video game—"you're gorgeous, but the last person I want to be around is someone who can't take a joke." He resumes playing the game. "I was messing with you."

I swallow the emotion threatening my tear ducts. I don't think he was, and that's reason enough to cut our date short.

"I'm going to go." At his nod, I dash out of the building, relieved when cold, fresh air hits my face. I walk slowly to my car, unlock it, and climb inside. The clock on my dashboard reads eight thirty. It's too early to go home. My mom will still be awake and ask for details of my date. She's like a bloodhound whenever I walk through the door, tracking me within seconds even when I've taken off my heels to tiptoe to my bedroom.

"Have a good time tonight," she'd said, catching me on my way out. She pops up out of nowhere when I leave, too.

"Thanks."

"Do you have a jacket?"

"I'll be fine, Mom." I gave her a hug goodbye. She's a great mom. She just likes to be in my business and offer unsolicited advice.

"You know for the evening, you could apply more makeup."

"I know." Much to her chagrin, I did not inherit her love of cosmetics. Mascara and lip gloss and I'm good to go.

"I could help."

I took a calming breath. "I'm good, but thanks."

"Maybe tonight's the night." She's still shaken over my wedding disaster. She had a picture of her daughter in her mind and I ruined it. In a way, she wants me out of the house as much I want to be out, only she envisions me married, while I see only freedom.

Hope, however, is something we could both agree on. "Maybe," I'd said.

"I can't wait to hear all about it."

Which is why when the dashboard clock changes to eight thirty-one, I decide there is one other place I can go. I hope it's not rude to arrive late, but I *was* invited.

On the drive to Mateo's house, I rehearse my speech. *My date was a jerk. End of story.* I'm not much for speeches. Plus, I hate the idea of going into detail about another awful date. Not that I'll be asked for any, since tonight is a celebration for Levi.

I lightly knock on their front door, second-guessing my decision to show up. From the sounds coming from inside the house, the movie has started. I'm already here, though, so when no one answers the door, I decide to try the handle. It's unlocked.

I slip inside. Sure enough, the kite-surfing film Levi worked on in Australia is showing on the flat screen above the fireplace. The glow from the television is the only light in the dark house. There's a small crowd of friends gathered to watch the movie for the first time, and I'm suddenly glad my date sucked. This is a much better place to be.

There's no room left to sit so I lean against the back wall.

"Hey, you made it after all," Elliot whispers, brushing my arm as he joins me. "It just started a few minutes ago. Don't move." He disappears around the corner, then returns with a chair from the kitchen. "Sit."

I smile in thanks. We've been nothing but professional since we got back from Seattle a few days ago. Correction: besides glances that keep us engaged longer than they should, we've been professional. It helped that the week was insanely busy. I've never loved working so much. The days fly by, and I have no trouble falling asleep at night. My brain needs the time off.

We watch the film with the rest of the rapt audience. When it's over, cheers and praise rain down on Levi. Harper hangs onto his arm, soaking up the compliments for her man with a gigantic grin on her face.

The group spreads out, some people keeping to the family room, while others go to the kitchen and the backyard.

"You're here!" Teague says, wrapping me in a hug. "Wait," she says far less enthusiastically. "You're here." Mateo, who's standing beside her, looks at me with his usual kindness. He knew where I was an hour ago, and now I'm here.

I wave away her concern. "The film was amazing. Especially the camera work." I notice Levi and Harper on their way over.

"It was, wasn't it?" Harper beams since I spoke loud enough for them to hear.

"Congratulations," I say to Levi.

"Thanks, Mad. I'm glad you got to see it."

"I think this calls for a round of celebratory shots," Elliot says.

The six of us move into the kitchen where Elliot pours us tequila. "To a future Academy Award–winning cinematographer," Elliot says, raising his glass.

"Here, here," we say before simultaneously tossing our drinks back. The alcohol slides smoothly down my throat.

"I think we need another," I volunteer. "For good luck." And because I've never asked for "another" before. It feels good to be less careful and more carefree.

"Can't argue with that." Elliot pours seconds.

I slam my shot glass down on the counter when finished. With my throat a bit numb from the first drink, this one slid down like honey.

"Excuse us," Harper says, taking Levi's hand and leading him away. I'm pretty sure they're headed toward Levi's bedroom to celebrate by themselves.

"Hey, Madison," the guys' good friend Van says as he walks into the kitchen. He settles next to me at the counter.

"Hi." I hope I'm not blushing. I probably am, though. Van always flusters me. He's gorgeous, and I've never been able to string more than a few words together when I'm around him.

"How's it going?"

"Good."

He smiles. He knows the effect he has on women. "What's new?"

"Dude," Elliot says, "what's with all the questions?"

"Ignore him," Van says. "He's jealous you'd rather talk to me than him."

I nervous giggle. Van is a total ladies' man with a long line of females wanting his attention, and here I am, not wanting it at all. To make it worse, a couple of people come into the kitchen and grab Mateo's and Teague's attention.

Elliot's phone rings. He pulls it out of his pocket. "I get to talk to her all week, have at it."

"What do you mean?" Van asks.

"Shit. I have to take this." Elliot steps out of the kitchen. "Hello?"

"What does he mean?" Van casts his movie-star eyes on me.

"We work together," I say.

"I didn't know that. I'm so sorry," he teases.

I laugh this time. "It's actually great."

"You know you don't have to say that when he's not in the room, right?" Van jokes.

Usually when I'm around the guys it's all of them and I can keep quiet during their banter, so with Van's undivided attention, I get even more nervous.

"I know," I squeak out.

"Huh," he says. I have no idea what kind of "huh" it is. "Shot?"

"Yes, please." I push my shot glass over to him.

He pours us each a couple inches of liquid gold and then we down them. Okay, so that probably was one shot too many, because all of a sudden, my head fills with butterflies.

A hand wraps around my waist. Warm breath tickles the side of my neck. It's not Van. I know it's not. "Can I see you for a minute?" Elliot whispers in my ear.

"Sure."

"I need to talk to her," he says to Van. Without waiting for a reply, he takes my hand, leads me down the hallway, and steers me inside his bedroom. "Sorry. I hope it's okay I dragged you away." He jams a hand through his hair as he closes the door.

"Is everything okay?"

He pulls the chair out from his desk and motions for me to sit. He rests his very fine ass on the side of his bed. There are only inches keeping our knees from touching.

"I was wondering if you would do me a favor?"

"Of course. Anything." Tequila = agreeable Madison.

"You might not be so inclined once you hear what it is," he says seriously.

"Do I have to steal something?"

He smiles. "No."

"Kill anyone?"

His smile grows wider. "No."

"Harm an animal?"

"Absolutely not."

"Then I'd say we're good. What is it?"

He drops his elbows onto his knees. "You'll probably think it's ridiculous." This is a new side to Elliot, one I'm not sure what to make of. He's not nervous, per se, but stressed out. I've seen him at work juggling multiple financial tasks and he's always calm, confident. He's neither of those things now.

I think about reaching out to comfort him, but I don't. Because it's then that it hits me where I am. We're alone in his bedroom. I take a quick peek around. It's neater than mine, clean, with a bed, desk, dresser, and, be still my heart... "You have a kitten?"

Elliot looks over at the tiny ball of black-and-white fluff curled up on a pet pillow in the corner. "As of three days ago, yeah. She showed up and won't leave."

"I can't believe you didn't mention it."

"We're not talking about personal stuff at work."

"Oh. Right." I look everywhere but at him. "Have you named her?"

"No. I keep thinking someone's going to show up to claim her or I'm going to see a sign posted with LOST CAT and her picture."

How cute is he right now? He's worried he'll get too attached, not that he'd admit it. "She picked you over Mateo and Levi, huh?"

"I am the best looking."

"Says you." And me. Thankfully, tequila does not = *gush over your boss out loud*. I watch the kitten, hoping she'll wake up so I can hold her.

"Back to why I brought you in here." Our eyes meet, and for a quick minute, I allow myself to imagine he brought me in here to strip me naked and do very bad things to me in bed, in the shower, against the wall...you know, wherever he wants.

"Yes?" God, I hope that sounded like a question and not permission.

"My parents are having brunch at their house on Sunday and I was hoping you'd go with me."

I rub my forehead. I didn't hear him right.

"You heard me right." *Gads*, it's crazy how we do that sometimes. "I just need a friend, Mads, nothing else." He says this with warmth and reverence, like I win the Most Valuable Friend award.

Lately, I've needed my friends much more than they've needed me, so this is a nice change. "Not as your date or anything? Just to clarify."

"Correct. The truth is I don't need to bring anybody, but I've avoided going over there for the past few weeks, and my mom basically just called to put me on the ultimate guilt trip, so I have to."

"You avoid your family?" My heart aches a little at that. My family means the world to me even when they drive me crazy.

"Sometimes, yes." He stands and paces around the room. "They don't expect me to arrive with anybody. I just...I'd like someone on my side for once. Will you come? Brunch is at eleven and we'll be there for two hours tops." He stops moving to look at me.

There's a lot he's not saying, but it doesn't matter. I'm happy to play whatever part he wants me to. "Yes, I'll go."

Chapter Twelve

Elliot

Madison baked banana bread. The girl not only looks hot as fuck every day, has a voice like a sexy angel, and a brain like a Wall Street banker, but she also *bakes*. I promised myself after I saw the hurt in her eyes, when I acted like an asshole in Seattle, that I wouldn't touch her like that again. But how the hell am I supposed to keep my hands off her now?

I love banana bread.

You love your job more. I need to stamp that on her ass or something.

The bread smells amazing—almost as good as her. We're in the car, a few blocks from my parents' house. She's holding a covered plate in her lap like it's a life preserver, and I can't say I blame her. I'm not at all sure this is a good idea. I just know having her with me today makes seeing my family infinitely easier.

I park in front of my childhood home. The two-story Bel Air mansion blends into the mountain and trees, giving it more privacy than some of the other houses. "Thanks again for coming with me."

"Would you please stop thanking me? I'm happy to be here."

"You sure? You've been white-knuckling that plate since you got in the car."

"I guess I'm a little nervous about meeting your family. I know it's not a big deal, but it kind of is at the same time."

Madison likes to make a good impression. She doesn't realize she couldn't make a bad one if she tried.

"I get it." I hurry around to her side of the car and open the door to help her out. "But you've nothing to worry about, okay? I think you're amazing and that's all that matters."

She casts her eyes downward, avoiding my compliment. That's for the best. Sometimes I can't keep my thoughts about her bottled up, and if she ignores them it makes me feel better about my lack of self-control. I reach into the back seat and grab the small bouquet of peonies.

"Wow," she says when the house comes into full view as we trek up the driveway. There's always been something special about the classic, old mission-style architecture.

"Back in the sixties some famous music producer lived here," I say. "And see that tree there?" I point to the magnolia on our right. "I had my first kiss under that tree."

Madison's face lights up like I'm telling her something top secret, which I guess I am, since I don't think I've ever told anyone else. "What was her name?"

"Kellie Simpson. She tasted like Girl Scout Thin Mints cookies. She'd just sold several boxes to my mom." I grin at the memory. "I'd seen Kellie walk up the drive, and I bet her my mom would buy at least four boxes. Mom bought six, so Kellie had to kiss me."

"How old were you?"

"Twelve. What about you? How old were you when you

let some boy kiss you?"

"Older than twelve," she says with a tone that begs I drop the subject. So I do. Even though we're firmly in the friend zone today, there's still a line we need to keep drawn.

The front door is unlocked and we walk into the house right on time. My mother is a stickler for punctuality, something I often disregarded when younger. Of course my brother and sister are already here. "Hi, Mom," I say as we enter the expansive kitchen.

Mom puts down the soufflé she just pulled out of the oven. "Elliot, hello." Her eyes dart to Madison, then back to me before she takes me in a hug. "I'm glad you could make it today."

"Me, too. These are for you." I hand her the bouquet. Now that I'm here, it's not so bad. My parents do like to see me, and the familiar comfort and smells of home remind me it's usually the anticipation of seeing my family that bothers me more than being here.

"Thank you." She sniffs her favorite flower around a faint but appreciative smile.

"This is Madison, the friend I left you a message about. Madison, this is my mom, Lynn."

"Hello, Madison. It's nice to meet you." Mom assesses Madison's shin-length skirt, V-back sweater, and heels with a quick, but obvious once-over.

"Nice to meet you, too. I also brought you something." She hands the plate to my mom. "It's banana bread. I baked it this morning."

"Elliot's favorite. Thank you."

Madison's eyes flit to mine. "Since I was a kid," I say like it's no big deal.

"We'll be eating in a few minutes. Please make yourself at home," my mom says to both of us. Like I'm a guest, too.

The rest of my family is within view, the floor plan open

and spacious. "Hey, Dad."

My father stands up from the couch and shakes my hand. "Hello, Elliot."

"This is Madison," I share with everyone. My brother, Evan, and his wife, Sierra, smile and say hello. My sister, Emma, and her fiancé, Lance, do the same. I introduce Madison to everyone. She's friendly and congratulates Emma and Lance on their engagement.

As we sit thigh to thigh at the short end of the L-shaped couch, my brother and sister stare at us like we're the sideshow at a carnival. It *is* the first time I've brought a girl to brunch. For the past couple of years I've been happy not to have a significant other, because it set me apart from my siblings. It was an easy way to rebel against my parents' desire for all their children to be paired off.

I have a feeling Madison is taking in my family with the same surprise. It's only when we're all together that my biracial parentage becomes obvious. My brother and sister favor my mom with lightly freckled complexions and upturned noses, while I've inherited more of my father's coloring. The one thing we all share is light-colored eyes.

"Madison and I work together," I say to dispel any notions that this is more than what it is.

Em is the first to speak up and ask about my job. I have just enough time to tell her it's great when my mom calls us to the dining table.

I pull out a chair for Madison. Since we have regular seats, it's the spot across from me. She doesn't seem to mind sitting between my dad and sister, but I wish she were close enough to touch. The one advantage is this position gives me a perfect view of her beautiful face.

"How's cash flow at ZipMeds?" my father asks, passing me the maple-sage pork sausage my mom likes to cook.

"It's good."

"Just good?"

"Great, actually."

"Elliot recently secured five million more dollars in funding," Madison says. "And key investors who are impressed with his management skills are helping to grow his circle of influence." She takes a blueberry muffin and passes the basket to her left.

Every person at the table pauses for a moment to look at her. When she realizes all eyes are on her, her lips press together in a shy, but assured smile.

I'm hit with a sudden warm sensation that fills my chest. She's proud of me and it feels amazing. I don't work my ass off because I want compliments, but I can't remember the last time someone heaped praise on me like that. It makes me want to share more about work and clue my family in on what fills my days and gets me excited. I'm about to bring up the new markets ZipMeds is planning to move in to, when Emma hijacks everyone's attention.

"Lance and I have some news," she announces. "We've set a wedding date! December twenty-third, and we were thinking it would be fun to do it in Aspen, since we both love the snow."

Immediately, my mom and sister-in-law think that's a great idea and wedding talk flies back and forth across the table. Lance nods like the good fiancé he is while the rest of us guys shovel in food. Madison keeps her head mostly down. I suppose weddings might still be a sore subject for her.

"You heading to the Final Four?" I ask my dad. Then to Madison I add, "He's a big college basketball fan." He played, and my brother played. It was expected I would, too, but I chose to play baseball year round.

"Of course. Evan and I have floor seats."

"Cool." While I have no desire to go, an invite would be nice. Just once.

"Do you have a favorite team?" Madison asks my dad.

"I do. North Carolina. I'm hoping they add to their collection of wins."

"He was born there," I tell Madison. "And remains a fan even though he's been here since he was a teenager."

The conversation around the table dies down and Evan clears his throat. "We have an announcement, too." He looks lovingly at Sierra before putting his hand on her stomach.

"We're having a baby," Sierra shares.

A second round of excitement ensues. "Congratulations, man." I slap him on the back. Speaking all at once, everyone else offers congrats, too. The smile on my mom's face is blinding.

I'm really happy for my brother and my sister, but once again, my life is relegated to nothing more than a passing thought. I should be used to it, yet I'm not.

I look across the table at Madison. Under long lashes, she's watching me. Her focus is on *me*. Her regard relaxes the tightness in my shoulders and dulls the resentment I've tried to let go of but find difficult to do. My family dynamics aren't going to change, of that I'm certain, so it's best to forgive and forget.

We finish brunch and Madison and I offer to clean up while my parents and siblings go outside to sit on the covered patio.

"Your mom is an amazing cook," Madison says, her hands in soapy dishwater. She didn't hesitate to roll up her sleeves and get busy. "Everything was delicious and so bad for my diet."

"Do not tell me you're on a diet." I take the pan she hands me and start drying it.

"Not exactly. Just trying to eat better since I've put on a few pounds."

"They look good on you." She's sexier than I ever thought

before. I've daydreamed about wrapping my hands around her curves.

"You really think so?" she asks, surprising me with her candor.

"I really do."

"Thanks. I feel like this is more my normal weight but…"

"But what?" I nudge her hip with mine. "Scoot over, let me get that." I reach into the sink to take over scrubbing the soufflé dish.

She rinses her hands, then reaches around me to pick up the dish towel. Her side brushes my back, and I almost groan. Which is all kinds of messed up. We're doing dishes and a quick graze gets me riled up?

"Henry liked—"

"Stop right there. Your ex was a fucking loser who treated you like shit, and you should disregard everything he ever said to you. You're more gorgeous now than you ever have been, and it's because you dumped his ass."

"Tell me how you really feel," she teases.

"You want me to cop a feel?" I tease back, pretending I didn't hear her correctly. I've mentioned her insane body, right? And while I've been on my best behavior since Seattle, I can't forget the taste of her on my tongue or the glimpse of her cleavage covered in light-blue lace.

"You want a cup of tea?" she says with a terrible British accent. It's so bad it's good, and I crack up. Then I continue the play on words.

"Climb a tree? You mean the one out front, right? The one I dub the kissing tree?" I just can't stop my mind from going there. I've wondered more than once what it would be like to kiss her.

She dips her fingers in the sudsy water and flicks bubbles at me. "No, I don't mean that, *Mr. Sax*."

I know she said my name, but all I hear is Mr. "Sex." And

no, it's not the first time I've taken that leap. It started around the time I noticed girls had tits and I couldn't stop looking at them. Alone in my room, I'd say, "Sex. Elliot Sex," like I was James Bond. Don't laugh. I thought I was the coolest.

I lift my hands out of the water and blow bubbles at her. Suds go everywhere. She squeals and splashes bubbles back.

"Oh, it's on," I tell her.

We're laughing and having a great time with the bubbles when I grab her wrists to put a stop to it. In that moment, everything in the room seems to stand still. I'm so aware of Madison and nothing else that I'm desperate for more from her. I swear I can hear her heart pounding as hard as mine. Only a few inches separate us, and I'd bet my car we're both thinking about the same thing: crashing our mouths together until we need to catch our breaths.

I'm a second away from saying fuck it and kissing the hell out of her, when my mom clears her throat. *"Ahem."*

I slowly let go of Madison. There's a bubble in her hair, one clings to her cheek. She's so pretty it hurts to look at her for too long.

"Sorry," I say to my mom. "We got a little carried away." This isn't the first time my mom has interrupted me with a girl, but it is the best timed. Kissing my assistant would be a monumental mistake. When am I going to get that through my thick skull?

"I can see that. Leave the rest for later and come join us on the patio for a game." My family loves to play games to torture me. This time, however, I'm happy to take part because I'm partnered with Madison for...wait for it... Pictionary.

We annihilate the competition. I correctly guess all of Madison's pictures almost immediately with her insane artistic skills. Somehow she identifies my childish drawings under the time limit, too, and it's safe to say this has been the best brunch I've ever had at my parents' house. I want to leave on a high note, so we say our goodbyes.

"Does your family do brunch every Sunday?" Madison asks after we walk out the front door.

I fight the urge to reach for her hand. "It's a semi-regular thing. Thanks for coming with me. I haven't enjoyed being here this much in forever."

A few feet from my car, a red double-decker tour bus drives by. Madison waves back at the people on the top deck. I think one of *The Real Housewives of Beverly Hills* lives a couple of streets over. I can't believe I know that, but believe it or not, my mom keeps up with the TV show.

"Have you ever done that?" Madison asks.

I open the car door for her. "A tour of stars' homes? No. You?"

"No, but I think it would be fun to play tourist for a little while."

Once she's comfortable in her seat, I walk around to my side. "Do you have to be anywhere this afternoon?"

Her eyes sparkle. "No."

"Let's buy a map and drive around. I'll be your tour guide. I'm sure there's an app, but doing it old school seems more fun." I have no idea where to buy one, but we'll find a place. I don't want our time together to end.

"I'd love that." She wiggles in excitement.

We hit Sunset Boulevard and drive toward Hollywood. I know tours take off near the corner of Hollywood and Vine, but we luck out and see a place to buy a map sooner. I illegally park on the street, hop out to grab a map, and jump back in the car all in less than two minutes. I hand Madison the map, then start the car. "Okay, point me in the right direction. I want to see some big-time movie-stars' homes."

"Umm…"

"Did you change your mind?" My stomach drops. She

had a couple of minutes to decide she's had enough of me for one day. We're stuck with each other during the week. There's no reason to be stuck today, too.

"No, it's not that. My motion sickness applies to cars, too, and reading makes it a hundred times worse."

That's right. I turn off the ignition. "How about you drive, and I read the map?"

"You'd let me drive your car?"

"True or False? You drive like a lunatic and it's no wonder you've been pulled over by the police more than once." My truth is I've never let anyone drive my BMW, but Miss Hastings makes it easy to try things I've never done before. One soft look or smile or happy lilt to her voice and I'm toast.

"False. And FYI, I have never been pulled over."

I'm not surprised. "Looks like you're our driver then."

"Okay!" She drops the map, leaps out of the car, and goes around the hood. I purposely go the opposite direction and round the trunk so my mouth doesn't accidentally bump into hers.

She takes her time to adjust the driver's seat and rearview and side mirrors. I appreciate the care to keep us—and my baby—safe. This sleek black two-door driving machine is only a year old. When Madison is satisfied and comfortable, she puts on the blinker to move into traffic. I stifle a smile. My little rule follower probably signals when she pulls out of her driveway.

I could totally close my eyes and take a nap. My car is in good hands.

"Where to first?" she prompts.

Or I could open the map and captain this adventure. "How about Bruce Willis's house?"

"Sounds good."

We quickly discover that most of the houses on our tour are behind big gates. The houses without gates belong to stars from the past, like Katherine Hepburn and Charlie Chaplin.

"There's another tour bus," Madison says. "Want to follow it?"

"Sure." So that's what we do. Sometimes we can tell from our map whose house we're slowing down for, and sometimes we can't. When the bus stops to let passengers off for pictures, we pull over, too, and jump out.

No one from the tour pays us any attention as I take a picture of Madison posing in front of the gate to Channing Tatum's house. She strikes a pose like she's blowing me a kiss. It's sexy and sweet, just like she is.

"Let's get both of us," she says, waving me over for a selfie of the two of us. With one arm around Madison and the other extended with the phone in my hand, Madison counts us down. "Three, two, one…"

I hear her, but holding her against my side feels so incredibly good, I forget why she's counting.

"Elliot? Are you going to take the picture?"

Right. *Stop enjoying the hot female beside you and snap the picture.* I have a feeling I'll be looking at it often.

"I think my eyes were closed," she says immediately after I snap the shot. "Will you take another?"

"I'll take as many as you want. One, two, three…"

"Cheese!" she says this time.

"Better?" I ask.

"I think so but let me see." She pulls the phone from me like it's the most natural thing for her to do and opens the picture. "It's good."

More than good, I think, when she passes me back the phone. She looks beautiful. I look like I just hit a million-dollar jackpot. Which I have. Only it's with my assistant, and if I continue to straddle the line of safe behavior, one or both of us will be burned.

Chapter Thirteen

MADISON

"He doesn't shave on the weekends," I say, striding into the guesthouse Teague and Harper rent from Harper's aunt and uncle and plopping down on their couch like my life is over.

"That was your emergency?" Harper asks without judgment. She and Teague are already sitting, and there's a tray of s'mores fixings on the coffee table. I almost cry at the sight. I'm so grateful to have these girls.

After Elliot dropped me off at home and I spent a couple of restless hours holed up in my room, I texted them I had a crisis and needed their help. They immediately invited me over for a pajama party.

"He's even more hot with stubble, and that's saying a lot because I sometimes can't breathe when I look too long at his clean-shaven face."

"You've seen him on weekends before," Teague says.

"Yes, but today was different. Why can't he be someone I'm not attracted to? Plus he's considerate. He let me drive his car when we drove around looking at stars' homes so I wouldn't get car sick."

"Wait. I thought you just went to brunch," Teague says.

"I did, and then we saw a double-decker tour bus and I made the comment that I thought it would be fun to play tourist and check out the stars' homes, so Elliot made it happen. And look." I take my phone out of my purse and pull up the picture of the two of us he texted to me. "How cute is this?"

"Very cute," Teague says.

"You guys do make a striking couple," Harper says.

"What am I going to do? I'm crushing on my boss!"

"I don't think it's one-sided. I've seen the way he looks at you," Harper offers.

I've told them about our flirting, but I haven't told them about all the things Elliot has said to me. *If things were different, I'd fuck you in the back seat of this car so good you'd still feel it tomorrow.* Or about what happened in Seattle, because I know I'll turn red-faced. I'm also a little ashamed. Elliot is my boss first and foremost and I don't want to lose my job. Does he like me back? Yes. But I'm not experienced enough to know if his playfulness is more than just a passing thing. Because I do know his job means everything to him, too.

"What are you thinking about?" Teague asks.

"He loves his job and I love mine, so I need to let go of my silly infatuation."

Teague gives my forearm a squeeze. "You could look for another job if you really think there's something strong between you guys."

I shake my head. "It took me six months of temping before landing this one, and I don't want to give it up. For the first time in my life I feel like I'm doing something that's all mine and that I'm good at. The company is amazing and I've made friends there, too. Plus, the pay is great and I'm going to start looking for an apartment."

"You are? That's fantastic!" Teague claps her hands.

"I have a solution for you," Harper says.

Harper runs her own nonprofit to bring awareness to swim safety and help those who have lost someone to drowning. If she's got a solution, I'll take it. The notes Elliot and I write to each other help, but only temporarily.

"Tell me."

"Any time you look at Elliot, picture Henry's face instead. That way you'll want to punch him in the mouth instead of kiss him, and it will give you the incentive to prove to your douchebag ex that you're strong and independent and kicking ass in the workforce."

I think about her suggestion. "That could work." Lord knows I hate Henry more than anything.

"Another thing you could do," Teague says, "is join a boot camp or boxing studio. Working out your frustrations with some high-intensity exercise could help keep your mind focused."

"I like that idea, too, but they're probably expensive."

"I know a guy," Harper says. "I'll hook you up if you want."

I rub the corner of my eye. "Thanks, you guys. I don't know what I'd do without you."

"Lucky for us, you'll never have to find out." Teague jumps to her feet.

Harper rises to hers. "It's time for Marshmallow Spears." She picks up the tray of s'mores ingredients while Teague picks up my hand.

At the confusion on my face, Teague says, "It's our own special brand of fun, going back to when we were college freshmen and I put on Britney Spears and Harper cooked marshmallows with a lighter, and the combo cured the injustice of us not getting into the same sorority. Since then it's been our go-to for any bumps or blessing in our days, and you are the first person we're initiating into our ritual, so come on."

The three of us walk to the backyard fire pit that sits between the pool and the guesthouse. "Toxic" blares through outdoor speakers. Harper flips the switch on the fire pit. Teague hands me a skewered marshmallow to roast. We gorge on s'mores and dance around the backyard in our pajamas. It's wonderful.

I glance up at the night sky and thank the hundreds of twinkling stars for putting me right here, right now.

• • •

The next morning I start work with a whole new perspective. From a single girl's standpoint, Elliot is good-looking, sexy, and attentive. But from an assistant's viewpoint, he is shrewd, businesslike, smart, and has a face I hate. This new plan is just right.

And so far it's working.

Elliot rings me from inside his office. "Yes?" I say, phone to my ear.

"Have you finished that financial report for my meeting tomorrow?"

"Finishing it now."

"Great. Thanks." He disconnects. If asked what it's like to work with Elliot, I'd say after a tense start where he was demanding and unapologetic in his requests, we've found a groove that's a little less stressful. "Little" being the key word. There's a lot of work to be done and Elliot gives me a lot of responsibility. I'm doing things a financial assistant with years, not weeks, of experience would do. I'm not invisible, but truly part of a team. There's a definite learning curve, but it's exciting. Challenging. I love waking up every morning to come here.

"Madison," James says, stopping at my desk, "great job on last week's revenue and expense spreadsheet."

"Thank you."

"I know Elliot appreciates it, too. He can't stop singing me your praises. Keep up the good work."

I nod, worried if I speak I'll blurt out how amazing Elliot is and sound like a girl in lust rather than a girl in appreciation.

Closing my eyes for a quick second, I revel in the praise before finishing the report. Good jobs are hard to find, and I'm lucky I landed this one.

"Hey," Auggie says.

"Hey." I swivel my chair to fully face her. "What's up?"

"Can you help me with something for about half an hour?"

I peer around her. Elliot is on the phone, zoned in on his laptop, and probably wouldn't notice if I walked into his office naked. Okay, bad analogy. He might notice that. But I think I'm safe to step away for a little bit. "Sure."

Auggie links arms with me and we go in the direction of the kitchen. Once there, she says, "It's prank day."

"Is that an official holiday?"

"No, but Mondays are so blah, I thought we could shake it up a little."

"Will we get in trouble?"

Auggie puts her hands on her hips. "Where's your sense of adventure?"

"Way behind my need for a paycheck."

"Well, shenanigans are important to my well-being so are you in or out? I promise no humans will be harmed in the execution of this little joke. Unless you consider smiling harmful, which in the case of your boss might be a problem."

"Elliot smiles," I say in his defense. It's an amazing one, too.

Auggie crosses her arms and brings her fist to her chin in

contemplation. "Hmm, I guess I have seen him smile more since you got here."

"Oh, he doesn't smile because of me."

She narrows her eyes in contemplation. "Not you, per se, but you being the first assistant to stick with him."

Shit. Obviously she meant like that. "Right, of course." I titter. Crap, I hope she can't see how nervous she's making me. "I'm helpful and good at my job. I really love working here. And I love working with you, too. I'm learning so much from everyone and it's not a chore coming here at all and—"

"Madison."

"Yes?"

"Is there something going on between you and Elliot?"

Crap on a crab cake. This is bad.

I walk over to the floor-to-ceiling chalkboard along the back wall. I don't want to lie to Auggie, but I can't tell her the whole truth, either. Elliot thought it best not to mention that we knew each other before I started working here. Friends don't always make the best colleagues, and it seemed easier to keep our connection out of the equation. But maybe if we'd acknowledged we had mutual friends and saw each other outside the office, I wouldn't have to be so careful with my feelings. I pick up a piece of chalk. "No," I say, as I write the word "maybe" and then erase it.

"You know James has a zero-tolerance policy for office romances," she whispers.

"I know. And that's why nothing will ever happen." Nothing beyond Seattle.

"I get it," Auggie says with understanding. "Elliot is super attractive and has this aura of power around him that makes him even hotter."

It's my turn to narrow my eyes. "Are you crushing on my boss?"

"Not anymore, but I admit when he first started here I was

kind of enamored. I got over it quickly, though. I love my job, too. And besides, Elliot never spared me a second glance."

"So there's hope for me." I tuck away the knowledge that he sneaks glances at me all the time.

She wraps her arm around my shoulders and leads me to the long hardwood table. "Definitely. Now take a seat and help me stick googly eyes on stuff." She pulls a small bag filled with various sizes of googly eyes from her pocket. "I thought we'd start with things in the refrigerator."

I laugh. "This is your prank?"

"Yes. Look." She sticks a large pair of eyes on a bottle of water she pulled out of the fridge.

"That's really cute."

"It won't be so cute when there's eyes everywhere."

"Only one way to find out," I say, jumping on board with my first-ever prank. The two of us google-eye condiments, the toaster oven, the coffeemaker, and blender. We leave the kitchen and covertly stop by desks to put eyes on calculators, pencil holders, staplers, and tape dispensers. When we get back to the second floor, Elliot and James are in the conference room, so we put googly eyes on their phones, the corner of their computer screens, and anything else on their desks that needs a pair. We giggle at that. And rest assured, the eyes peel off easily, so really there's no harm in having some fun like this.

We high-five when finished and go back to our desks like nothing's happened. A half hour later I'm working on another report when my phone rings. It's Elliot's extension. "Hello?"

"Why are there googly eyes all over my office?"

I try not to grin. "I have no idea what you're talking about."

"Really?" He doesn't buy it for a second, and I burst out laughing.

The giggles won't stop. I lean back in my chair to look into his office. He's shaking his head in dismay, but the pull on his closed lips tells me he isn't angry. Then I hear James yell, "Auggie!" and Elliot's brows arch in amusement. I shrug and hang up the phone.

For the rest of the morning I handle some correspondence for Elliot and schedule him a haircut. *Shame.* At a little after noon, I grab the lunch I brought and head to the roof to eat. I've been up here only one other time, and with spring just days away, the weather is warming up.

I imagine this is what rooftops are like in New York City, only with a ton more high-rises. And traffic noise. And city smells. Okay, so this isn't really like NYC at all, but it does feel different. More *real*. Like this is true life, not the insulated version I grew up living. There's blue sky for miles and in the distance, the ocean. But there are also homeless people in the alleys. Garbage cans filled with trash and who knows what else, buses making stops. I sit on a cushioned bench to eat, enjoying the sunshine and this slice of L.A.

"Mind if I join you?"

I startle at the sound of Elliot's voice.

"Sorry. I thought you heard me."

"It's okay." I scoot over to make room for him even though I'd prefer to keep my distance. His wavy black hair and rolled-up shirt sleeves are a distraction I don't need during my lunch break. "Have a seat."

"You haven't seen us fly drones yet, have you?" he asks.

"No. Is one scheduled for today?" I bounce up and down, excited by the idea.

"Later this afternoon, but let's see if I can get Tony to bring one over now so you can check out how it works." He brings his phone to his ear. "Hey, Tony. It's Elliot. Think you could come to the rooftop now? Great. Thanks." He disconnects the call. "He's on his way."

"You didn't have to do that."

He lifts one shoulder. "This way you get a private

showing."

"Here." I hand him half my PB&J with bananas sandwich. "I notice you don't have a lunch."

"What is this?" He scrunches up his nose like a little kid as he eyes the food.

"Just try it."

"Bananas on peanut butter and jelly is gross. No thank you." He hands the sandwich back.

"You've had it before?"

"No, but—"

"Then you don't know it's gross."

He plucks the sandwich back and takes a bite. "As I suspected," he says around a mouthful. "It's gross."

I crack up at the look of disgust on his face. "Good on you for trying."

"You want to know what would look really good on me?" His eyes shine with hunger and I'm fairly certain he's referring to me. I immediately tingle between my legs, imagining him naked in bed, his hands on my waist as he lowers me onto him.

Peanut butter gets stuck in the back of my throat. I shake my head. My "no" can be interpreted in many ways. No, I don't know. No, don't tell me. No, I don't want to know. No, but tell me anyway. See what this man does to me?

Thankfully, the door to the roof opens before he ignores my "no" and tells me. Tony steps onto the roof holding a drone and some other equipment. He greets us, Elliot chats with him for a minute, and then I get an up close and personal look at ZipMeds' fixed-wing drone, launcher, and landing rig. That technology is available to deliver lifesaving medical supplies to people who desperately need it is amazing, and once again I'm so grateful for this job.

I tell Elliot as much when the demonstration is over. This time when he looks at me, it's with a mix of regret and understanding. In another time and place we could explore this crazy pull between us.

But for this future, we have to keep our distance.

Mr. Sax,

You really should consider a different hairdresser. Or at the very least, one who isn't inebriated when she cuts your hair. (I mean what other explanation is there?) Don't worry too much. It's only when someone is staring at the back of your head that the uneven cut is noticeable. Face-to-face, the sloppy cut is noticeable only in daylight. It's a shame we've turned our clocks ahead and "sprang forward." Anyway, I'd like to suggest a barbershop next time rather than a salon. Barbers, like finance assistants, are always a cut above.

Sincerely,
Miss Hastings

Miss Hastings,

I'm sorry to tell you this, but the skirt you're wearing today? It does make you look bigger than normal. Don't blame the messenger on this one, Mads. I heard you ask Auggie if it made you look fat, and friends never tell friends the truth in that situation. So, you're welcome. If you need to leave work a few minutes early in order to change clothes before your date tonight, please feel free.

Sincerely,
Mr. Sax

Chapter Fourteen

Madison

I'm still fuming over Elliot's note when I get to the Burger Lounge to meet Brooks for our dinner date. I didn't leave work early. I didn't change my clothes. My butt does not look fat in this skirt. Elliot wanted to piss me off and it worked.

I barely interacted with him for the entire afternoon. Granted, my note made him angry with me, too, so he was happy to keep his distance. This strategy of ours is working better than I think either of us thought it would. Even though we know we're both joking with each other, it still can sting.

It's for the best, I remind myself for the tenth time today.

Opening the glass door to the burger joint, the casual and brightly colored counter-serve restaurant with a delicious smell quickly cures my irritation. I didn't eat lunch because I was super busy, and I'm starving. I'm a couple of minutes late so I glance around the room until I find a really cute guy with light-brown hair smiling at me.

"Hi, Brooks?" I say as I approach his table.

"Hey, Madison. How are you?" He jumps to his feet to pull out my chair. He's tall and solidly built. "Thanks for meeting me here."

"I'm good, thanks, and I love this place." When Brooks suggested we meet here, I agreed without a second thought. The food is great and the prices reasonable. This particular spot also told me he wasn't pretentious, but preferred a comfortable setting where we could get to know each other.

"Me, too." He sits on the edge of his seat, his green eyes on me with friendliness and warmth. He likes what he sees. I have to admit, I like what I see, too. *Poof!* My bad mood is completely gone. "What can I get you to eat?" he asks.

"A quinoa veggie burger with mozzarella and a hibiscus lemonade, please."

"Fries?"

"Umm…"

"We could share?"

"That sounds great," I say around a smile.

He smiles in return. It's the nice, approachable kind, like he's the type of person you could tell a secret to and trust he'd keep it. "I'll be right back. Don't go anywhere."

"I won't." The tiny flutter in the pit of my stomach makes sure of that.

"Oh, wait," I say as he walks away to place our order. He turns. "No grilled onions." He nods with another amiable curve of his mouth before striding to the counter. I like onions, but they give me horrible breath for hours and well… right off the bat, I got a good vibe from Brooks and I don't know, maybe he'll want to kiss me good night later.

My cheeks heat at the thought. I miss kissing. When Henry and I first started dating, we'd kiss for hours. Those memories with him are my favorite. They're the ones I hold onto, not the others that cause me pain and grief. Despite what he did to me, the beginning of our relationship was magical.

The sound of male voices in happy conversation interrupts my recollection. Normally, I wouldn't turn around to check out whom they belong to, but I know these voices. One of them I've heard for as long as I can remember since our moms are best friends, and the other one I hear during work hours and at night when he whispers dirty things in my dreams.

Glancing over my shoulder, my guess is confirmed. Mateo and Elliot are walking up to the counter to order food. Mateo knew I was going to be here, per my promise to share my first date whereabouts with him. After he pried the details out of me about my date with Jesse, he'd been upset and asked if he could show up tonight. I agreed because 1) this isn't a "real" date in the sense that I'm here because of Brooks's mom and 2) he's a protector by nature and thinks of me like a sister. He knows I can take care of myself. I handled Jesse, and I'll handle Brooks if need be, but backup never hurt anyone.

I'm not sure why Elliot is with him.

"Here you go," Brooks says, placing my food and drink in front of me. He puts the fries in the middle of the table, his hamburger at his spot, and deposits the tray atop a nearby trash container before sitting down across from me.

"Thank you. I missed lunch and this looks really good." I bite into a french fry.

Brooks grabs a couple for himself. "Long day at work?"

"You could say that. What about you? Were you on duty today? I'm not sure how your shifts work." Brooks is a paramedic. Which means if I choke on this burger, he can save me. There's something very nice about that.

"I finished a twenty-four-hour shift this morning and slept until about an hour ago when I had to get ready for a date with a beautiful girl."

I feel myself blush. It's not just the compliment. It's the

way he says it. With genuine kindness that is refreshing after my last few dates. There *are* still nice guys out there. "Well, I have it on good authority that your date thinks the same about you. I mean, not that you're beautiful, but that you're handsome." My face is on fire. "I'm going to stop talking now and eat my burger."

"Me, too," he says, having the good grace to let my blabbering go.

We eat in somewhat easy silence. It's clear we want to know more about each other, but we're giving it some thought first. In my limited dating experience, this is another considerate quality. So different from guys quick to judge me, or talk about me like I'm an object, not a person. I haven't always been a good judge of character, but I'm getting better at it, and Brooks exudes good character, which makes sense given his occupation.

In my periphery I see Elliot and Mateo sit down at a table. I'd forgotten about them for a minute, but now I feel them watching me and I wonder if I should give Mateo some kind of signal to let him know everything is good and he can eat and run. I turn my head to try and make eye contact with him. He's engrossed in conversation with Elliot now and looks like he's in no hurry.

Damn it. I will him to look at me but he doesn't. Maybe he'll leave quickly if I make a public spectacle of myself by climbing over the table to make out with Brooks.

Do I want to do that?

Or is it the guy a few feet away wearing gray slacks and a dark-blue button-down with the sleeves rolled up to reveal strong, capable forearms that I want to do that with?

I 100 percent lied about his haircut. It's perfect. Shorter, but not too short, the jet-black strands are still long enough for a girl to comb her fingers through. The curl at the base of his neck is gone, but I bet within two weeks it will be back. Not that I've given much thought to his hair today or anything.

"So, you mentioned you recently moved back here from up north," I say, focusing back on my date.

"That's right. I was pre-med at San Francisco State, but changed my mind about med school. I liked it up there, though, so stayed to train as an EMT and first responder after graduation, finished both my basic and intermediate training, and got hired down here as a paramedic."

"How's it going so far?"

"Great." He offers me the last french fry. I shake my head and he picks it up. "I'm the new guy, so there's some jokes at my expense, but the team is dope. What about you? How do you like the finance world?"

"I love it." I wipe my napkin across my mouth. "Can I tell you a secret?" I ask quietly.

"Absolutely. Secret keeping is part of my paramedic's oath."

I smile, then clear my throat. "I have this recurring dream where my boss and I switch places and he's my assistant and I'm sitting behind a massive desk and I look at him and I say, 'You're fired.' Is that weird?"

"Not at all. Sounds to me like you've got big aspirations. Nothing wrong with that."

Or I want to get naked with Elliot.

"What was the last dream you had?"

Brooks thinks about that, his eyes roaming around the restaurant before settling back on me. "I don't know. I don't often remember them."

"Really? I always remember mine and they're super vivid." Like the one of Elliot—

"Hey, do you know that guy? He keeps looking over at you." Brooks tips his head in the direction of Elliot and Mateo, and because I have to know which one of them has been staring at me, I turn my head.

Elliot's bright-blue eyes meet mine, wiping out everyone else in the room. For a split second it's just him and me, and my breath catches. This isn't the first time he's stolen my surroundings, but each time grows more intense. I force myself to blink and turn back to Brooks.

"Umm"—I shake my head to try and clear it—"yeah, actually, I do. He's my boss."

"Seriously? That's a weird coincidence."

If he only knew. "The guy he's with is one of my good friends and his roommate. I've been here with him before and well, I mentioned to him I was going to be here tonight, so he probably thought it sounded good, too."

Brooks studies me. I have no idea what he's thinking, and he doesn't get the chance to tell me, because Elliot and Mateo arrive at our table. "Hey, Mad," Mateo says.

"Hi, Mateo." I drop my chin and mouth *sorry* to Brooks.

"How's it going?" Mateo asks.

I want to be mad at him, but I know he means well. "Great, thanks." Hopefully that will get him to be on his way. He checked in with me, got his answer, and he can go now. Brooks seems like a smart guy, so I'm pretty sure he realizes what's going on here. Instead of having a girlfriend call me with an emergency to bail me out of my date if I needed it, my overprotective guy friend sat nearby like a bodyguard.

"Hey, I'm Elliot." The last man I want to talk to right now puts his hand out to Brooks.

"And Madison's boss, I hear. I'm Brooks. Nice to meet you." While they shake hands, Elliot cuts me a surprised glance. I notice Mateo give Elliot an annoyed look. What's that about?

"I'm Mateo," he says to Brooks, shaking hands.

"I heard that," Brooks says good-naturedly. He's taking this invasion really well and I wonder if it's because he's lost interest in me, or if he's just being nice about it. "Madison mentioned you're friends. Want to sit for a minute?"

Looks like Brooks has lost interest *and* is being nice. The one time I wish a date wouldn't be polite…

"Do we?" Elliot says to Mateo.

I watch Mateo waver between leaving me alone and satisfying his curiosity a bit more. "Sure," he decides.

They sit down, Elliot to my left and Mateo to my right. Elliot's knee rubs against mine under the table. It's accidental—I think—but distracting and I forget what I was going to say to get rid of these guys. I'm safe with Brooks. They can go.

"What do you do for work?" Elliot asks.

Oh no. They are not going to give him the third degree. I find my voice. "You guys. We're in the middle of a date, so…"

"It's fine," Brooks says. His nice eyes land on mine before turning to Elliot. "I'm a paramedic."

"A buddy of mine is a firefighter," Mateo says, and before I know it the three of them are talking like I'm not even there.

I rest my chin in my hand and think about what I should pack for the company retreat this weekend. I'd be a lot more upset if I wasn't here to scope out Brooks's behavior first and foremost. Mateo knows this is the "third guy," so maybe that's why he felt like he could sit down with us.

"Excuse me?" One of the restaurant's employees stops at our table. "We have a private party happening tonight. We apologize for any inconvenience, but will be closing in five minutes."

"Thanks," Brooks says. "Madison, can I take you out for dessert somewhere? Just the two of us."

I perk up. He is interested and doesn't want our date to end. "I'd love to."

"Are you sure that's a good idea?" Elliot pipes in. "We've got to leave early tomorrow morning." He looks at Mateo and Brooks. "We're driving to Lake Tahoe for a company retreat."

"You're heading to Tahoe tomorrow?" Brooks asks.

"Yes," I say.

"I am, too. I'm doing a search and rescue training camp up there."

"Wow. How funny," I say. Is this the universe's way of saying I should definitely see Brooks again?

"I'm not sure what the schedule is, but I could check in with you?" he adds.

"Okay."

"I'm pretty sure we've got a packed agenda," Elliot says, reminding me that this weekend is about my job, not another date.

"Right," I say. "I wasn't thinking. Sorry."

"No worries, I get it. So, dessert or no dessert?" Brooks asks, as the four of us stand to leave.

As much as I'd like to grab something sweet to eat with him, I haven't packed yet. I'm also feeling a weird vibe from Elliot. Does he see something in Brooks I don't? Is he trying to silently warn me away from making a mistake? Is he jealous? Mateo seems normal, so I don't know for sure.

"I should head home, but thank you anyway." I hang back a moment so Elliot and Mateo can leave before us and I can walk out beside Brooks privately.

"I'd like to take you out again. Is it cool if I get in touch with you next week?"

"Yes." It's the first time a guy has asked for a second date and I've wanted to accept.

Brooks stops before opening the glass door of the restaurant. "It was really nice meeting you, Madison."

"You, too. Thank you for dinner."

An awkward moment passes before I decide to kiss him on the cheek. His return smile is nice, more comforting than stimulating, but at least it's something.

We step outside, Elliot and Mateo thankfully not anywhere in sight. "Are you parked close by?" Brooks asks.

"Just across the street."

"I'm down that way." He thumbs over his shoulder, down the sidewalk.

"Good night then." I smile.

"Good night." He smiles.

We stand in happy stillness for a beat before I break the connection. My steps are light as I turn around and walk to the intersection so I can use the crosswalk. To my surprise, Mateo and Elliot come around the corner. I roll my eyes. I should have guessed they'd be lurking around here somewhere.

"Seriously? You waited for me?" That's taking it too far. "You guys are unbelievable. I was okay with you keeping to yourself and keeping an eye on me, Matty, in case I needed you, but you should have noticed I was totally fine and left without approaching us. I had a good time with Brooks. He's a nice, normal guy, so what gives?"

Mateo shoots Elliot another annoyed look. "You're right. Brooks is a good guy, and I'm sorry we interfered."

"Thank you."

"You have my blessing if you want to go out with him again."

I give Mateo a little push in the upper arm. "I don't need your blessing."

"That's true," he says, again looking at Elliot, but this time I'm not sure what his expression says.

"You parked close by?" Elliot asks, echoing Brooks. His eyes have been on me this whole time and he sounds like he's both relieved and in a hurry to leave. There's something he's not saying.

"I'm right across the street. I lucked out with a metered spot."

Elliot nods, noticing my car. "I'll see you in the morning." He's picking me up at five for the sevenish-hour drive to Lake Tahoe. I'd wanted to ride with Auggie and Hazel, but they left today in order to make sure things were ready at the resort when everyone arrives. Yesterday, Elliot put a small box of over-the-counter medication to treat my motion sickness on my desk and told me I could drive his car whenever I needed to while on our way.

"I'll be ready," I tell him, then I give Mateo a hug goodbye. "Bye," I say softly in his ear.

When I get home, I gather my stuff for the trip. The weather calls for sunshine but cold temperatures, so I bring clothes I can layer. Once my bag is packed, I hop in the shower to save time in the morning. While standing under the hot stream of water, I think back on my night. I enjoyed being with Brooks. He's attractive, smart, friendly. But the person I really want, the person I can't stop thinking about, is Elliot. I cover my face with my hands and drop my head. I can't have Elliot. He's off-limits as long as we're working together, and I hope to be working together for a long time. Which means I need to get over him, and the best way to do that is to spend time with someone else.

Someone like Brooks.

I wash, shampoo, shave my legs. I finish with my loofa, scrubbing it over my entire body. I think about rubbing it between my legs, but I don't. Because the person I'd be thinking about while I got myself off is the one person I have to stop picturing all the time.

Climbing into bed, I power up my laptop to send an email to Brooks's mom. I'm really glad to have my three paid dates over with. The report I gave to Liam's mom had been easy. He was a decent guy and if it hadn't been for Elliot dating his sister, I'd like to think he would have asked me for a second date. Jesse's report was harder. I didn't want to bash the guy, and I didn't want to hurt his mom, so I tried to stay mostly neutral, pointing out good things—he bought me a drink and picked a unique place to meet—with areas where I thought his manners could use improvement. I owed it to her to be truthful and I was, to a safe degree.

Easiest of them all is the report I'm typing now. I sing Brooks's praises and assure his mom she has nothing to worry about. Brooks is definitely boyfriend material. (Insert happy face.) I don't mention we might see each other again. I typed it, then deleted it.

Because I'm not sure what I'll do if he does get in touch.

I'm not sure about anything.

"Having perfected our disguise, we spend our lives
searching for someone we don't fool."
—Robert Brault

Sax/Hastings
Workplace Strategy
Scorecard

Sax – 1
Hastings – 3

Chapter Fifteen

ELLIOT

After a long drive to get to Lake Tahoe, I wasn't about to say no to the optional hike, even though I should have. There's eight of us following a guide through the giant pine trees, the dirt trail an easy walk with inspiring views of the deep blue lake in the distance. More stimulating to me, however, is the female body in front of me. I can't take my eyes off Madison's long legs and round ass covered in black skin-tight workout wear.

I've tried. Trust me, I've tried. But I've been to Tahoe before and the sight right in front of me is so much better.

The agenda for the weekend is very loose, with only three mandatory sessions beginning tomorrow morning. It's James's goal that those meetings, combined with unstructured free time, will give his employees a chance to bond away from work and build deeper relationships.

I'd like to bury myself deep inside Madison.

Dude, breathe in the fresh air and take in the snowcapped

mountains, not your assistant's sexy backside.

Madison glances over her shoulder at me. She's so damn adorable, checking to make sure I'm still behind her. We're the last two in the single-file line. Drake is up at the front with a couple of other people from the San Francisco office.

Discussion between the group members has centered on what everyone plans to eat once we return to civilization. Auggie, in the middle of our line, makes it sound like we're so far from the hotel we may starve first. She's a natural-born leader and jokester and has no problem poking fun at herself.

"Okay everyone," she calls out. "Time to break into song. This is to the tune of 'These are a Few of My Favorite Things,' so sing with me, people: when your stride breaks, when your foot aches, when I'm moving too slow, I simply remember my favorite things, and then I don't feel so low." She repeats the refrain until we all join in. She's got a killer voice. I can't say the same for the rest of us. Then someone shouts out, "How about 'Ain't No Mountain High Enough'?" Auggie gives a "Yes!" and we change songs.

I've just managed to get my eyes fixed on the sway of Madison's ponytail when out of nowhere she goes down.

"Ow!" she cries out, but no one else hears her over the singing. She rolls onto her butt, holding her left leg at the knee.

I immediately kneel down to help her. "What happened? You okay?"

"I twisted my ankle and hit my knee on the way down."

The guide notices we're not following and directs Drake to continue leading while she hurries to us. Of course that leads all eyes to Madison and the group stops, like any tight-knit team would.

"I'm okay," Madison says, sounding embarrassed. "Please keep going and we'll catch up."

"You sure?" Drake calls.

"Positive!"

"Can I take a look?" the guide asks, lifting her backpack off and unzipping it.

Madison nods and pulls up her legging to expose her ankle. "It's just a twist."

The guide puts on protective gloves, then, with a gentle touch, examines Madison. "Does that hurt?"

"A little."

"It could be a sprain. Walking down the mountain is harder than walking up, so I think you should definitely turn around here. Let me call for someone to come help you down." She pulls out her radio.

"No need. I've got her," I say.

"Elliot, you should—"

"It's not up for discussion," I interrupt. Like hell I'm letting anyone else help her. Sure, if it was something serious, but I can manage this.

"Are you sure?" the guide asks me.

"Yes."

"Okay, let's get you up," she says to Madison.

I take one arm, the guide the other, and we help Madison to her feet.

"Can you put any pressure on it?" The guide lets go of Madison to lift her backpack off the ground.

Madison takes a tentative step. "A little, yes."

There's no need for her to put any pressure on it. I scoop her into my arms. I've got a good seventy-five pounds on her, most of it muscle, and can carry her downhill no problem.

"Elliot! What are you doing?"

"We're good," I tell the guide. "Thank you."

She smiles, whether it's because I said thanks or because I've swept Madison off her feet, I'm not sure. Maybe both. "Put some ice on it when you get back to the resort and try to stay off it for the rest of the day."

"She will."

"I can answer for myself," Madison grumbles. "I will. Thanks."

The guide jogs back up the mountain while we walk down. Madison loops her arms around my neck. Her Wint O Green Life Savers breath fans the side of my neck. She loves the hard candy. I do, too, now. "You should be with everyone else, not me," she says.

"No. I shouldn't. I take care of what's mine."

"I'm not yours."

"You're my assistant. Ergo, my responsibility." It's way more than my duty, but I can't say that out loud. I can't feel it. I can't think about it. But I can act on it, at least in this scenario.

"I'm sorry. I didn't see the pothole."

"There's no reason to be sorry. If anything I should be thanking you for getting me out of more singing."

She giggles. "You do kind of suck."

"Oh yeah? Just for that I'm going to sing all the way down the mountain."

She vigorously shakes her head. "No, no. Please don't."

I open my mouth to belt out something, but she presses her palm to my lips to stop me. I'm reminded of my lips on other parts of her and my dick twitches. I close my mouth. She withdraws her hand, looks away.

Holding her like this, laying claim, and enjoying it, probably wasn't my smartest move, but when it comes to Madison, I can't stop myself.

"If you're getting tired of holding me, I can walk."

"I'm not tired." And even if I get there, I'm not letting her put any weight on that ankle until we're back at the hotel so she can ice it.

"Okay." She lays her head on my shoulder. For a moment, the gesture makes my legs weak. Having her relax in my arms and trust that I've got her feels like I've won something rare.

A few hikers pass us on their way up the mountain, and a few more pass us on the downslide. Several people ask if we're okay. I tell them yes. Then a large group, all wearing navy blue shirts and running, comes into view. There's a medic symbol on the front top left corner of their clothing. As their heavy footfalls and deeper breaths get closer, Madison's head pops up.

"You good?" The guy leading the pack asks us.

"Yes, thanks," Madison says. "Hey, I wonder if…" She trails off because she can stop wondering the same thing I was the second I saw the troupe—Brooks is right there in the middle of the pack.

He stops. "I'll catch up," he says to the person behind him. "Hey, fancy seeing you here. Are you okay?"

Madison tells him what happened. I tell him I've got her. After a quick glance at her ankle, he says he hopes she feels better and takes off.

"I had a feeling I'd run into him this weekend," Madison says once we've resumed walking.

I hate the tone of her voice, like she's been thinking about him and willing a run-in to happen. There's got to be at least a dozen trails around here and this is the one his team picks? It's a beginner's trail. Shouldn't they be running up advanced routes?

It sucked seeing her on a date with him last night. Contrary to what I said in my note, she looked hot as hell. She wears a skirt like nobody's business, and all I can think about is sliding my hands underneath the form-fitting material. I hadn't aimed to tag along with Mateo to the restaurant, but Teague—who happened to be on the phone with him when I got home—suggested it, thinking it was a good idea because it would be less obvious. I still had my doubts, given I'd planned to hang out with Socks. The four-legged furball has purred her way into my heart and at the end of the day I like petting her. Talking to her. She's a great listener.

Teague can be persuasive, though, so I loved on Socks for a minute, then left with my roommate. He made me promise to behave myself. Reminded me that I could not hook up with Madison. I agreed, since logically I know he's right, and feel like I did a decent job in spite of the confusing emotions taking up space in my thoughts.

"Can I ask you something?" Madison says now.

"Sure."

"I got a weird vibe from you last night. Do you think Brooks isn't as nice as he seems?"

Fuck me. The last thing I want to discuss with Madison is her dating life. It's none of my business. We've tried to keep our personal lives separate, only neither of us has had much luck. Me especially. I *want* to get to know her better. I want to know things nobody else knows.

"It doesn't matter what I think." If we get into this, I'm going to say something I'll regret.

"It does to me. Please, I just need someone to confirm he's not like all the other jerks I've gone out with."

"I haven't met those guys, so I don't know." I'd like to bash all their faces in, however. What dickhead treats a girl like Madison poorly?

"You're no help."

No shit. The second to last thing I want is to help some guy catch the girl I can't get out of my head. "Dating advice to my assistant isn't on my list of job requirements." I adjust my arms, situating her closer to my body to alleviate some of the strain on my forearms.

She tries to wiggle out of my hold. "Just put me down."

"Nope."

"This is stupid. My ankle feels better."

"Does it really?" I ask sincerely.

She stops fidgeting. "I don't know for sure, but if you put me down I can see."

"I'll do it once I get you back to your room. We're almost there. How's your knee feeling?" The hotel's steeple rooftop is in view.

"It's okay." From her tentative tone, she's full of crap, but I let it go. "I think I'll go out with Brooks again if he asks."

Why is she telling me this? I thought I made myself clear that I didn't want to discuss the paramedic, who for the record, is a nice guy and would probably treat her well. Which is why I act like a complete douche and say, "Just be sure he doesn't find out you only met up with him because his mom *paid* you." I'm not proud of myself for emphasizing paid. Mateo mentioned it, and I should have kept my mouth shut.

Her body tenses, making me feel even worse. "That's a really mean thing for you to say."

"How is it mean? It's the truth." *Annnd* I don't know when to quit.

"That you're using to hurt me."

"Fuck, Madison. The very last thing I ever want to do is hurt you. Ever. I'm saying that because I'm jealous. I'm jealous, okay? I want you, and I don't want anyone else to have you."

Shit. I can't believe that all came tumbling out of my mouth.

"Elliot," she whispers. My name hangs between us. Her big blue eyes are heavy-lidded. Her mouth is inches away from mine, and I want to kiss her. No matter the consequences, I want to fit my lips with hers until my kiss is the only one she remembers.

The trail opens up, the manicured grounds of the resort only a few hundred feet away. I'm two seconds from kissing her.

"Hey," Hazel says, jogging up to us. "We got word Madison was hurt."

Madison blinks away our connection as I jerk my head back. Our office manager knows everything back at the office, so I should have assumed the same would apply here, or that protocol dictated the guide radio the situation to the front desk.

"I twisted my ankle and hit my knee is all."

"Let's get you inside so you can elevate and ice it. James has a local doctor on his way to check you out."

Madison's cheeks turn bright pink. "That's really not necessary. I'm sure it's nothing serious."

I carry Madison into the lobby. James is waiting near the fireplace and high-back chairs. There's a towel and two bags of ice on one of the ottomans.

"This is so not necessary," Madison mutters for my ears only.

"Hang in there," I whisper. I sit her down on a chair, then step back so Hazel can tend to her. James asks what happened, and once again she tells the story. The doctor arrives and establishes it's a slight sprain and should feel better tomorrow but to take it easy for the next few days. Madison admits her knee hurts worse than her ankle and when she pulls up her legging she almost passes out at the sight of the blood.

She turns her head and looks up at me. A deep line bisects her eyebrows; worry clouds her usually crystal clear eyes. She reaches her hand to mine, and I don't hesitate to take it. If James doesn't like it, we can hash it out later. The fact is he wants his employees to have one another's backs and that's what I'm doing.

"You must have landed on a pretty sharp rock," the doctor says. "You need a few stitches."

She visibly shakes. I squeeze her hand. I'm not going anywhere.

"Okay," she says, her eyes glued to mine. "As long as I don't have to look."

"Not at all," the doctor says. "I'll tell you what I'm doing so there's no surprises, though. Sound good?"

"Yes." Her eyes skirt over to James. "Thank you for the special treatment."

James nods. "You're welcome." He looks between the two of us, but I can't make out what he's thinking. At the moment it doesn't matter. I'm not leaving Madison's side.

True to his word, the doctor gives a step-by-step rundown. James steps away but Hazel stays. She tells Madison about the many times she's been to the ER because her rambunctious twin boys have needed to be stitched up. The stories seem to keep Madison's mind off her own stitches.

When the doctor is through, Hazel and I get Madison back to her room. She's sharing a two-bedroom villa with Hazel and Auggie, so there's no reason for me to stay. I tell her I'll see her later.

Then I land in my one-bedroom villa and take a shower. One guess who I think about while I jack off.

• • •

"To sum up, I hope spending a couple of days away with coworkers, talking, eating, and sharing a couch brings you closer and creates a special feeling similar to gathering with extended family," James says. "It's been proven that teams who act like a family tend to have better communication, trust and appreciation for one another, and increased productivity. I value each and every one of your personal contributions and the energy you bring to ZipMeds. Thank you." He smiles at everyone in the small conference room. "Now I'm going to turn things over to Hazel, who has an exercise planned for us."

"Thanks, James. And I think I speak for all of us when I say we're honored and proud to be part of your company."

I applaud my agreement along with other clapping and verbal praises. When I quit my corporate job before having other employment lined up, I was worried I'd made a mistake, but it turns out it was the best decision I've ever made.

"For this exercise, I want you to separate into your department groups. Go ahead and do that now," Hazel instructs.

Madison is at the next table over and I motion for her to stay put. Drake, Drake's assistant, Peter, and I can come to her. She's moving a little slower than usual today but insists she's perfectly fine.

"On the center of each table," Hazel says, "are index cards. This exercise is called Worst Nightmare, and I want each of you to write down your worst department or industry-related nightmare. Once everyone has done that, you'll each take a turn sharing what you've written. The goal is to openly discuss your fears and stressors with your team's support and then talk out steps that can be taken to solve the issues or at the very least help prepare you for worst-case scenarios. Any questions?"

I have a question. Can I sit this one out? My worst nightmare is someone discovering I want to have slow, blow-her-mind sex with my assistant. And there's no fucking way I'm sharing that. I know how it ends. With my ass kicked out the door.

"What if my nightmare is sharing my nightmare?" someone jokingly calls out.

"Then you get to go first," Hazel says with a smile.

Drake gives me a funny look from across the table. After he met Madison, he asked me how in the world I was going to keep it in my pants. I told him I had plenty of other options, which was a lie, but he seemed satisfied. This entire morning

I've been trying my damnedest not to look at her like the sun rises and the moon sets with her. Maybe I'm not doing a very good job and he's noticed my infatuation.

I ignore Drake's attention and pick up an index card. My fingers brush Madison's when she reaches for one at the same time. Her eyes flash to mine before racing away and I'd bet money sparks shot up her arm, too. Is her worst nightmare on par with mine? I've been with enough women to know she has dirty thoughts about me, too. The signs are all there: the hitches in her breath when we accidentally touch, the peeks in my direction when she thinks I'm not looking. I've seen her check out my ass more than once.

I also know this job means everything to her.

"What do you say we break the rules a little bit?" Drake asks.

Now he's got *my* attention. And Madison's and Peter's. Speaking of Peter, if he keeps sneaking glances at my assistant like he's picturing her naked, my fist is going to accidentally meet his jaw.

"We know we've got the best jobs in the company and the only thing we worry about is keeping our focus metrics-driven, so unless I'm off base, let's exercise our minds and get to know one another in a different way."

"Sounds good to me," I say. That I've already broken the rules with Madison weighs heavily on the back of my mind, but it's like I forget every goddamn thing but her when we're alone together.

"Me, too," Madison says, seemingly as relieved as I am. I imagine this thing between us also plagues her, and I'm mad at myself for making her worry. I'm the senior employee here and I should have listened to my doubts and let her go on her first day. But at the time, I had no idea I'd grow this undeniably attracted to her.

"I'm in," Peter agrees.

"All right. Instead of nightmare, we'll answer a few out-of-the-box questions about one another. First one: look at the person to your left and write down what animal they remind you of."

Drake is to my left, Madison to my right, and Peter across from me. I jot down falcon for Drake. The bird is fast, super chill, and doesn't sweat the small stuff. At least that's what my falcon brain is saying.

"Next look to your right and write down what type of fruit comes to mind."

Madison better not be thinking "banana" about anyone else at this table but me. She quickly looks at Peter before writing down her answer. I can think of a few fruits when it comes to my sexy assistant. Apple—they are synonymous with carnal sin after all. Cherry, obviously. Coconut—not that her pert, round tits define her, but they are hard to ignore. Strawberry. Melon. Passion fruit. I settle on writing down peach. It seems the most innocent—*Madison, you're a peach of an assistant.*

"Third and final question, look across from you and write down what genre of music they are."

Peter is clearly country.

I know this is a team building exercise, even given Drake's impromptu change, but the only answers I care about are the ones that concern Madison and me, so I pretty much tune out everything else.

She turns the prettiest shade of pink when I tell her she's a peach. I puff out my chest when she tells me I'm a panther—fierce, strong, and unafraid.

I can't let anyone see the truth about her last description. I am afraid. I'm terrified of *her* and the things she makes me feel. I imagine what my days would be like if Madison wasn't in them and a shudder runs through me. Then I imagine what my nights would be like if she starred in every one of them and fuck, it's a pretty stellar picture.

When Hazel announces we're free to leave for lunch, Drake and Peter take off in different directions, leaving Madison and me alone.

"Let's grab lunch," I tell her.

"Thanks, but I was thinking about putting my leg up and ordering room service."

"Sounds good. Come on." I pull her chair out and help her get to her feet a little easier. It's not my fault she twisted her ankle and hurt her knee, but a part of me still feels responsible, since I was right behind her and didn't see the pothole to warn her.

"Did you not hear what I said?"

"I heard you, and we can eat in my room."

"I'm not sure that's a good idea." She follows beside me despite her objection, my steps slower than normal so she can easily keep up.

It's a terrible idea, but I can't stop proposing we spend more time together even though I know we shouldn't.

"That makes two of us, but upstairs we're in the friend zone, and what's that saying? Two wrongs make a right?"

Chapter Sixteen

MADISON

There is nothing wrong with the view from Elliot's room.

"Here," he says, carefully lifting my leg off the small table on the balcony and putting a pillow under my ankle. "How's that?"

"Good. Thank you."

"Are you cold? Can I get you a blanket?"

Elliot's villa faces the lake in the distance and while the sun is shining, we're seated in the shade. There's a chill in the air, but I'm not cold. I'm the total opposite of cold. Elliot's fussing is making me warm, and I hope my complexion isn't giving away just how much. "I'm fine."

He sits next to me on the cushioned love seat, and suddenly I'm a statue, afraid to move. He's being way too sweet and attentive, acting like a boyfriend, not a friend, and it's freaking me out.

We avoided each other all morning until Hazel's activity, when all I could think about was him. Animal: panther. Fruit:

banana. (I've checked him out *there* when he wasn't looking.) Genre of music: hip-hop. It had taken all my concentration to keep my eyes on Drake and Peter. Not only does Elliot smell better than should be legal, but he's got the stubble thing going on again.

"Lunch will be here in ten."

"Sounds good."

He nods. I nod. Neither of us really knows what to say to each other next. There's this crazy energy around us where one ill-considered word could change everything.

"Did you know the French don't call someone 'idiotic,' they call them 'as dumb as a broom'?"

I chuckle. "I didn't know that. Are you saying we're being dumb as brooms right now?"

"*Etre con comme un balai,*" he says in that delicious accent of his, and I don't care what he calls me when he speaks like that.

"That doesn't sound bad at all."

He turns his head. "*Really?* You like it when I speak French?"

"I didn't say that." I keep my attention forward and wave off his question like he's talking crazy.

"Your face says otherwise, *mon cheri,*" he whispers.

Damn blush. I cover my cheeks with my hands. Then someone moans and I resume my frozen state, not sure what exactly I just heard. There's another moan, and this time there's no mistaking what kind. It's a male moan—a *happy* male moan.

I peek at Elliot out of the corner of my eye. He's peeking back at me. "Is that...?" I trail off because I can't say it out loud. *Is that someone getting off?*

"Is that what?" Elliot teases.

"You know."

"I do?" he asks like he's Mr. Innocent. Ha! The last time

he was squeaky clean was probably when he was two.

The moaning gets louder. I break eye contact, my body temp rising higher, and look to my right. I'm pretty sure the sounds are coming from the room or balcony beside ours.

"That's it, baby," the guy says. "Keep sucking just like that."

I squirm. I can't believe the guy is getting a blow job right on the other side of the wall! I've never heard anything like this before. Henry didn't make noises when we were together. Maybe an occasional grunt, but he certainly never talked. He never told me he liked something I was doing or gave me instructions. Sex with him was like…a chore. A task with a reward when finished and the quicker he got to the finish line the better. More often than not, he got to the end before me and didn't care about my happy ending. I've stayed up more nights than I care to admit wondering why he didn't make sex with me a priority.

"Mmmm…fuck yeah," the guy next door groans. "Your mouth is fucking heaven."

Half my brain is telling me to get up and pretend I have to use the bathroom. But the other half is keeping me right where I am. I'm intrigued. Curious. And I don't want to be the one to chicken out and go inside. I can handle sex sounds with Elliot right next to me.

Long, deep sighs of sexual pleasure continue to float to my ears. I didn't know ears could tingle, but mine are.

I venture a glance at Elliot. He grins at me like he hears this kind of noise all the time, and granted both his roommates are in committed relationships so maybe he does, but—

"This isn't my first rodeo, Pink Cheeks."

Pink Cheeks! Great. I'm blushing and overheating, and Elliot has named my predicament. Well, I'll show him. "You like to eavesdrop on people having sex?" I ask quietly so that the couple getting busy doesn't hear us. Not that they would with all the action going on between them.

He chuckles. "Good idea whispering. We don't want them to know we can hear them. And no, I don't eavesdrop, but sometimes sounds travel through walls, or you know, across a dark freshman dorm room. Didn't you ever hear things you didn't want to when you were in college?"

"I lived at home."

"The whole time? You didn't ever stay in the dorms or with friends?"

"No, I commuted all four years." I've never lived anywhere but at home, which is why I can't wait to get my own apartment. I'm long overdue.

Elliot puts his elbows on his knees. "Okay, listen carefully."

I lean toward him, ready to commit to memory whatever words of wisdom he's about to impart. I respect his knowledge on all sorts of topics and resolve not to be embarrassed by this one.

Tiny lines fan out from the corners of his eyes and mouth. "I meant listen to our neighbor, not me."

"Oh." I press back. "Right. Of course."

"Little did you know you'd be getting some sex education along with your company education this weekend, but we ought to take advantage of it, don't you think?"

"This is teaching me something?"

Deep, guttural hums come from next door. "Baby, that feels amazing, but I want to blow my load inside your pussy, not your mouth."

Oh my God.

More than my ears are tingling now. Can Elliot tell?

"I'm guessing you and your dick-for-brains ex stuck to missionary and the bed. The couple next door is either on their balcony or up against the open sliding glass door and the guy is standing."

"How do you know?"

"Because having a girl on her knees while she sucks you off is, to quote our neighbor, 'heaven.'"

I did wonder that, but more so I wanted him to elaborate on the first part of his comment. "I meant how did you guess that about Henry and me?"

"I met the guy once, and after hearing about what he did to you from Mateo, I figured he was the kind of asshole who cheated because he didn't want to dirty his perfect and wholesome bride-to-be." He brushes the hair off my shoulder, then slides his fingers down my arm a few inches before pulling his hand back.

My body is on fire, my breasts instantly heavy. I wish he'd run his fingers across them, around, over, and under them.

Bad wish. Bad. Bad. Bad. I keep waiting for this feeling of desire to fade, but every time Elliot touches me, it grows worse. I want to get dirty with him, wherever, however, and whenever he wants.

"Hands on the glass, baby," the guy next door says. "That's right."

"So," Elliot murmurs, "this is teaching you how desperate and top priority sex can be."

"Hurry," the woman says, sounding beyond eager. "I need you inside me now."

The couple joins together—I know this from the explicit language the man uses and the cries of pleasure the woman lets out. From the sounds of it, they aren't making love but fucking. I'm not sure I've ever been fucked. Certainly not like the woman next door, who couldn't care less if anyone hears her, and whose sighs and groans sound like she's on the edge of ecstasy the entire time.

I squirm again.

"Does it turn you on to hear them?" Elliot whispers in my ear.

"Yes," I admit.

"Me, too."

I close my eyes. "This is wrong."

"We've already established that, but look at it as another bonding experience. I'm learning that you like some dirty talk, and the idea of being watched or listened to turns you on."

My eyes fly open. Elliot is so close, yet so far. If he was anyone but my boss, and I was anyone but his assistant, we'd be all over each other right now. I gaze into honest blue brilliance fringed with dark lashes, knowing that thought is true.

"Yes! Oh my God. Yeesss!" The woman being thoroughly fucked screams.

"What am *I* learning?" I whisper.

"That it's not just the back seat of a car I want to fuck you in. I want you bent over this love seat, up against a wall, on your back, on all fours, and every other way we can think of."

I feel his words between my thighs, making me wet. I bet I could come just from listening to him talk. "Maybe we should kiss," I blurt out. I know it's wrong and I could get fired, but just saying aloud what I've been thinking is the emotional release I needed.

"You read my mind again, Pink Cheeks, but..."

"It could be awful and then we can put this whole insane attraction thing to rest and forget about it."

"It wouldn't be awful."

"How do you know?"

"Because I'm an amazing kisser and I have a hunch you are, too. You've just been kissing the wrong guy."

I lick my lips. I can't help it.

Elliot groans. "The thing is we won't want to stop at just a kiss. And every day at work we'll know what we're missing until we can't take it anymore and I put you on my desk and bury my face and fingers in your pussy, making you come *twice*, before I bury my cock so deep inside you I'm touching a place no man has ever touched before, and you come a third time."

My heart stops. Literally stops. Then it pounds harder than ever before. His certainty is as sexy as the words themselves.

Knock. Knock. "Room service!"

"Fuck, you feel good. I'm coming, baby. I'm..." Next-door guy grunts through his release.

I giggle. It's an involuntary defense mechanism. My nerves are at an all-time high level of restlessness. This situation isn't anything I could have imagined, and laughing is necessary if I want to maintain what little professionalism and calm I have left. When James said he wanted his team to fortify bonds and build deeper relationships, he didn't mean by having—or listening to—sex.

"I'll get the door," Elliot says, adjusting himself as he stands.

I follow him inside, relieved to leave the lust drenched patio behind us. It's unfair how much I want more with Elliot.

"Oh, hey, Madison," the room service guy says. He brought dinner to my room last night and we'd spoken for a couple of minutes. "How are you feeling today?"

"Hi, Dante. I'm much better." I stand in the middle of the room as he pushes the food cart into the sitting area.

"That's good right there, thanks," Elliot tells him gruffly. He picks up his wallet and pulls a few bills out to give to Dante. Is he mad I know Dante's name?

"Have a good day," Dante says, looking at me.

"Thanks. You, too."

He stays focused on me for a few seconds longer than he probably should. Dante is a couple of years younger than me, I'd guess, and he wants to work in hotel management eventually. He was really sweet last night and brought me extra bags of ice after delivering my dinner.

"You can go now," Elliot instructs. He steps in front of me, blocking me from Dante's view. I suck in my bottom lip. I think he's jealous. Again.

I lean sideways and give a little wave goodbye. Embarrassment crosses Dante's face before he turns to leave without another word.

Elliot grabs two chairs from the dining table and situates them across from each other at the linen-covered rolling table. He holds my chair for me. "Have a seat."

"Thank you. You know, Dante was really sweet to me last—"

"I don't want to talk about Dante."

"Okay." I play it cool when I'm secretly happy about his clipped response. I unwind a linen napkin, pull out the silverware, and put the cloth on my lap. I couldn't decide what I wanted to eat, so Elliot ordered all three of the meals I was having a hard time choosing from and said we'd share. He lifts the metal lids off the plates, and the yummy smells of pesto, garlic, and cheese hit my nose.

"About what I said…" Elliot puts half of a grilled cheese sandwich in front of me. "I—"

"Please don't take any of it back."

"I'm not." He relaxes in his chair and closes his eyes for a moment. "I meant every word I said."

"But it ends there, I know. So let's move past it and eat." I pick up the sandwich. "I bet you can't guess my favorite kind of cheese."

He arches a brow in playful amusement, his shoulders visibly relaxing. "What do I get if I do?"

Cheddar oozes out the side of my grilled cheese, so I pinch it off with my fingers and put it in my mouth while I think about what to wager. Elliot watches me, his eyes lingering on my lips before he looks away and dishes some pesto pasta onto his plate.

"Guess it right and I'll buy you a new tie. Guess it wrong and you buy me a new skirt."

"Mozzarella," he quickly answers, "but I'm buying you a skirt and you're not buying me a tie."

My jaw drops.

"Thank you anyway," he adds.

"How did you know?"

"I pay attention, Mads. I know what kind of cheese you order on your veggie burgers and sandwiches and how much you love pizza." He digs into his pasta.

His notice is one of the nicest things ever. Henry never remembered my favorite anything without asking me— sometimes twice. I almost argue about the tie, but I have a feeling if I try to fight him on this, he'll refuse no matter what I say, so I bite into my sandwich instead.

We talk about regular things after that. When we're finished eating, I go back to my room. I have to get ready for my presentation. This morning James exposed hidden talents in a few of his employees and asked us to share them later today. My talent wasn't so hidden since almost everyone saw my drawing that one Friday on the hill at ZipMeds, but the other secret skills were surprises. Besides my drawing lesson, we get to watch a cooking demonstration and listen to a guitar player. These discoveries about one another are great ways to connect as friends.

Before I get my drawing plan together, though, I write Elliot a note. We're not at the office, but after the dirty things he admitted to me, I need to make him hate me for a little while.

Mr. Sax,

I'm not sure if you're aware of your bad manners

when eating, but as your assistant I feel it's my duty to inform you that you chew with your mouth open. How in the world your business meals are a success, I don't know. More than once I almost threw up in my mouth. No one wants to see masticated salmon or pesto pasta or—I shudder to think about it—any type of meat. Perhaps you should practice chewing in front of the mirror.

Sincerely,
Miss Hastings

I fold the note in half and slip it under his door. Two hours later when we assemble in the conference room again, I know he read it because he glares at me as I stand in front of everyone.

Auggie hands out large drawing pads to everyone while Hazel hands out boxes of colored pencils for tables to share. Obviously, they had a heads-up about this plan today. I wish I'd had one. I've never taught anyone anything, so I have no idea if my instruction plan will work.

"Hi, everyone!" *Good start, Madison.*

Hellos fly at me in return.

"Thank you to James for appreciating my drawing talent enough to ask me to teach you guys something." I smile at my boss's boss. "And since I'm most comfortable drawing people, I thought we'd draw the man who brought us all here."

James raises his eyebrows, a mix of flattery and worry on his face.

I turn to the easel set up beside me. "Step one is to start with a circle…" I continue to give step-by-step instructions for the eyes, nose, eyebrows, and mouth. With each step, I impart my thoughts on eye shape, eyebrow angle, and nose length and width. Ears come next, then the hair. James has a thick head of brown hair, so I give him a good hairline. When finished, I glance over at James and consider my drawing a pretty good rendering.

With the "teaching" part over, I circulate around the room to help anyone who would like my assistance. My coworkers are talking, laughing, and enjoying their newfound skills—or lack thereof.

"Is that James or one of the stars from *Planet of the Apes?*" someone jokes.

Elliot is sitting in the back of the room with Drake. Drake's drawing is good. He picks up a brown pencil to color the hair. Elliot's drawing is...nonexistent.

For a moment, I'm so hurt he didn't have the courtesy to draw something that I almost hurry past him without a word. But then I'm mad at his disregard and decide he doesn't get a free pass.

"Is that invisible James?" I ask, my tone unpleasant enough to make Drake notice.

"I don't draw," Elliot says.

"Neither do I," Drake counters, "but Madison's instructions were easy to follow." He gives a small shake of his head and goes back to his drawing.

"I could help you," I offer, my anger dissipating. Elliot sounds a little...lost maybe?

He looks up at me, ready to tell me no if the flash of irritation is any indication. But just as his mouth opens, his eyes soften. "Okay," he relents.

I sit down next to him and start my instructions from the beginning. His hand isn't exactly steady as he follows my directions, so I lean over and cover it with mine. He's a leftie, though, and I'm right-handed, so the angle is weird. When I try to pull my arm back, his other hand captures my wrist, signaling I should stay put. "Let me switch hands," I whisper. If he just needs my touch, I can do that, and at the very least help stabilize his hand.

Our position brings me close to his side, my breasts pressed against him, my mouth only inches from his stubbled jaw. I'm well aware of everyone else in the room so I'm sure to throw off the vibe like this is no big deal. Nothing to look at here! I'm just helping Elliot draw. I'd be in this position with anyone else in the room if need be.

Body language can lie, right?

I continue to quietly instruct him until the bare bones of his sketch is complete. He takes a deep breath as he studies what he's drawn. "Not bad, Mr. Sex," I say. Shit! "I mean Sax." I yank my arm back and practically kick the chair away in my haste to stand.

Elliot grins for the first time since he entered the room. This is not amusing. This is dangerous. I can't believe that slipped out of my mouth. Did Drake hear?

And now my ankle hurts because I landed on it funny.

I hobble away before either one of them can say anything. Auggie is at my side two seconds later. "Are you okay?" she asks.

"I'm fine. Totally fine."

"I don't think so."

"You're right. Can you ask Tony to play guitar now? I don't want to draw any attention to the fact that I stood up wrong. Maybe I can sneak away to ice my ankle for a few and then come back?"

"Of course."

"Thanks." I keep walking, but before I exit the conference room I look over my shoulder to see if Drake appears to have heard what I said. His head is down so I've no idea, but Elliot is staring at me, an unreadable expression on his face. I wince, my ankle throbbing, and focus back on my steps.

For the rest of the weekend, I vow to keep my distance.

Chapter Seventeen

ELLIOT

"Let her go," Drake says.

I sit my ass back in the chair. "It looked like she might have reinjured her ankle." When I grinned like a jackass at her mispronunciation of my name and she jumped to her feet.

"And you want to kiss it better?"

I jerk my head to look at him directly. Shit. I should have lived with the hurt in Madison's eyes and skipped the drawing like I'd intended. Was I aware of Drake sitting right next to me while she had her tits pressed against me, and her small, soft hand on top of mine? Yes. But he looked engrossed in his drawing. And I thought I'd done a good job of schooling my reaction to her. I think about lying to him now for all of five seconds. Drake is the reason I got this job and I owe the guy the truth.

"Am I that obvious?"

"Yes."

"Fuck," I say to my lap. Then raising my head, I say, "We

haven't crossed any line in case you're wondering." I think more seriously about that statement. "Fuck. Yes, we have." Even if I hadn't had her half naked in my lap and my finger in her mouth in Seattle, the flirting I've done far exceeds innocent. "If things were different and I wasn't her boss, I'd want to date her," I admit.

"That's a problem," Drake says.

"I know."

"It sounds like there's enough grounds to let her go."

His laying blame on Madison rubs me the wrong way. I clench my fists under the table. He has no clue what he's talking about. "She's not at fault. Not by a long shot."

"Look, I know I've joked around about her, and I shouldn't have done that. If I put you at ease with your relationship with her, that's on me, so if you can move forward in a professional manner only, I'll forget we had this conversation."

"She's a phenomenal assistant and I don't want to lose her."

"Looks like you have your answer then."

Tony starts playing the guitar in the front of the conference room, bringing my conversation with Drake to a stop. While my coworker strums the instrument like a pro, I think about Madison. Am I that hard up that I'd risk my job to what? Fuck her once? We can't have a relationship *and* work together, so that leaves giving in to temptation then forgetting it ever happened? That's fucked up and Madison deserves more. I just have to suck up this feeling that it's inevitably going to happen.

And keep my hands to myself in order to make sure it doesn't.

My mind drifts to my future and my five-year plan. I eventually want someone special to share my life with, but work comes first. It always has. I'm afraid I'll be worse off if I veer from my work goals. Yes, there's been the occasional girl to spark more than my passing attention, but it hasn't panned out. That Madison is the brightest spark I've come across is a cruel joke. And she's been right under my nose for years.

Not for the first time, I wonder why we didn't connect after she ditched her groom and before she walked into ZipMeds. Then I answer my musing with *because the job was meant for her.* I wasn't stretching the truth when I said she was a phenomenal assistant, and maybe it's not what I needed, but what she needed.

Which means I will not screw it up for her.

There will be no screwing.

Of any sort.

No more flirting.

No more fantasizing, eye fucking, staring, or teasing. Anything that ends in –ing is stricken from our association. Even eating.

Goddamn note of hers.

• • •

"Hey," Madison's gentle tone is music to my ears after the phone call I finished with Drake a few minutes ago. I lift my head from my computer to see what's up as she slips all the way into my office. "I just emailed you the final trending forecast for Indonesia and Rwanda, so if that's all, I'm going to head home now."

I glance at the time. Jesus. It's nine o'clock. I kept her late because James has been breathing down my neck about the expansion project. She's been amazing helping with it, her contact in Indonesia a big plus.

"Okay. Thanks, Mads. I really appreciate all your help. Good night." Damn it. I quickly drop my gaze. It's the first time I've slipped and called her Mads in a while. Ever since we got back from Tahoe a little over a week ago, we've been nothing but appropriate with each other.

It hasn't been easy.

Every time I look at her, I feel connected to her beauty and intelligence in a way I've never felt before, and I tell myself in order to keep her, I have to let her go.

"You should head home, too," she says, taking the chair across my desk and drawing my helpless gaze, because there is nothing I'd rather rest my tired eyes on than her. "You've been working late every night."

I reach over my shoulder and rub the knots there. "Some weeks are like that."

"Is there anything else I can do so you get out of here quicker?"

"No. You've done enough. Thanks for the extra hours you've put in." It hasn't been a hardship working late when Madison is on the other side of the glass wall.

"Thanks for trusting me with so much responsibility. I've learned a lot from you."

"We make a good team."

"We do." She stands and moves around my desk toward me.

In typical pulse-pounding fashion, my heart beats a little faster. What is she doing?

"Friend to friend, let me at least help with that?" She lifts my hand out of the way and starts massaging my upper back and shoulders.

I'm an idiot, because no way in hell am I about to refuse a massage from her. I don't tell her *no, that's okay.* Instead, I drop my chin and let my head loll forward. She did put us in the friend zone.

She kneads my muscles with perfect pressure, using the heel of her hands and fingers in flawless coordination. Add back massage to her list of extraordinary qualities. It feels so good that when I sigh in total surrender, I don't give a shit.

"You're really tight," she says.

I'd like to find out how tight she is.

"I've been told I carry my stress there."

"I think a lot of us do." She digs a little deeper. I had no idea her small, delicate hands contained so much power.

"Feel free to stop as soon as you get tired."

Her hands still. "Do you want me to stop?"

"Not even a little."

She resumes rubbing my knots away. "You played baseball growing up, right?"

"I did."

"Did you play in college?"

"For two years, yeah. I had to give it up when I tore my ACL." Behind my closed eyelids, I remember the green of the grass and standing in the outfield hoping the ball would be hit to me in center. With every pitch and hit, I wanted in on the play.

"Ouch. So you know all about knee pain."

"More than I wish I did, that's for sure. How's your knee feeling, by the way?"

"Good. The stitches are out and there's a small scar, but I don't mind it."

"And the ankle?" She's been wearing heels again for the past few days, today's pair the black ones with a thick bow at the back of each ankle.

"It's good, too." She leans against my chair, pressing more firmly into the spot just below the curve of my neck. The knot there is almost gone.

I make a mental note to buy her a gift certificate to a day spa for a massage or facial or whatever she wants to relax and feel good. I'd offer to personally return the favor, but I don't trust myself to limit my hands to her back and shoulders.

"Okay, turn around," she says, lifting away.

"Turn around?" I ask, raising my head, but making no

other move. My mind immediately goes to a sexy-as-hell picture of her down on her knees unzipping my pants. I concentrate on keeping my dick in a polite position.

"Yes, if you don't mind facing me, the new angle will make it so I can grip your shoulders and use my thumbs to press into your front deltoids while the rest of my fingers massage your rear deltoids, and I should be able to break down the rest of those knots."

I run my hand over my mouth and jaw as I turn. *Grip, press, massage.* She can do whatever she wants to any part of me she wants. I'm putty in her hands. "Is there anything you're not good at, Miss Hastings?"

"Probably."

"Such as?" I automatically spread my legs so she can step between them. Big mistake. This puts my face just below her mouthwatering chest. She's wearing the short black dress I bought her with those sexy heels of hers. The dress is fitted on top and flares out at the bottom. The short sleeves, neck, and shoulders are crocheted, revealing a hint of skin. The outfit is sweet and sexy, just like my assistant. I couldn't resist. I felt the gift was about giving rather than claiming ownership of a bet.

"Hammering," she says, gripping my shoulders. "I'm terrible with a hammer. I tried to hang a picture in my room once and missed the nail entirely and put a hole in the drywall." She squeezes her hands, pressing her thumbs and fingers into my skin.

I can think of a few things I'd like to press against her. *Focus on the massage, man.* I close my eyes and drop my head.

"At least you didn't hit your finger," I say.

"Oh, I did that the next time." She stops for a moment, as if feeling the pain all over again. "I was so worried I put a hole in the wall that I moved slightly to the right and tried again, thinking I could cover the hole with the picture. Instead, I hit my thumb."

I open my eyes, intending to look up, but get stuck on Madison's bare legs. Her skin is smooth and the color of cream. The light scent of strawberries reaches my nose. All of a sudden, I don't know what to do with my hands. My fingers itch to touch her. To slip under her skirt, palm the backs of her thighs and work my way up to her ass. What color underwear is she wearing? What style? What would she do if I dipped a finger inside them?

"Ouch," I give back to her before slamming my eyes shut and clutching the arms of my chair. Is it against office policy to undress my assistant with my mind? I don't think so.

"Needless to say, coordination has never been one of my strong suits."

"You've got plenty of others."

"Thanks."

For the next few minutes, we're silent. She's got me so relaxed, I'm finally able to clear my mind. My muscles are loose. My jaw is slack. I doze off. I dream…about C-cups encased in a light-blue bra, long, sexy legs wrapped around my waist while I sit in my desk chair. Matching light-blue panties fit snugly against the growing bulge in my pants as she grinds against me and…

"Elliot?"

Damn, I love the voice saying my name.

"Elliot?"

I jolt awake. My cock is hard, my breathing a little shallow. And my hands are underneath Madison's dress. Shit. I look up. Her chest is rapidly rising and falling, her face is flushed. Do I immediately remove my hands from the fantastic curve where her ass meets her thighs? Nope.

Not yet.

Because I've never touched a sweeter curve than this one

in my life. (By my estimate, she's wearing a cheeky panty.)

And I'm a selfish prick.

To my credit, a mixture of longing and greed shines in her eyes. She isn't upset about where my hands are.

"I got the knots out," she whispers. Her arms are at her sides and I wonder how long ago I started copping a feel.

"Thanks. And uh"—I reluctantly release my hold—"sorry about that. I've never acted on a dream before. At least none that I'm aware of."

"You were dreaming about me?"

"Yes," I tell her honestly. Trying to be the good guy is exhausting. I'm tired of fighting with myself.

"I dream about you, too," she admits. She combs her fingers through my hair, sighs in pleasure, then pulls her arms back. My scalp tingles from her touch. "I've been dying to do that, and I figured since you got to feel somewhere, I could, too."

I glance down at my lap. She does, too, and my best intentions completely abandon me. "Can I pick the next place you feel?"

Her eyes widen.

"Don't get shy on me now, Mads."

She smartly scoots around the desk, out of reach. I contemplate standing, but remain in my seat and swivel my chair around. If I get to my feet, I'll chase after her until I catch her.

"And don't tell me that massage was completely innocent on your part."

She plays with the hem of her dress. "I don't know what it was, but I genuinely wanted to make you feel better."

"You did."

"This back and forth is confusing, Elliot." She lets go of her dress and pushes her shoulders back so she's standing at her full height.

"Agreed."

"I love this job. It's given me confidence I've never had before, and I think that's spilling over into my personal relationships, too. You're easy to like as a boss and as someone more, but I've worked too hard to throw this job away for a night of mind-blowing sex."

"Mind-blowing?"

She waves the description away. "Whatever. You know what I mean."

"I do. And I'm completely out of line here and apologize for flirting with you again. You're an outstanding assistant and I don't want to lose our working relationship. These feelings will pass and we'll laugh about it one day."

"I hope so." The vulnerability in her voice kills me, and I should have realized what an ass I was being.

"I'm sorry if I've made you uncomfortable in any way. It wasn't my intention and you can be sure I'll back off completely."

"I'm sorry, too."

"You've got no reason to be." It's not her fault she's beautiful, smart, kind, and a host of other qualities that get me in trouble when I think about them. "Let me shut down my computer and I'll walk you out."

"Okay. Can I say one more thing?"

"Absolutely. I want us to be able to talk about anything."

"Even if there wasn't a nonfraternization policy, it would be really dumb for us to get involved. If we were sleeping together and had a fight or things went wrong, we'd bring it to the office and things would get awkward really fast. And if we ever broke up, I don't think I could keep working for you. How could I when you..." Her gaze darts out the window behind me. "I also want—"

"Back up. When I what?"

She takes a second. "When you found someone else."

"Do you mean cheated on you?"

She crosses her arms over her chest. "Maybe."

"Jesus, Mads, that you even think that about me hurts like hell. I would never do that to any girl I was dating. I've been cheated on, too, remember, and I know how it feels." A sharp ache settles in the pit of my stomach. Her uncertainty tells me she still isn't over what her ex did to her. I stand but stay on my side of the desk. "Not all guys cheat."

"I know," she says, like she regrets dropping her guard and saying what she did.

"Despite some of my behavior this evening, I am one of the good guys."

"I know that, too, and I'm sorry for implying otherwise. I shouldn't have."

"Thanks."

"What I started to say was I also want to be recognized for my work here because I earned it, not because I was sleeping with my boss. I want my coworkers' respect and to prove myself valuable for no other reason than my work performance, not any performing I do in the bedroom. So even though the rule seems stupid when we get caught up in each other, it's not a bad thing. At all."

"No argument from me."

She lets out a breath. "I guess I needed to get that off my chest."

"I'm glad you did."

"Me, too."

"So, we good?" I'll stay and talk all night if she needs to.

"Yes."

Five minutes later, I watch her drive away before I get in my own car. Everything she said tonight is true, but there's one thing I'm still stuck on.

Her.

"I never realized until now how hard the brain has to work to make the body do what it asks. Or maybe how hard the body has to work to ignore the brain."
—Thalia Chaltas

Sax/Hastings
Workplace Strategy
Scorecard

Sax – 1
Hastings – 4

Chapter Eighteen

Madison

On Thursday morning, I call in sick to work. I can't face Elliot today. Not after everything that happened last night. I'm embarrassed to admit his hands up my dress was the most erotic thing I've ever experienced. If he'd asked to finger me, or lick me, or fuck me, I would have immediately said yes to any and all of it. But things got real when I looked down at his lap and saw how hard he was. I panicked, straightened out my sex-rattled brain cells, and swiftly put distance between us by moving back to the other side of the desk. My self-protective mode kicked in.

After that, I somehow got everything off my chest that had been bothering me. But what I didn't—couldn't—tell him was that I'm half in love with him, and turning off those emotions is going to be the hardest thing I've ever done.

How do you stop falling for someone you see forty-plus hours a week?

You start with calling in sick, then returning another

guy's text to let him know you're playing hooky for the day and would he like to meet up?

Brooks has texted me a few times since our first date. He checked in to see how I was after my fall in Tahoe and sent me a link to the cutest baby panda video to cheer me up. He's texted to say hello. Yesterday he tossed out a few dates to get together again.

My phone chimes with a text back. While my heart isn't pitter-pattering or anything, I like the idea of spending more time with him. *How about lunch?* he asks. *There's something I've been meaning to try. Are you up for some walking and taste testing?*

I'm up for anything to get my mind off Elliot. *Sounds good!*

Can I pick you up?

My mom is home and I'm not ready to introduce her to Brooks so I text, *Is it ok if I meet you?*

Sure. Give me 5 to confirm we can get in and I'll text you the address.

Okay.

When Brooks texts back it's a date and to meet him in two hours at the corner of Hollywood and Vine, my mind immediately goes to Elliot and our fun afternoon finding stars' homes. That corner is full of tourists visiting Hollywood, which makes it an unusual meeting spot for locals.

I read for a little while, shower, then dress in a comfortable heather gray ruffle sleeve T-shirt dress and my bow platform sneakers. The colorful floral-print, mini shoulder bag I finished sewing over the weekend completes my outfit.

"Hey, sweetheart," my mom says when I step into the kitchen to tell her goodbye, "where are you off to? I thought you weren't feeling well."

"I'm meeting a friend for lunch." I kiss her cheek. "I'll see you later." I hurry out the door before she questions me further.

Brooks is easy to spot at our meeting place. He's got the all-American football quarterback look going on in jeans and a well-worn New Orleans Saints T-shirt.

"Hi," he says. "It's great to see you again." His eyes rake over me in an appreciative way.

"You, too."

"It looks like our group is right over there. Come on."

The "group" is eight other people and a tour guide. "Hi, everyone," the guide says. "I'm Cynthia and for the next four hours you're going to be treated like a VIP while we explore a bit of Hollywood and visit several different restaurants for some unique tastings."

"I hope you're hungry," Brooks whispers, his arm brushing mine.

"I'm always hungry."

"We'll cover roughly seven blocks," Cynthia says, taking backward steps to begin the tour. "If you look down, you'll notice we're on the famous Walk of Fame…" She shares some fascinating history, past and present, talking nonstop. This is exactly what I need today—the sun on my face, some culture, new foods to taste, and a cute guy with dating potential at my side.

Brooks's hand grazes mine, but he doesn't try to hold it. We joke and laugh as we put our feet and palms in several of the famous movie stars' concrete prints. Actresses had really small feet fifty years ago. I feel like a giant.

I eat like one, too. The first two restaurant stops offer amazing crepes, artisanal pizzas, and mac and cheese potpies.

The third stop on our eating tour is a charming hole-in-the-wall and organic herb garden serving vegetable and corn tostadas and salt cod churros, which sound gross, but are delicious.

"There's a breakfast tour in Santa Monica we'll have to

try next," Brooks says.

"Because breakfast *is* the most important meal of the day," I say, not sure how I feel about *next time.*

"Damn right. And it's pretty much the only meal I know how to make."

I laugh. "Good thing you can eat it anytime of the day then."

"You have no idea how often I eat french toast for dinner."

"I love french toast."

He smiles at me. "Good to know."

I'm flirting with him and it's unintentional. I love bread. Period. I *like* Brooks. There's nothing about him that isn't likeable. He's handsome, attentive, sweet. But he's not pushing thoughts of a certain someone else out of my head.

On our next two culinary stops we indulge in gelato pops dipped in dark chocolate, then old-fashioned milkshakes.

"Mint chocolate chip shakes are the best," I argue, drinking very loudly from my straw, as if slurping will prove my point.

Brooks's eyes drop to my mouth. "I can tell you think so, but try this." He nudges my shake away and puts his Oreo cookies and cream shake under my chin. I wrap my lips around his straw and take a sip.

"It's okay." I scrunch my nose to tease him. "Try mine." I reach my arm out so he can taste the best. I watch his lips circle my straw. Lips should inspire a desire to kiss, right? After nearly four hours of eating, drinking, talking, and flirting, kissing should be a high priority.

"It's okay," he mimics.

"Okay, okay? Or just okay?"

"I didn't know there were varying degrees of 'okay.'"

We follow our group out of the shake shop. The sidewalk is crowded, and I feel like we're walking upstream, against the majority of pedestrians. "All 'okays' are not treated equally," I say like it's a legit thing when I'm making it up on the fly. "There's the 'satisfactory' okay and the 'tolerable' okay, neither of which you could possibly mean about my delicious shake. Then there's the 'fine' okay and the 'good' okay. Should I continue?"

"Absolutely. I'm curious to see how many you can come up with."

"Umm..."

He puts his arm around my shoulders. "Just kidding. You can stop. It was the good kind of okay."

"I know." I lean into him. The two of us share a similar ridiculous sense of humor. He makes me feel comfortable, like my brother does.

Not like someone I want to kiss.

There's only one person I want to make out with. He also happens to be the one person I can't think twice about.

Brooks walks me to my car when the tour is over. If there were even a tiny spark, I'd be all over kissing him and making plans for another date.

"Thanks for a great afternoon. I really enjoyed it." I lean against my car door and look up at him. *Come on, spark... ignite, flash, glint—something. Please.*

"I did, too." He leans closer, cants his head. He's in no rush. He's giving me time to say "no."

This is slow motion torture. Kiss him? Don't kiss him? That I have to debate it gives me my answer. I will never treat someone with even the tiniest bit of disrespect. Brooks is great and deserves great in return. It's not right to be with him if my thoughts are with someone else.

I turn my head so he kisses my cheek.

He awkwardly pulls back. I sag against the car in relief. "I'm sorry. I think you're awesome and I really like you, but not in a romantic way. I wish I did, I really do. It would make my life so much easier if I could fall for you," I ramble. "Plus there's something I need to confess to you about your mom."

His brows wrinkle. "My mom?"

"Yes, it's a funny story I'd like to tell you the next time we meet. As friends?"

He stays quiet.

"I know this really good breakfast place." I take his hand and lace our fingers, swing our arms in a sign of friendship. "My treat."

"Has any guy ever said no to you?" He squeezes my hand before breaking contact. "Honestly, I'm not happy you're friend zoning me, but I like you enough to deal with it."

"There's a lot you don't know about me."

"I'm getting that."

"I'm glad we can be friends."

"You sure you don't want to at least give me a shot at kissing you into changing your mind?" he teases.

I glance at his mouth. Not even the tiniest tingle of anticipation runs through me at the prospect, even though I can appreciate he has very nice lips. "I bet you're a great kisser, but...but I'm kind of hung up on someone else even though—"

He holds up a hand. "Got it. I thought there might be something going on with you and Elliot...was that his name?"

"*What?* There isn't anything going on with Elliot and me. I mean, why do you think that? Is it obvious there's some tension between us? Do you think anyone else has noticed it? Why would you say that?"

Brooks laughs. "Slow down there, speed talker. It was just a hunch. But I recommend you stay silent on the subject until you're more chill about it."

I press my lips together and nod.

"Workplace relationships can be tough. I've been there and it didn't end well."

"I'm afraid this one won't, either," I admit.

"Then it's a good thing you've got a friend to lean on."

"Thank you." I wrap my arms around him. I'm grateful to have someone to talk to who doesn't know Elliot.

He hugs me back until I let go. "See you around," he says, helping me into the car.

"Definitely."

I get home and go straight to my room. I take a long bath, read some more, and skip dinner because I'm still full from lunch. I pass on *Jeopardy!* with my parents, instead logging into my work email to see if I missed anything important. My inbox is oddly empty of new messages. I expected to see at least a couple from Elliot, since he likes to email me daily notes so he doesn't forget things. I also imagined he'd send a text or two to see how I was feeling and he didn't do that, either. He must have had a busier than normal day without me there. I waste the next two hours on the internet, trying not to feel guilty for missing work. When I lay my head on my pillow, I get a fitful night's sleep.

The guilt isn't strong enough to get my butt to work in the morning. I need another day, plus the weekend, to lock away my emotions before I see Elliot. I call Hazel to once again feign illness.

A half hour later, my phone rings. It's Auggie. Concerned there's something she needs from me right away for work, I don't hesitate to answer it. "Hi, Auggie."

"Hi, Madison. How are you feeling?"

"Okay." I'm feeling the "so-so" kind of okay, so total truth right there. Elliot has me lightheaded and a little overheated at times. Ergo, a good argument for sick.

"Is it the stomach flu?"

"Not exactly."

"The reason I ask is Elliot called in sick yesterday and today, too, so I thought maybe you guys ate lunch or dinner together and both caught a touch of food poisoning or something."

"Elliot is sick?" My pulse picks up. Is he the same kind of "sick" as me? "Does he know I haven't been at work, either?"

"You haven't been in touch?"

"No."

"I don't know if he knows. He talked to James this morning, but you know men, they don't always share like girls do. Madison?" My name comes across the phone line softer than the rest of her words.

"Yes?"

"I hope you know you can talk to me off the record about work stuff."

I can't believe Elliot and I *both* called in sick to work. I bite my lip in worry. He must *really* be sick, not faking it like I am because I need time away from his gorgeous face. "I know." I do. Auggie is someone I can trust, but I can't burden her with a secret like this when her boss is the head of the company.

"Well, feel better and I'll see you on Monday."

"Thanks. Have a good weekend."

Leaning against my headboard, I toss my phone to the side and imagine Elliot at home in bed, his shirtless ex-baseball player's body, his long muscular legs, his athletic shorts tied loosely around his hips as he goes over financial reports. He's insanely hot when he's in work mode.

I pick my phone back up. I'll send him a quick text to make sure he's okay. *Hey, just wanted to check in and see how you're feeling.* I stare at the screen, hoping to see those three tiny dots wave at me right away. They don't. After a few minutes without a response, I try one more time. *Hi Elliot. I hope you're okay. Lemme know.*

When an hour passes and I still haven't gotten a reply, I wonder if instead of being shirtless and going over financials, he's in sweats and shivering under the covers with a fever. And if he's at home, he's home alone. Mateo is out of town with Teague on a road trip up the California coast for work. Levi is on location for a TV shoot. I know this because I'm supposed to spend the weekend at Harper's for some girl time.

I quickly throw on clothes and put my hair in a bun on top of my head. I can't wait another minute thinking Elliot could be sick with no one there to help take care of him.

I'm at Elliot's front door ringing the doorbell fifteen minutes later. Relief washes over me when he opens the door looking fit and healthy. Athletic shorts hang down from his trim waist, a white T-shirt stretches across his chest. His hair looks like he recently rolled out of bed and ran his fingers through it. "Madison? What are you doing here?"

"I came to check on you since you called in sick."

"I'm fine. I told James I was exhausted, not sick, and asked if I could work from home for a couple of days." His eyes slide down my body, slowly, like I'm a road map and there are lots of places he'd like to visit. "Did you go to work like that?"

I glance down. I'm wearing white capri leggings and a pink hooded cropped sweater with white Chucks. I'd fit right in at work—especially for a Friday, but he knows my nine-to-five attire is dressier. "No, of course not. I called in sick. Yesterday, too."

His head pops up, his focus on my face. "Are you okay? What's wrong?" His brows furrow in concern. "And sorry, come in and sit down."

He sweeps me inside before I have a chance to decline. Not that I would have. Now that I'm here, we might as well talk, even though being alone with him in such a casual way sets off flutters inside my chest.

"What's going on?" he asks, sitting next to me on the couch, his elbows on his thighs. "I'm happy to say you don't look sick."

We've been honest with each other so far, so there's no reason not to be now. "I'm not. I, uh, just needed a couple of days to myself." He cocks his head, seeming to ask for more so I add, "After what happened in your office."

His eyes close for a moment. He leans back into the couch. "That's why I stayed home, too. Exhaustion had little to do with it, but I couldn't exactly tell James I'm having dirty thoughts about my assistant and needed some time to rein them in."

I'm dying to ask what kind of dirty thoughts. Instead I say, "Once again we're on the same page. I mean with the staying home, not the X-rated thoughts."

He runs his fingers along the stubble on his jaw. He has nice, big hands. I bet he knows exactly what to do with them to make a girl—

"X-rated? I didn't say that, Pink Cheeks. You sure you haven't—"

"I should go." I start to stand.

"Don't." He stays me by gently gripping my wrist. "I... Let's change the subject."

I wiggle back into the couch cushions. "Okay, why didn't you answer my texts?"

"I didn't know about them. I dropped my phone in Socks's water dish. It slipped out of my pocket and I didn't notice right away. It's drying in a bowl of rice, but I'm not optimistic about it surviving."

"That a bummer. I'm sorry. Who's Socks?"

"My cat."

"You still have the kitten?" I ask excitedly.

"I do," he says, his eyes softening at the mention of her. "We've hit it off, so I took her to the vet to get checked out and adopted her."

I catch movement out of the corner of my eye. Sure enough, Socks is walking lazily into the room. She is so cute.

Black with white paws and pointy ears. She curls right up next to Elliot. I know nothing about cats, but it's obvious she's in love with her owner.

"I've never had a pet. My brother has really bad allergies, so we couldn't get a dog or a cat. And the idea of any kind of reptile in the house freaked my mom and me out. I did win a goldfish at a carnival once, but it died after a day. I was so sad, I refused my dad's offer to get me an aquarium." I look down at Socks, her little whiskered face on Elliot's thigh. "I did get to bring a mouse home from school for the summer, once. I was so excited when my name was picked. We all wanted to bring Minnie home. She died, too, though, after a couple of weeks. We buried her in the backyard and bought a new mouse for the class. After that, I was afraid if I brought any kind of animal home he or she would die." I take a breath to stop my rambling. Kitten on Elliot's lap = he's hotter than usual. "Can I hold Socks?"

"I don't know." He wraps a protective hand around her small body. "I'm kind of worried after that story." He's joking, the glint in his eyes telling me so.

I make a sad face, pushing out my bottom lip.

He laughs softly. "Okay, pouty face. Here you go." He puts Socks in my lap so I can pet her.

"She's so soft."

"Like someone else I know."

"Are you comparing me to a kitten?" I feign irritation.

"Sorry." He turns so he's facing me and gently caresses a finger across my cheek then around my ear lobe. Rather than keep my attention on Socks, I drink him in. His thin T-shirt clings to his broad shoulders and bulging biceps. His neck is more thick than long, and I want to lick my way up the slope to where it meets his angular jawline. Is the stubble there soft? Rough? Would I even notice which one if he kissed me with his full lips and slid his warm tongue inside my mouth?

"Not sorry," he adds, referring to his lingering touch, I think.

Said mouth quirks up on one side. His eyes shine with unshared knowledge, like he knows the secret to making all my fantasies come true. Mine and no one else's. His laser-sharp focus always makes me feel special. When I gaze into those depths of uncommon blue, I'm more hopeful than I've ever been before that there are smart, intelligent, sexy men in the world who believe in soul mates and cherishing one person above all others.

"Because it doesn't matter how many times we reason through this situation, I can't stop dreaming about you, Mads."

"What are you saying?"

"Stay with me this weekend. Mateo and Levi are both gone. It can be our secret."

My heart is about to pound its way out of my chest. This is a big deal. Bigger than I may be able to handle, my head is saying. My body, though, is already straining to get closer to his. "I'm supposed to hang out with Harper this weekend."

"Tell her you can't."

"Because..."

"You're spending it with me. I don't want you to lie to your friend."

"But you said—"

"We'll keep it a secret at work."

Socks scurries off my lap as I twist to fully face Elliot and bring one leg under my bottom. I've followed the rules my whole life. Always been the good girl no one has given a second thought to worrying about. And all it got me was broken dreams and broken promises.

I'm tired of playing it safe.

Elliot isn't asking for anything serious. He's asking me to live in the moment, to feel alive and desired, and maybe that's what I need in order to fully take on the world again. Maybe this forbidden liaison will further boost my confidence and propel me to take chances.

There's just one teensy, tiny problem.

My heart is engaged already. If I spend the weekend with my boss, there is a very real chance he'll hurt me. He won't mean to, but he will.

"What are you thinking about?" Elliot asks.

"Truth?"

"Always."

"I'm worried you'll break my heart."

"You're assuming I have the power here, Mads, but you're wrong. If anyone has the power to break a heart, it's you. I've never wanted to touch anyone as badly as I want to touch you, and if I don't get to make love to you, I'm going to lose my mind."

I rub my lips together and shake my head "no." I've never had power over anyone like that. He's crazy.

"No, you're not going to stay?" he asks, like the thought is a stab to the chest.

"No, I won't hurt you," I say softly, the words true, but scary. I'm telling him I want this as much as he does, that I don't hook up, and being with him means something to me. Is it smart? Probably not, but I want to do something unpredictable and out of my comfort zone. And I want it with Elliot. Henry never looked at me the way Elliot does, with genuine admiration, like he'd chase me until his legs gave out.

Like I truly matter.

Elliot puts his hand on my knee. "So that's a yes?"

My eyes shoot to his hand on my leg. For one weekend, can I let it be that easy?

Chapter Nineteen

ELLIOT

"Yes," Madison says quietly.

It's the best goddamn "yes" I've ever received, but— "Are you sure?"

Intense blue eyes, fragile, yet stronger than she gives herself credit for, meet my gaze. "That you asked me that makes me even surer."

"We can't go back."

"I know."

Moving my hand back to her cheek, my body tightens when she tilts her head into my touch. The kind of trust Madison gives is beyond anything I've experienced before. It's potent. Rare. I've never felt like I held a woman's entire body and soul in my palm like I do right now, and I silently vow to protect this girl's heart no matter what.

The workings of the female heart are immensely complicated to say the very least, though, and I'm certainly no expert. I rub my thumb over her bottom lip, then lift my hand away.

Madison grabs my wrist, eyes still locked with mine. "I want this."

My own heart beats heavily inside my chest.

"I want you," she adds.

No matter the consequences, I want her, too.

I know I shouldn't do this.

I know it's stupid. Dangerous.

But I'm going to do it anyway.

"I can't wait a second longer to kiss you, Madison."

"Then only wait half a second."

I wrap my arm around her waist and lay her back on the couch. She complies easily, scooting down so she's lying flat underneath me. She stares up into my eyes with such trust it almost steals my breath. Madison isn't some girl I'm hooking up with. She means something to me, and if we only have this weekend, I want to make every moment special for her. I toss the pillows off the couch to give us more room.

"Your idea of a second and mine are very different." She wraps her arms around my neck to bring me closer. "I'm way past it." The sultry sound of her whisper drives me to action.

I position my elbows on the sides of her head and crash my mouth to hers. Soft, pliant lips open underneath mine. She tastes like coffee and cinnamon. Her small, wet tongue tangles with mine and it's good.

Beyond good.

I like to kiss, but this is a whole other level of kissing. Her eyes flutter closed. So do mine. We kiss.

Moan.

Kiss.

Hum.

Kiss.

Tight sounds of *more* pour out from the back of her throat.

What I'm doing is wrong for several reasons, but it's right for one: Madison is melting underneath my attention.

She gently rakes her fingers through my hair, cranking up my nerve endings in an unexpected and awesome way.

I move my hips against hers. She wraps one leg around mine, bringing me tighter. My cock grows stiffer as she makes no secret of grinding against me. I love this assertive side of her, this feisty part she normally holds back. I slide my hand down her side and underneath her sweater. She lifts her arms above her head. Perfect. I'm dying to get her clothes off, too. I release her mouth and pull the sweater up and off.

She shivers as I take a minute to enjoy the view. The white lace bra is one of those half-cup styles, putting the swell of her breasts on amazing display. My mouth waters. Seriously waters like I've never seen a pair of tits before. It's true I've never seen any wrapped so pretty. The lilac straps are velvet, and the same velvet trims the cup. There's a tiny lilac bow in the center. I will never look at another bow again and not think of Madison.

"*Tu es la plus belle chose que j'ai jamais vue*," I say.

She sighs. "I love when you speak French."

"That's why I did it."

"What did you say?"

"That you're the prettiest thing I've ever seen. Have I mentioned I love how you dress?"

"Not really."

"I do. Every day you come to work, I admire every sweet, sexy inch of you."

"I like the way you dress, too. All business sexy."

I grin. "Ever since Seattle, I've been picturing in vivid detail what you're wearing under your clothes, too."

"Today you don't have to picture it." She wiggles her hips, signaling her impatience. Normally, I'm not this patient, but I want our first time to be memorable for more reasons than

I made her come with my fingers, mouth, and cock. That's right. She's getting the newly devised Sax Hat Trick this morning.

"I am anxious to see the rest of it."

She kicks off her shoes. "I'm anxious for you to see it, too."

I tug her leggings over her hips and down her legs. It's like unwrapping the best present ever and discovering the something you've wanted for so long is even better than you imagined. There's a freckle on her hip, and one on her inner thigh. At the sight of the lilac bow centered on her thong panties, I lose my shit and have to kiss her there.

Starting at her belly button, I drop a featherlight kiss. On contact, Madison sucks in a breath, presses her hands into the couch. I open-mouth kiss my way to the edge of lace and groan when I smell her arousal.

I lift up, tug her leggings the rest of the way off, and look my fill. The scar on her knee is pink, but small, a badge of pride by the comment she gave me about it. I'm staring at beauty that is so much more than skin-deep and give a silent thank-you for the gift.

Then I'm on her, lips, tongue, hands. I kiss her mouth, drinking in her sweetness while I clasp the edge of her bra, pulling it down until her nipple is exposed. I rub the pad of my thumb over it, feeling it tighten. Madison bucks against me, moans from the back of her throat.

I kiss down her neck, breathing her in, enjoying her hot skin. I reach behind her back to unclasp her bra. One flick and I'm able to pluck it off her body. Holy shit, her tits are gorgeous. Round and full with pale-pink nipples begging to be sucked.

So I do. She arches, giving me full access, and moans loudly.

"Do you like that?" I ask. I want to know everything that

turns her on.

"Yes," she answers breathlessly. "I can…I can…"

"You can what?" I move to her other beautiful, stiff nipple and suck.

"I can feel it between my legs."

I'm happy to do something about that. While I continue to pass my tongue and lips over her nipples in equal time, I cup her over her panties and rub my thumb against her clit.

This earns me a louder moan. She bucks against my hand. Her wetness seeps through the thin material, making my dick impossibly hard. I slip a finger underneath the triangle. Feeling her bare pussy is hot as hell. She's swollen and in need of release, because of me.

"Can I finger you? Would you like that?"

Her eyes fly open, mere inches from mine. They're bluer than just minutes ago and full of lust and…uncertainty? "You can do anything you want to me," she murmurs.

"That doesn't answer my question. This isn't about me. It's about you, Mads."

Embarrassment has her lashes sweeping down.

"Hey." I touch my nose to hers, then give her an Eskimo kiss. "This is a no-shame zone. My entire house is, and for the next three days, I don't want you holding anything back. I want you to share everything going on in that beautiful head of yours, or there will be consequences." That last part is a joke.

Her throat moves as she swallows. "You mean like spanking?"

"Do you want me to spank you?" I ask with surprise. It's not really my thing, but I'm game if that's what she wants.

"No." She couldn't have a more adamant tone. I laugh softly.

I've gathered from our conversations that sex with her ex was very vanilla, and I've also sensed she wants more—

within reason. I rub noses with her again. "There is no embarrassment in asking for exactly what you want so I can give it to you. If it's something new, tell me. I'm yours to command until we discover what gets you off."

She crosses her arm over her eyes. "I've never talked like this before."

"Should I stop?" The idea of just fucking her doesn't sit well, but if it's all she wants...

"No."

I toy with the edge of her panties. "You have had an orgasm before, right?"

She drops her arm and gazes up at me with such vulnerability, I vow to make this weekend the best of her life. "Kind of. I mean yes, but nothing earth shattering or anything."

Her ex is a piece of shit.

"I'm guessing he never fingered you to climax?"

She shakes her head.

"Did you ever come on his face?"

Another shake of her head. "He didn't like oral."

What the fuck? The guy is a unicorn. "You never gave him head?"

"I did. He just didn't like to go down on me." She thinks about that for a moment. "He probably did on other girls, though, right?"

My jaw clenches. Am I happy that Madison is untouched in so many ways that I can be her first? Yes. But I want to fucking use her ex's face as a punching bag. "I'm going to say this once and then we're moving forward, okay?"

"Okay."

"Your ex was a despicable human being and you should never think about him again. Starting right now, I'm going to show you how a real man acts toward a woman he cares about. If at any point I do something you don't like, please tell me. And if I do something you really like, tell me that, too. Your body is incredible, Madison, and it's a privilege to be the guy to show you what it can do."

She blinks her agreement. I suspect she's too emotional to speak given how sincerely charming I am.

I reclaim her mouth, this time starting with a gentle glide of my lips over hers. She immediately surrenders. And takes the initiative to slip her tongue inside my mouth, where I let her dictate how hard and fast she wants to kiss.

My hands are another story. One slips back inside her panties, while the other cups her tit, kneads it. I rub my thumb over her nipple. I work her back up, until she's bumping and grinding, then slowly, I insert a finger inside her. She's tight, warm, and so wet. She pushes into my hand, telling me she likes what I'm doing. I add a second finger. She moans some more before her breathing grows shallow. I break the kiss and sit up.

I nudge her legs apart and sit between them on my knees as I continue to work her pussy. I'm fascinated by her. Gaze down at her with reverence, happy I'm the guy who gets to make her orgasm. Her lips are swollen from our kisses. Her mouth is slightly open. Her firm tits barely move, but the muscles in her stomach visibly clench as I make her feel good.

She sighs in pleasure when I hit the right place inside her. I take my free hand, move her panties to the side, and stroke her clit. Her hips lift off the couch. "That feels so good," she croons.

Two hands are always better than one.

I keep up the double dose of attention. She's close. Her fingernails dig into the couch. She presses her shoulders back. Her chest rises and falls. "Oh my God, Elliot."

"Let go for me, Mads. I want to hear you come."

She peeks at me under heavy-lidded eyes. "You're already watching me," she says, like that should be enough.

"Almost the best view ever."

"Almost?" she breathes out.

"Watching you come when my cock is buried deep inside your tight pussy will be the best."

My dirty words work like I hoped they would. Madison clenches around my fingers and then she falls apart, coming hard, screaming unintelligible words through her orgasm.

I slowly withdraw my fingers. She watches me lick them clean, her eyes going wide. "Delicious, but I think I need a better taste."

"You—"

She bites her lower lip when I curl my fingers around the sides of her thong and tow the small piece of lingerie down and over her ankles. Then I hook her legs over my shoulders and bury my face in her pussy.

Her musky scent is intoxicating, but when she moans my name and threads her fingers through my hair, it's electric. Tingles race down from my scalp to my dick. I latch on to her clit and suck, lick up and down her slit. She thrusts against my mouth, cups the back of my head, and holds me more firmly against her. I love that she's taking what she wants from me.

"That feels amazing," she says. "I can't believe you're going to make me come again."

I had no doubt. I reach my arms up and massage her tits, scraping my thumbs over her nipples.

"Holy stairway to heaven," she manages in between sexy-as-hell pants. "Don't stop."

No problem. I taste and tease, using my mouth and hands in tandem.

She starts to vibrate. Her legs squeeze my shoulders, while her hands keep my head in place. If I wasn't so good at this, I'd probably need to come up for air, but Madison inspires more from me. I want to feel her come against my face, taste her sweetness directly on my tongue. Make her lose control at *my* ministrations. That no man has brought her pleasure like this sparks fire in my blood.

I keep at it until her body stiffens, until she's screaming my name, and pressed firmly against me. Until she starts to float down, her body relaxing with satisfaction. She lets go of my head. Her hips sink into the couch.

Her cheeks are flushed, her body covered in a thin sheen of perspiration. She's glorious. I could stare at her for hours.

Our eyes meet as I lower her legs. "I'm really, really glad I decided to come over and check on you," she says.

"You have no idea how happy I am you did."

"I'd like to make you happier." She scrambles onto her knees and wavers when upright, reaching for the back of the couch for balance. "Whoa."

"Careful." I lift her into my arms and situate her on my lap. "Two orgasms will do that to you."

The smile she gives me is pure bliss. "I didn't know that until just now." She drops her chin and buries her face in my chest. "And I can't believe I'm completely naked in your arms right now, either."

I kiss the top of her head. "Believe it, baby." I get to my feet.

"Where are we going?" she asks.

"My bedroom. You're due one more orgasm."

She raises her head. *"What?"*

"It's time for number three, only this time I'm coming with you."

Chapter Twenty

MADISON

Elliot slowly sets me down inside his bedroom, my back to his front. The hardwood floor is cool underneath my feet, offering a welcome reprieve for my warm body. The left side of his bed is untouched. The right side is rumpled, and I know where I'll be sleeping this weekend.

I feel my cheeks flame. I'm sleeping with Elliot! Having sex with Elliot. Experiencing multiple orgasms with Elliot.

This is the biggest mistake of my life, but right now I don't care.

His hands gently untie the bun on top of my head. My hair spills down my bare back, his fingers combing through the strands before sweeping them to the side to expose my neck and shoulder.

I roll my lips tightly together in anticipation of his next move. Electricity hums between us. His breath is hot on my prickling skin. I've never felt more alive.

He places a soft kiss on my shoulder and a current of

unforgettable pleasure coasts down my spine. "You have the prettiest skin," he whispers. His warm, wet lips trace every inch of my shoulder. He kisses me there for a long time before moving to the curve of my neck.

It's sweet, wonderful torture. That he's taking so much time with me and my body is so entirely new for me, I'm about to turn into a puddle at his feet. Sensing my jellylike state, he puts one hand on my waist and the other on my upper arm to steady me.

His full lips are like velvet as they smooth over my sensitive flesh.

"And you smell unbelievably good," he murmurs. The tip of his tongue joins his lips in the simple, but amazing pressure to my neck. My head tilts to the side without thought.

My breasts feel full and my nipples are hard. Once again my body begins to strain for more, to go higher and higher. I can't believe it's possible to have these sensations again so quickly.

Elliot's hand slides over my hip down to the curve where my butt meets my thigh. He palms my bottom, squeezes, then gives a little push as he whispers in my ear, "*Monte sur le lit.* Get on the bed."

God, his voice. I do as I'm instructed, adding a little extra wiggle in my hips. I told him I couldn't believe I was naked in his arms, but not because I'm shy about my body. I'm comfortable naked, and am dying to find out if Elliot is, too. I toss him a look over my shoulder. His eyes jump from my bottom to my face. He licks his bottom lip.

"I'm going to leave bite marks on that ass," he growls.

I quickly turn my head back to hide my smile. That sounds…thrilling. My spine quivers thinking about it. I climb onto the bed, turn, and kneel in the center. He's still standing by the door, watching me. His eyes travel all over my body, while mine zero in on the huge outline of his hard cock underneath his shorts. I want to make him even harder. Do something sexy and unexpected. So for the first time ever, I touch myself in front of another person.

"Fuck," he says huskily.

I tweak the nipple on my left breast while my right hand slides down my stomach to rub between my legs. My fingers slide easily through my wet folds.

Elliot's expression goes taut, like he's waging a battle with himself. Then he reaches behind his neck and yanks his shirt over his head, tosses it aside. The move is hot, his body a thing of beauty. I swallow hard at the smooth muscle outlining his chest, abs, and arms. The clearly defined indentations at his hips that disappear into his low-riding shorts halt my movements.

"Are you for real?" I ask.

He smiles. "One hundred percent pure grade Sax." His palm glides down his torso. "Want to see the rest?"

I nod vigorously.

"Don't stop touching yourself." He waits until my hands are in motion again before pulling down his shorts and boxer briefs in one fluid move.

Thank goodness I'm already on my knees. I've seen one guy naked in person. Harper and Teague had me watch porn with them one night. An emergency "your ex is a dick and a small dick at that" tequila and cupcake night with pornographic visuals, so I have *viewed* more than one penis.

But this one is perfect. It's large, thick, and seeing it inside Elliot's hand, his long fingers wrapped around the base, then stroking up to the darker tip where it's shining, puts me in immediate need for him all over again.

He stands there, gliding his hand up and down his cock. I kneel back, massaging both my breasts now, because I want him to quell the ache at my core. Need him buried inside me more than I need my next breath.

"Elliot." My voice is ragged. Pleading.

"I'm going to fuck you now. Is that okay?" He stalks toward me, blue eyes piercing and powerful.

I love that he hasn't taken anything for granted with me, but he can stop. I'm his for the taking. I trust him more than I've ever trusted anyone. My heart flips over at the thought. "Yes, please."

He stops at the foot of the bed. I reach out to put my palm on his chest. His heart is beating as fast as mine.

"You are disarmingly beautiful, Pink Cheeks." He covers my hand with his, pressing our linked fingers against his skin.

I feel myself flush further. Probably all the way down to my toes. "No one has ever made me blush as much as you do."

"Then he was doing things wrong."

I nod. I think everything I've done up until today has been all wrong.

"One more question, and you can absolutely say no. I want to feel inside you. Skin to skin. I'm clean and I've never had sex without a condom before, but I've got this intense need to make what we're about to do different. So, if you're already using protection and are okay with what I'm proposing..."

My breath hitches.

"Shit. I'm an idiot for even asking. Forget I—"

"No, I'd like that." I cup his cheek with my free hand. "I'm on the pill and clean, too." I had myself tested a couple of times after I left Henry and more truths were revealed than I realized. He and I didn't use condoms. I've been on the pill since I was eighteen and only with him. I shudder at my stupidity. Thankfully he swore to me he wore condoms with everyone else. Still, I had to make sure I was healthy.

Elliot has me on my back two seconds later. I giggle.

He quiets me by crashing his mouth to mine. Every kiss from him is better than the last. He explores with his lips, tongue, and teeth, giving more than he's taking, lighting me up inside with nothing more than his passion for kissing me.

I run my nails over his scalp, through the soft black strands of his hair, and kiss him back. The scruff on his chin feels better than I imagined.

Elbows braced on the sides of my head, he lowers his hips over mine and glides his cock against my folds. Holy foot long, this is really happening. I stiffen, excited for him to fill me, but nervous, too. Will he fit without hurting me?

He lifts his head, kisses the shell of my ear. "Don't worry," he whispers. "We'll go slow." Then he kisses up and down my body until I'm writhing and wet and going out of my mind with eagerness.

What happens next is nothing short of amazing. He straddles me, his cock fully extended and glistening, and lifts my hand to wrap around his shaft. He hisses when I grip him. "Guide my cock inside your hot, wet pussy," he says. I love when he talks dirty.

Everything inside me tightens as I bring the tip of him to my opening.

"Breathe," he says, and as I do, he slides inside me, stretches me, fills me. I close my eyes at how good it feels.

Then he's moving, bracing himself on his elbows again. "Straighten and press your legs together," he says. As I do so, he lays his legs outside mine and buries his cock deeper. "Fuck, you feel better than I imagined." He rolls his hips slowly, watches me. "You good?"

"Uh-huh," is all I can muster in response. I'm some place else, weightless, every nerve in my body lit up like the brightest star in the universe.

Our eyes stay glued as he rocks against me. His strokes are slow, a caress rather than a full-on thrust. He brushes a strand of hair off my face, then plants a kiss on my jaw.

"You're gorgeous, Mads. So fucking beautiful like this. I hope you know I plan to thoroughly take advantage of you this weekend."

I run my fingers over his shoulders and down his arms, feeling his muscles as he keeps me pinned beneath him. "Then we're even, because there are things I want to do to you, too."

He lazily strokes his hips against mine. I stroke back. "Yeah? What kinds of things?"

"Naked things," I mumble. He knows exactly what he's doing here, circling and pressing his hips to hit my clit just right.

"Excellent," he says in a raspy voice. All of a sudden, he's deeper, filling me to the extreme.

I move my hands to his lower back to help keep him right *there*. And he stops.

"What are you doing?" I hiss out.

"Patience, gorgeous." He starts up again. Moves inside me slowly, like we have all day.

Then stops.

Starts.

It's maddening in the best possible way. I'm so turned on I'm about to come no matter what. "Elliot," I whisper, "please."

His lips claim mine and we're kissing. The kiss is deep, intense, s-l-o-w. Our mouths move in time with our lower bodies. It's amazing, special, pulls on every fiber inside me, and I'm falling over the edge of bliss. Elliot pulls his mouth away, rolls his hips once, twice, and the two of us let go at the same time. I scream his name. He grunts, groans, and whispers mine.

He stays seated inside me until we're both completely still, then he rolls over so he's flat on his back. Despite our slow lovemaking, we're both out of breath. "That was amazing," he says to the ceiling.

"It was." I stare up, too.

"On a scale of one to ten, ten being best"—he rolls to his side and props his head in his hand to look at me—"would you say an eleven?" He traces a finger around my belly button.

I turn my head. "No."

"No?" He is ridiculously cute with his eyebrows scrunched up.

I smile at him. "I'd say a twelve."

That earns me a blinding grin in return. "Come on." He scoots off the bed and gives me a hand.

"Where are we going?"

"To get cleaned up in the shower."

"Together?"

He jerks to a stop. His eyes search mine for a moment before he says, "This weekend we do everything together."

• • •

"No!" I almost choke on the pizza Elliot ordered in for our "dinner date." We're sitting on the rug in front of the couch. I'm wearing one of his shirts since he refused to let me go home to get any clothes (stating clothing was not required this weekend), and he's got on navy sleep pants. He decorated the coffee table with a cloth and candles, and we're drinking sparkling apple cider from wineglasses. It's the most romantic date I've ever had.

"Yep. No one noticed I'd wandered off to use the bathroom when my dad went to pay the check at the register, and then they walked out the door, got back in the car, and left the diner without me," Elliot continues.

"I can't believe your parents didn't notice you were missing."

He shrugs. "I handled it well. When I got back to the register and realized I was all alone, I climbed up onto a barstool at the counter and ordered a piece of apple pie."

"You didn't!"

"I did."

"You didn't cry or tell someone what happened? You were six. Weren't you scared?" I wipe the corner of my mouth with a napkin. "I would have freaked out."

"I had five dollars in my pocket, so I wasn't too worried." He takes a casual bite of his mushroom-and-olive slice.

"*What?*" I ask, confused.

"I figured that would get me two slices of pie and by the time I finished the second one, someone would notice I was alone or my parents would be back." He says this with ease, but sitting next to the flickering candlelight, I catch a hint of pain on his handsome face.

I lean over and kiss his pec. "Which was it?"

"The waitress was on to me the second I sat down."

"Of course she was. I bet you were the cutest six-year-old. Kind of hard to miss."

"True." He flashes his white teeth. "But she let me think I was cool and grown-up until my mom came flying back into the diner looking for me."

"How long were you there?"

"I don't remember. Honestly, it was probably only a few minutes, but it seemed like a really long time to me."

"I bet."

"I did get a new baseball glove out of it."

"Like you ever wanted for anything anyway," I tease.

Once again a flash of discomfort mars his expression, and I feel terrible for saying that. I've met his family and he's said things here and there to imply he's always felt disconnected from his parents and siblings.

I crawl onto his lap, drape my arms around his neck. "Whatever upbringing you had, you turned into an amazing man."

He palms my bottom. I'm not wearing any underwear,

but as soon as I find where Elliot hid them, I'll be slipping them back on. Maybe. Quick, easy access has its benefits. Like right now. I wiggle and feel him grow underneath his thin pajama pants.

When I'm close to him like this, our noses almost touching, I can't help but fall deeper into the fire held in his vivid blue eyes. "You're smart, ambitious, super sexy."

"Go on," he says, inching his fingers toward my cleft.

Just like that, my pulse speeds up. I gently grind my hips against his. "Kind, giving, good with your hands."

"How good?" He dips his fingers farther, reaching between our bodies. I grip his shoulders and lift up to give him better access.

"I'll let you know in a minute."

"A minute?" *Not a chance, Pink Cheeks*, his tone says. He likes to prolong my pleasure.

"Okay, five." I'm kind of over the slow and steady and am ready for fast and furious.

He easily slips a finger inside me. No surprise there. I'm turned on just looking at him. It's a crazy sensation I both love and hate. What happens on Monday when we're back at the office? I can't get turned on when I see him. *Don't think about that. Focus on right now.*

"I can work with that," he says, *working me.*

"I think I should run the show this time." We're staring so hard at each other neither one of us has blinked.

His fingers stop moving. He moves his hands back to my bottom. "Go for it."

"You might want to hang on for this."

He laughs. It's a really great sound. "Don't worry about me, beautiful."

I push down his pants until his length springs free. Then without preamble I guide his tip to my entrance and sink down. I'm so ready he slides all the way in in one fluid motion, filling me so fully my bones tingle.

"God, Mads. You're so tight and wet. It feels so good." He catches his breath. His fingers dig into my waist, not too hard, but not soft, either. I like it.

I release my own pent-up breath. "I know. And you're so big and warm." The pressure he creates inside my body is exquisite. I want to freeze time and feel this for hours. I put my hands back on his muscled shoulders and shift, seeking the ideal position. He lets me control the tempo, so I start slow, because experiencing every inch of him is high on my list of pleasures. Unhurried drag up. Steady drag down. Then I speed up. He chuckles softly. I never knew sex could be so much fun, too. That two people could connect mind, body, and funny bone. For as serious as Elliot is at work, away from the office he's irresistibly playful.

He also likes me naked. He grabs the hem of my shirt and pulls it up and off to toss over the couch. His hands are on my breasts a second later. He knows my nipples are my trigger and he cups, kneads, tweaks. I grind, press, and push, angling to hit just the right spot between my thighs.

"Imagine there's a knock at the door," he says.

I swallow thickly.

"The pizza guy came back for something."

I start to pant, clench around Elliot's cock.

"When no one answers the door, he steps to the window to peek inside."

Everything inside me tightens. I grow wetter. Elliot's eyes are locked on mine. I dart a quick glance to the window. Oh my God. How did I not notice the curtains are open?

"He presses his nose to the window and sees us. He sees you riding my cock."

Crazy good vibrations, hot, intense, uncontrollable, steal over me. My body temperature rises.

"He sees your tits in my hands, the sexy slope of your

back, and his dick gets hard watching us."

I thrust my chest out, lift my chin, and quicken my pace.

Elliot moves one hand to my waist and the other to my clit, leaving my boobs exposed.

"When he gets to see your firm, round tits and pretty pink nipples, he grips his cock and starts to jerk off."

My entire body shakes, and the pulses where Elliot and I are joined together intensify. We talked earlier about what thoughts turned us on, and I told him while I didn't want it to ever *really* happen, the idea of getting caught—of having someone watch me—got me majorly aroused.

"His eyes are glued to you, Madison, and your naked body, as we fuck in the candlelight. As I ram my cock into your pussy and you milk me until I'm dry."

Elliot's words and the visual are too much and I cry out as I come. He pumps into me, strokes my clit with the pad of his thumb, and even knowing no one is at the window, the fact that there could be someone there peeking in, has me rolling right into a second orgasm. Elliot bucks, surges into me one more time, and groans through his own release.

I'm boneless and dazed when I collapse in his arms, our bodies slick with perspiration once again. He wraps his arm around me, keeping us connected. The smell of sex fills the room.

Best. Date. Ever.

Chapter Twenty-One

ELLIOT

I flip over a ten, hoping Madison has a face card or an ace. This is our fourth game of War and I've beaten her soundly each time. I keep wishing for the tide to turn and luck to be on her side. She tosses down a four, groans her annoyance.

"Seriously?" she chides in the cutest voice. "Are you cheating somehow? Because a run this bad is very suspicious." She looks at the few cards left in her pile. "You have to be. The highest card I have left is a seven!"

Have I mentioned how cute she is?

I lean across the bed to kiss her, distracting her with my tongue while I swap our card piles. She's been a good sport—a great one really—and I know she's just messing with me, but I've got this urge to right her wrongs, no matter what they are.

"Kissing me does not"—her lashes flutter as I scoot back to sit—"does not...I forgot what I was going to say."

"Magic mouth," I say, pointing at my lips.

She bursts out laughing. "That...is...the..." She grabs her

stomach, she's laughing so hard. And I can't help it, I laugh with her and watch her face as she notices one of her cards is right side up. It's a queen. *Oops.* Still giggling, she checks all the cards, then tosses them at me with a sweet shake of her head. "That is the funniest thing I've ever heard," she finally says. "And now every time I hear *Magic Mike* I'm going to think magic mouth. You've ruined Channing Tatum for me."

I hope I've ruined all guys.

Selfish, but true. Yesterday and today have been the best days I've had in a long, long time. She's definitely ruined me for other girls. I don't know what the fuck I'm going to do come Monday when we're back at work.

"Okay, you are the official card game champ. Now it's my turn to pick something."

Between rounds of sex, we're spending Saturday taking turns suggesting things to do for fun. We don't want to leave the house and this cozy, amazing sanctuary we've created. "I'm yours to command," I say. I'd do anything for this girl, a thought I quickly tuck away before she notices that anywhere next to her, doing anything at all, is my happy place.

"Do you have any art supplies?"

I groan, but it's halfhearted. "Not really. Paper and pens is all that I know of."

"Hmm…how about hand sanitizer?"

"I think there's some under the kitchen sink. Mateo bought a big container of it so whenever Zoe comes over her hands stay clean." Zoe is our six-year-old next-door neighbor and she likes to show up on mornings after we've partied a little too heavily.

And shit. It's the first time I've thought about my roommate and how I've ignored his warning to stay away from Madison.

Madison's eyes roll. "Okay, let's go investigate." She jumps off the bed and I get a quick flash of her mouthwatering ass. Immediately I forget about Mateo.

My most comfortable dress shirt is all that separates that lush skin from my hands. The soft cotton hangs down to the middle of her thighs and I want her to keep it. I want her to think of me when she's back in her own bed, and I'm here in mine with only Socks to keep me company. "Is hand sanitizer a secret art supply I don't know about?" I ask as I follow her out of my room. In just twenty-four hours, she's gotten very comfortable being here. Made herself right at home.

"It's my turn to teach you something," she tosses over her shoulder.

"What have I taught you?"

"A lot." She bends down to retrieve the hand sanitizer, puts it on the counter, then starts opening cupboards in search of something.

I put my hands on her waist and bury my nose in her sweet-smelling hair. "What are you looking for?"

She stops moving and shivers. I love how she responds to my touch. "Food coloring," she murmurs.

"I'm pretty sure we don't have that." I let go and take a step back. It's difficult—I like breathing her in—but I remind myself I want this weekend to be memorable for more than physical intimacy. "But if it's a requirement for whatever you have in mind, I could run next door and see if Abby has some. She and Zoe like to bake, and I seem to recall Zoe bringing over blue sugar cookies one day."

"Would you?" she asks with hope so sweet, I'd run next door during a zombie apocalypse for her.

I kiss her cheek. "Be right back."

"While you're there, could you ask for a few paintbrushes, too?"

"You got it." I quickly put on a shirt, then run out the front door. I'm in luck. Abby has a box of food coloring, as well as some paintbrushes. The always-curious Zoe wants to know what I'm making, and I tell her it's a surprise. She asks who I'm surprising. I tell her I'm the one being surprised. Her cute little nose scrunches up at the same time her mom tells her to stop asking me questions.

Brushes and food coloring in hand, I bend down and whisper to Zoe that I'll fill her in on the surprise the next time I see her. She wraps her short arms around my neck and says "thanks." Zoe and her mom have lived here for a while now, but it's the first time I look at this little girl with deep-rooted protectiveness. Her dad passed away a couple of years ago and my roommates—especially Mateo—have taken to doing things with her a dad might do and keeping a protective eye on her and Abby. At one time or another all three of us have commented on how hot Abby is, but Zoe is important to us, so we axed any MILF thoughts. *Us*. I'm not sure why I just realized that, but I'm glad I did.

I sweep Madison into my arms the moment I step back into the kitchen. Fuck, she looks gorgeous in my shirt, the material rumpled and only a few of the middle buttons fastened.

"What was that for?" she asks.

"No reason. Here you go." I hand her the supplies.

"Yay! Okay, so what we're doing is making body paint." She steps over to a muffin tin sitting on the counter. "I've filled each muffin cup with hand sanitizer and now we're going to add some color."

"Did you say body paint?"

"Uh-huh."

I whip my shirt off. "I'm ready." She can paint me from head to toe if she wants.

"Not so fast. We have to mix our colors first. For example, combining yellow and red gives us orange."

"And mixing red and blue gives us purple."

Madison's gaze jumps from my chest to my face. "That's

right."

"Don't look so surprised. Just because art isn't my thing doesn't mean I don't know my colors." Socks wanders into the room and rubs against my leg, so I pick her up.

"Sorry. You're right. I'm pretty sure there's nothing you don't know. And oh my God."

"What?"

Her cheeks turn pink. "You need to stop that." She's staring at Socks cradled in my arms.

"Holding my cat?"

"Shirtless, yes. It's distracting."

"I like distracting you." I pet Socks so she purrs. And okay, maybe flex my arm muscles while I'm at it.

Pulling a face that I think is supposed to convey annoyance, but is damn cute instead, Madison gets back to work on our homemade paints.

"Do you like to do all kinds of art, or just painting and drawing?" I ask.

"I like to sew, too. I've made a lot of my handbags."

"Wow. That's awesome."

She shrugs a shoulder in modesty. "It's kind of therapeutic, and I don't know, makes me feel accomplished at something that no one can take away from me. Auggie asked me to make her one, and I was so surprised and happy about it. She insists on paying me, but I told her no way."

I set Socks down on the floor. "You're a pretty cool person, Mads."

"Thanks," she says to the muffin tin.

I reach across the counter and gently lift her chin between my thumb and index finger. "You constantly steal my breath in the best possible ways," I confess, staring into her eyes.

"I could say the same to you."

"Go right ahead," I tease to lighten the mood. Serious talk will get me in serious trouble. Not that I'm not already waist-deep in complications with this gorgeous girl.

"And risk your head getting even bigger?" she teases back. "No, thanks."

She's smarter than I am. All this playful banter is a direct link to deeper feelings I can't afford to even consider.

"Would you like to mix a color?"

"Sure." I make green and then purple. A quiet minute later, we've got all the colors of the rainbow.

"Would you like to go first?" she asks.

"No. I think I need to study the master before I try anything."

"Okay. Have a seat at the table." She brings the muffin tin, paintbrushes, and some paper towels with her, putting them down on the tabletop. "Can I paint something on your chest?"

"You can paint wherever you want on my canvas." I spread my arms wide and give a slight jerk of my hips.

She steps between my legs. "There will be no penis painting."

I mock gasp. "Of course not. I'm shocked you even thought that."

"Shut up. You were totally insinuating that with your little hip thrust." She dips a brush into the orange.

"I've no idea what you're talking about. But now that you mention it, you know how much I like my dick *stroked*."

"Stop," she reprimands around a tiny smile. As she starts to paint on my skin, I put my hands on the outside of her thighs.

The bristles tickle for a second before I close my eyes and focus on keeping my shit together. Having her close like this, doing something she loves *to me*, has got my dick's attention. I mentally go to the one place sure to cool my jets: work. When we're working intently on something together, I've noticed she slips the tip of her tongue out of her mouth. It's sexy as hell, *and fuck*, this isn't helping me at all. I open my eyes, and sure enough her tongue is peeking out between her lips.

"You okay?" she asks.

"Fine."

"Your skin isn't feeling irritated from our paint, is it?"

"Nope. You're good to keep going." *Just ignore the growing bulge in my pants.*

She totally knows it's there, but she keeps working. She's focused, painting around my left nipple. The colors change to red, yellow, brown. I hadn't noticed her mix brown. I drop my head to take a peek, but she quickly catches my chin and instructs me not to look until it's finished.

I close my eyes again. She smells like my body wash. The side of her hand is warm as it brushes over my pec. Every so often I catch a whiff of her wintergreen breath. This innocent activity now ranks very high on my list of favorite entertainment.

"Done." She takes a step back. I look up at her for permission to see the finished picture and find her mouth stretched wide and her eyes sparkling. She's amused with her artwork.

It's impossible not to smile before I've even taken a glance. If she likes what she sees, then I will, too.

I look down. It takes me a few seconds to figure out what she's drawn, not because it isn't amazing, but because it catches me completely off guard. I pictured her drawing a horse or a sun or a tree and flowers—something girlish. But not my Madison. "Is that what I think it is?" I ask in awe.

She crosses her arms, still grinning at what she did. "What do you think it is?"

"A slice of pizza."

"Yep. And your nipple is a piece of pepperoni. Or as I like to call it, nipperoni."

We crack up. I've laughed more in the past six weeks than

I have in the past six months.

"All right, genius, it's my turn."

"Where do you want me?"

"That's a loaded question."

She pushes me on the paint-free side of my chest. "Later."

I stroke the stubble on my jaw. I'm the worst artist on the planet but really want to do something she'll remember. "Can I paint on your chest?"

"Sure," she answers quickly without any qualms. That she's eager to agree to all my suggestions is mind-blowing. There's a wild girl inside her. She's just needed to trust the person she was with to let loose. That I'm the person she trusts is a responsibility I don't take lightly.

She takes off her shirt, sits on the edge of the table, and places her hands in her lap, covering herself with the cotton material. "So you don't get any extra ideas," she says, wiggling her shoulders and straightening her back.

I'm stuck on her tits, so no worries there. What I have in mind is nowhere near as creative as her pizza, but I think it's a drawing I can manage with my very limited skills.

I dip a brush in the red paint and start work on her right tit. She shudders, her nipple stiffens. "We should finger paint next time," I say. I swear her boob gets heavier at the suggestion.

She closes her eyes while I work. I finish her right side and then move to the left, switching to blue paint. She sucks in a breath when I brush the underside of her tit. I've been holding my breath the whole damn time, touching her like this arousing as hell. Once I'm done, I step back to examine my work. In my haste to finish, the two sides aren't a perfect match, but close enough to be respectable.

Madison waits for me to give her the okay.

Instead, I clasp her hand and lead her to the bathroom, so she can look in the mirror. I stand behind her as she takes her first look at the five-point stars I painted on her breasts, her nipples the center of each one. "I call this American Dream because I seriously want to fuck your celestial body, between those stars if you're willing."

She smiles. "I'm definitely willing." She reaches back, slides her hand inside my sleep pants, and grips my cock. "Excellent job, by the way."

I grin back, and for the rest of the weekend we readily please each other in every way we can think up.

· · ·

Being out of the office for two days last week cost me. Monday and Tuesday are insanely busy. Wednesday morning is the first time I'm able to take five minutes at my desk and stare out the glass wall at my assistant.

That's a lie.

I've checked her out one million eight hundred fifty-four thousand times, but that's between you and me.

She and I agreed we wouldn't talk about the weekend. We agreed there wouldn't be any repeats. When I kissed her goodbye on Sunday night, we settled on keeping what happened in my house out of the office.

Being swamped has helped us transition back to coworkers after the most intense, amazing weekend two people could have. I know she feels the same way about our three days, because before lunch even hit on Monday, we started leaving notes for each other.

Mr. Sax,

Just because you overheard me tell Auggie I had an amazing weekend does not mean you had anything to do with it. If you listened carefully, I told her it was because of a new art project I did, which led to u discussion on handbags and an idea I have for a new one. So there was no need for you to look smug. FYI: you actually look constipated when you smile like that.

Sincerely,
Miss Hastings

Miss Hastings,

You're looking very tired today and I have to ask: too much exercise? I know you don't normally work out, so if you need a break at any time today, please let me know. I'd hate to be accused of overworking my assistant. By the way, I noticed the purse you carried this morning looked like it was very well made.

Sincerely,
Mr. Sax

Not my best note there, but I couldn't think of anything really negative to say so soon after being inside her and feeling like I'd found exactly where I belonged.

Mr. Sax,

How many wrinkles does it take to make a finance manager look like an amateur? Take a look in the mirror. Honestly, did you pull your clothes out of the laundry basket today? I almost want to shield you from anyone's notice. Almost. I'm not sure I'd be very effective anyway, since you're almost double my size. There is a dry cleaner just down the street I recommend you look into.

Sincerely,

Miss Hastings

Miss Hastings,

Your smile made my day today. Thank you.

Fondly,
Mr. Sax

I've got nothing. I can't even make shit up like she does. I'm so screwed. We need to talk and figure out a new strategy. What the hell was I thinking when I invited her to stay the weekend? She's an invaluable assistant, and I've jeopardized everything—our working relationship, our friendship. Maybe more.

Because as I look up from my desk, I see she's leaving for the day without saying goodbye for the first time ever.

"A heart worth loving is one you understand, even in silence."
—Shannon L. Alder

Sax/Hastings
Workplace Strategy
Scorecard

Sax – 3
Hastings – 6

Chapter Twenty-Two

MADISON

"He changed our plan of action without asking me," I say semi-softly. "He can't do that. He can't start writing nice notes at work and think that's okay. I was totally unprepared. I'd been busting my butt trying not to look at him as Sex God Elliot and only Boss Man Elliot. *I* was perfectly capable of continuing with our normal strategy, albeit I had to think for a long time to come up with something even halfway decent. But the point is, I didn't break our deal. He did. And I'm really pissed at him. So, now that I think about it, I guess you could say his note actually worked better—"

"Shh!" a lady near me admonishes.

"Miss," the yoga instructor says, cruising around the studio like she's floating on air, "there's no talking."

Sorry, I mouth. Then I whisper, "—than mine" to Teague and Harper. They've dragged me to six a.m. yoga boot camp. I'm not even in the right pose. How in the world do people bend like that?

"What am I going to do?" I ask.

"First, you're going to clear your mind and finish this class," Harper says so quietly, I fall over while straining to hear her.

"Fine." I do my best to follow the teacher's instructions, but when my mind goes to Elliot doing poses with me in X-rated positions, I give up. I grab my towel and leave the room to wait in the hallway.

Not even a minute later, Teague and Harper have followed me out. "You guys didn't have to quit early," I say.

"Yes we did," Teague says. "Come on, let's get coffee and talk this through."

Coffee is thankfully two doors down in a small Italian pastry shop. We sit at a table near the floor-to-ceiling window, the first rays of sunshine brightening the sidewalk outside. The smell of freshly brewed java fills the café. I think about spending the rest of the day right here in this spot pretending I really am in Italy.

"What do you think this means?" I ask, taking a sip of my vanilla latte.

"It means he wants under your skirt again," Harper says straightforwardly.

"This is bad, you guys."

Teague puts her hand on my arm. "You had to know things would get messy before you agreed to spend the weekend with him."

I slouch down in my chair. "Of course I did, but I pretended otherwise."

"At least you didn't have to pretend to orgasm," Harper says.

"If she had to do that, she wouldn't be feeling like this," Teague points out.

"I'm so confused and worried. I don't want to lose my job." And I don't want to admit what is really bothering me —

that Elliot is good in bed, good in the office, good everywhere. Does he think I'm good enough? We agreed to move on from our weekend, but I can't stop thinking about everything leading up to it. His thoughtful gestures, encouraging words, the times we've thought the same things, his genuine care for me—and his friends. He may only like to share his top layer with people, but I've seen deeper. Experienced more. And no matter how hard I've tried not to fall all the way in love with him, I've failed.

"I get why it's never a smart idea to have an office romance," Harper says, putting down her espresso. "If things go badly it definitely affects the workplace vibe, but shouldn't that decision be up to the two people involved and not mandated by company policy? That's kind of not fair. What if Elliot is your soul mate?"

I think he might be.

"And you guys are able to work together *and* be together?" she continues. "You can't tell me there aren't companies with coworkers who are dating or married."

"I asked Elliot about the policy and he said it was because our CEO, James, got burned big time when he married his business partner. His ex-wife got their company because he just wanted the pain to stop. He's a really nice man, and I'm ashamed of myself for breaking a rule that's important to him."

"It's an unfair rule," Harper says.

"What if you guys talked to James?" Teague asks.

"The person I need to talk to is Elliot, but I'm not sure what to even say. Maybe I'm reading more into this than he is, and I don't want to look like a fool." I feel the familiar weight of Henry's deceit crushing my chest. Elliot is nothing like my ex, but sometimes it's hard to trust my feelings when for years they didn't matter to the person I held in my heart.

"You're not a fool, Maddy, and he's an idiot if he doesn't

fall madly in love with you." Teague, our happily-ever-after captain, crosses her arms like the subject is closed.

"But here's the other thing," I say. "What if we did start seeing each other and James magically says it's okay. I don't want people to look at me differently. Or think I'm not earning my keep because of my intelligence and hard work. I've been whispered about behind my back and it sucks. It sucks the life out of you, and for the first time *in my life*, I've got something that is mine and that I've earned, and I don't want that jeopardized because I'm sleeping with my boss."

"You guys could just do it and not tell anyone," Harper offers.

"You mean sneak around?"

"Yes. Personally, I don't see the harm in it since it's not hurting anybody else."

"So, is a lie really that bad if some people know the truth?" I don't want to keep Elliot a secret away from work. I want to triple date with Teague and Mateo and Harper and Levi. I want him to meet my parents and my brother. I want to brag about him to the person in line in front of me at the supermarket. Does it make me a bad person that I'm willing to hide our relationship at work if that means I get to keep him?

"I think you know the answer to that, you just don't want to admit it." Teague takes a sip of her coffee.

I hate that the right thing to do isn't what I want to do. "I'm a horrible person."

"You're not," Teague and Harper answer at the same time. "You're just a girl who's falling for the one guy she isn't supposed to. People do a lot worse than work together when that happens," Teague says.

"I guess. Hey, what time is it?" I ask.

Harper looks at her phone. "Seven."

I get to my feet. "I've got to go. Thanks for everything

you guys." I give them each a hug.

"If you do go down that rabbit hole," Harper says, "remember you've always got us no matter what."

• • •

As I knew he'd be, Elliot is already at his desk when I get to work twenty-five minutes early. I stow my purse in my desk drawer and knock on his open door. "Good morning."

He swivels his chair so he's looking at me rather than out the window. "Morning."

"I was hoping we could talk for a few minutes before everyone gets in?"

"You read my mind. Come in and close the door."

I do as asked and take the chair in front of his desk. As I smooth down my black pencil skirt, he stands and walks over to lock the door and close the curtains. My stomach flutters the moment we're hidden from view and safe from anyone barging in.

I'm not sure what to make of his locking us away until he reaches my side and takes my elbow to help me to my feet. He stands before me, staring into my eyes. Searing me with too many emotions to name. Does *he* see how hard I've fallen for him? A second passes. Then another. He's giving me time. Time to back away and keep to our agreement or hold my ground. The decision is easy—I stay glued to my spot. Stuck to him no matter the consequences.

He cants his head and pulls my bottom lip between his teeth. His hesitancy is tender, thoughtful. I gently kiss him back before he retreats, and his forehead touches mine. "Madison," he whispers, my name his pleasure and his pain.

"Yes," I say softly. A question. An answer. Whatever he wants it to be. Good or bad, we crave contact from each other.

His hands slide to the back of my waist. Mine go to his

elbows. And we're kissing again, still tentatively, like one wrong move will set off a bomb in the room. Our noses rub, his lips play with mine, tease and dance until he tilts his head to the right, I go left, and he deepens the kiss.

He brushes the hair off the side of my face, traces the shell of my ear with his fingertips, and cups my neck. "I've been going out of my mind thinking about kissing you again," he says, a breath away from my lips, his eyelids heavy.

"Me, too. I've missed us like this."

His hand moves slightly down my neck. I sense his chest rise and fall. "You make me rethink everything I thought I knew I wanted."

"I do?" Our breaths are ragged, the air thick and warm. I bring my arms up to cradle the back of his head.

"You do."

I smile, and he crushes his lips to mine. Urgent, openmouthed kisses follow. I feel our connection all the way down to my toes. Every cell inside me responds to Elliot's unique touch. I press my chest against his. More. I need more.

Groaning, his hold moves to my butt. Without breaking our kiss, he moves me atop his desk. Something clatters to the floor, his stapler, I think. Next, he's hiking up my skirt. I'm going for his belt. When I feel how hard he is underneath his dress pants, I fumble with the buckle. *I do this to him.*

I lose *all* dexterity when he rubs his fingers over my panties, slips underneath the lace, circles my swollen skin with his thumb. His kisses move to my jaw, my chin.

"I need to taste you, Mads. Please tell me that's okay."

"That's okay." I'm not thinking right now, just feeling. Everything.

All of it.

In case it never happens again.

With care and attention, Elliot works my thong down my legs, kissing inside my thigh, my knee, my ankle, as he goes.

"I've imagined you here in my office in nothing but these fuck-me pumps wrapped around my waist, more times than I can count," he rasps, sliding my underwear over my black-bow stilettos.

Then he's kneeling in front of me, nudging my legs wider so they bracket his shoulders and burying his face between my thighs. He licks, sucks, fingers, and pleasures me until I buck hard against his chin and press my lips together so I don't yell out his name. As always, he sees me through every last pulse before backing away.

"Take your clothes off," he says, helping me off the desk.

"Even the shoes?"

"You can leave those on." He unbuttons his shirt, lays it over the back of the chair. God, he's beautiful. In one impressive stroke, he pulls his belt free, then unbuttons his pants. The large, thick outline of him is easy to see.

I drop my skirt, blouse, and bra on the chair cushion.

His eyes caress me from head to toe. "Stand in front of the window," he instructs.

My eyes widen. "What?"

"No one can see in." He takes my hand and leads me to where he wants me behind his desk. "Arms above your head, palms on the glass." He helps me get in position, then presses his chest to my back.

I lean back into him. My heart is racing as I look out at the blue sky, buildings, and cars. "Are you sure no one can see me?" I ask.

"Yes, but imagine if they could," he says in my ear. He stretches his arm above me, cradling my hand against the window. His other arm wraps around my waist. "Imagine someone across the way seeing your tits and pussy on display, watching me get you off with my fingers."

And just like that I'm wet and needy all over again. Elliot kisses the side of my neck and shoulder while his very talented fingers roam up and down my torso. When I'm panting and nearing climax number two, he spins me around and pushes down his pants and boxer briefs. "Wrap your legs around me and hold tight."

He thrusts inside me two seconds later. "Fuck," he hisses out and stops moving.

"What's wrong?" I loosen my grip on his shoulders.

"Nothing's wrong. Everything is perfect. I just wanted to take a second to memorize how good it feels to be buried deep inside you like this."

I don't know whether to smile or cry. Is he confirming this is our last time? Luckily, before I can think too hard on that, he starts moving again. He surges into me hard and fast. His powerful legs handle my weight like I'm featherlight. I'm lost to his body joining mine, taking me somewhere only he can.

Our breathing quickens, our eyes close. My back is plastered against the window as Elliot fucks me in his office. He adjusts his stance, presses our bodies closer so he can rub just the right spot to set me off. I bite his shoulder to keep from screaming. He buries his face in my neck. I feel his jaw clench as a low guttural sound falls from his beautiful lips as he spills inside me.

He holds me afterward. I hold him back.

"We better hurry and get dressed," I whisper, breaking the spell.

"Shit," he says. He cups my cheek. "You're right and this was—"

"Perfect. Remember?" I unhook my legs from around his waist and stand. I don't want to hear it was a mistake. We both know it was foolish and inappropriate, but some mistakes are worth moments of bliss, and I won't regret this one.

"We still need to talk." He hands me a box of tissues to

help clean myself up. "Can you do lunch tomorrow? Today is pretty busy, as you know because"—he walks around the desk to grab his shirt—"I'd be lost without your assistance."

I give him a sidelong glance. "Sure. Tomorrow works."

"Hey." He lifts my bra strap off my arm and slips it over my shoulder. "We'll figure this out, okay? I promise."

There's a rustling sound out in the hallway, so I nod and rush to get my clothes back on. Elliot resumes his seat behind his desk. I smooth down my clothes and pray my high ponytail is still high. "Do I look okay?" I ask.

"More than okay."

With another nod, I turn to go. My hand is on the doorknob when Elliot says, "I'll be thinking about this morning all day."

I smile at him over my shoulder. "Me, too." I leave the door ajar after I step out. Sitting down at my desk, I take a slow, deep breath.

"What's with the secret meeting?" Auggie asks, making me jump out of my seat. "Sorry. Didn't mean to scare you. So?" She thumbs over her shoulder. "What was that? Is everything okay? Elliot's seemed off all week and if he's thinking about firing you because he's got a grumpy bug up his ass again, I'll have to kick said ass. Because he is never going to find a better assistant than you."

"It wasn't… He…" I stammer.

"Are you feeling all right? You look flushed."

"I'm… He…" *I look flushed?* I rub my cheeks like that will get rid of my after-sex glow. I think I might pass out. I can't lie or pretend with Auggie. She's my friend.

Her eyes widen and her jaw drops. She comes inside my cubicle and sits on the corner of my desk. I swivel in my chair to face her. "Did you just fool around with Elliot?"

"*Shh.*"

"Oh my God."

"We didn't think anyone was here yet."

"You've done this before?" She's surprised, not judging me, and I relax the tiniest bit.

"No. Not here at work."

She wiggles her butt like she's trying to get more comfortable and ready herself for an in- depth conversation. "You've been with him outside the office?"

"Yes. We're friends, actually." Auggie frowns in confusion. "I knew him before I started working here," I confess. Then I tell her how we've known each other casually for years and how we spent the past weekend together being much more than that.

"Oh my God," she says again. "This is crazy."

"I know."

She eyes me closely. "You really like him."

I nod. More like love, but if I ever get to voice that out loud, the first person to hear it will be Elliot.

"Madison." Her tone is sympathetic and laced with regret. She doesn't need to say anything else. She's reminding me about the nonfraternization policy.

"We're going to work it out."

"How? If James learns about it he'll be furious, and you could both lose your jobs."

"I'm not sure how. We're having lunch tomorrow to talk about it."

"Madison, can you—" I spin around at the sound of Elliot's voice. His intelligent blue eyes bounce from me to Auggie then back to me. I'm trapped. Caught. Unable to look away. With the curtains still closed in his office, he had no idea Auggie was here. His gaze is pleading then resigned then offended. It feels like an eternity passes, but it's only a few seconds. His shoulders stiffen. *He knows.* He knows I've just told Auggie about us. "Never mind. I'll take care of it." He turns on his heel, strides into his office, and shuts the door.

I twist to face Auggie. "What just happened?"

"I'm not sure, but..."

"But he's not happy with me. He knows I told you and he's mad and he has every right to be." I drop my face in my hands.

Auggie nudges my knee with her foot until I look up. "He'll get over it, and you know you can trust me, right? I won't say anything."

"I know. Thanks."

The sound of heavy footsteps grabs our attention. "Good morning," James says, stopping at my desk.

"Morning!" *Take it down a notch, Madison.*

"Hey, boss," Auggie says in a normal tone of voice as she slides off my desk. "You've got a conference call in five, notes are already on your desk, see you later, Madison"—she squeezes my shoulder—"Elliot's report is attached to..." the sound of her voice trails off as she walks out of my cubicle and down the hall with James.

I power on my computer with shaking hands. This is terrible. I'm so mad at myself for lasting all of five seconds with a straight face after I had sex with Elliot in his office. His office! I know how deeply Elliot affects me and should have walked out before we got carried away. Did James think I looked flushed? Did he notice the high pitch of my voice?

The thing is, if I could rewind the last hour, I'd do things exactly the same. I've thought about having sex with Elliot on the other side of that glass wall numerous times. Pictured his hands and mouth on me, him moving inside me. The reality far outweighed my fantasies. And the element of risk—being seen through the window *and* being caught by someone knocking on the office door—only heightened the experience.

For my whole life I've been the good girl and this morning I wasn't.

I'm sorry Auggie caught me right afterward and I spilled

everything. I'm not sorry Elliot and I did what we did, though. No one has ever made me feel the way he does. What if I never find that again?

I startle when the phone on my desk rings. It's Elliot's extension. "Hi."

"Hi. Can you come into my office, please? We need to talk now."

Chapter Twenty-Three

ELLIOT

"Fuck." I run my fingers through my hair, tugging at the roots. If I read the situation right, and I'm pretty damn good at reading situations, Madison told Auggie about us. I don't know exactly what she shared, but I need to find out.

Madison enters my office with a sheepish expression on her face.

"Could you close the door, but open the curtains, please?"

"Sure."

I watch her, the graceful way she carries herself, the small steps she always takes like she's never in a hurry. Although with four-inch heels it's hard to walk fast. *Fuck*. What was I thinking fucking her here at work? Fucking her at all. I knew she was off-limits. Knew I had to quit imagining the two of us together, but she makes me forget myself. I lose track of time when I'm with her. I lose my mind thinking about being with her. Inside her.

At this very moment, my cock is twitching for more, the

greedy pecker not listening to a goddamn thing my mind is telling it.

When Madison's eyes meet mine, though, it's much more than a physical response. It's visceral and that throws me even more off-balance.

"I'm sorry," she says, sitting across the desk from me.

Suspicion confirmed.

"Auggie caught me off guard right after I sat down at my desk. She asked what was with our secret meeting and when I didn't answer right away, she could tell by my face what kind of meeting it was. I was flustered and nervous and she's my friend, so I spilled everything. I shouldn't have, I know, but—"

"Slow down, Mads."

She lets out a breath, her soft pink lips parting.

"You told her *everything*?" I ask, doing my best to stay calm when I feel anything but.

"Without going into detail, yes." Her gaze moves over my shoulder and I wonder if it's because she doesn't want to look me in the eyes, or if she's remembering what we did against the window twenty minutes ago.

I'm a moron. Every time I look outside *I'm* going to see Madison coming all over my cock, not the ocean in the distance.

"What were you thinking?" I ask, no longer even-tempered.

"Obviously I wasn't."

"Obviously."

She flinches. "You don't have to worry about Auggie. We can trust her."

"We?" My anger is rising and I don't like myself for it, but I'm pissed at her for sharing our secret. Rational or not, she had no right to compromise my status at ZipMeds like this. "There is no *we* in this case. I don't know Auggie that well and she's my boss's assistant. What if she says something without

thinking? James is smart as hell and can read between the lines. This could cost us our jobs."

"She won't." It's a delicate whisper, filled with regret.

"You don't know that," I say with less annoyance. She may have told Auggie about us, but I put her in the position of having something to tell. This is just as much my fault. The only difference is I know how to keep my mouth shut.

"I'm sorry," she says again.

Elbow on my desk, I drop my head and rub two fingers across my forehead. This is my dream job and I can't lose it. I can't lose respect, either. "I know you are, but you've put me in a really bad position. I'm glad you think you can trust Auggie, but there's more than trust involved. Do you think she'll look at me the same way now? I don't. And that fucking sucks."

"I'm sure—"

"You can't be sure about anything, Madison. You've worked for a high-level company for all of what? Seven, eight weeks? You know nothing about the cutthroat world of business. There are a hundred finance guys waiting to take my place if I get let go."

Apology, remorse, innocence, all play across her face. "What do you want me to do?"

"You don't need to do anything. Ultimately, this is on me, and I'll think of a way to fix it. In the meantime, we should keep our distance."

"Okay. Is that all?"

"Yes."

She hurries out of my office without another word. Her feelings are hurt, and I feel like shit for it, but I've got two and a half years of experience over her. I'm sick to my stomach thinking about how to put this to rights—because at the top of that list is firing her.

Hear me out.

I think I'm in love with her.

And if it's Madison in my personal life or Madison in my work life, I choose personal. I can find another assistant, albeit he or she will suck in comparison, but I won't find anyone else I want to be my girlfriend.

There's a catch, of course. She loves this job and I have no idea if she'll forgive me if I fire her. She's the one losing something, while I get to keep everything. I squeeze the back of my neck. *Fuuuck*.

Am I a total asshole for even thinking this way? Yes, which is why I have to give Madison the choice—the job or me. Because I can't in good conscience continue to break office policy. The guilt is eating at me.

My phone dings with a text. It's Michaela. She's flying into town tonight for a friend's wedding this weekend and do I want to meet up for a drink tomorrow night? Yes, I want to meet her. She's a corporate HR wiz and maybe she can help me sort out my situation with Madison. Michaela won't be happy I don't want to fuck her ever again, but I'd like to think we're friends despite the occasional hookup.

We text back and forth and set a time for seven o'clock at Donahue's.

I set my phone down a moment before James walks into my office. "Got a minute?" he asks, closing the door behind him.

"Sure." It's not like I can say "I don't." But given what's transpired this morning, his presence is a little nerve-racking.

He takes the chair Madison always sits in. "I just got off the phone with Alan Reitkerk and he's thrilled with the new strategy we're taking and happy to help us work on the big picture," James says.

"That's great." Alan is one of our biggest investors.

"In light of that, let's make sure we discuss product vision this afternoon with Drake."

"Will do."

"If I haven't told you lately, I really appreciate your hard work and forward thinking. I'm not sure Drake or I would see the company's metrics as comprehensively as you do. Which makes our humanitarian efforts that much more worthwhile."

This is the kind of praise that feeds my soul and makes me beyond grateful to be in the position I'm in. "That's nice to hear. Thank you."

"I need to bring something else up." He pauses but continues to meet my gaze head-on. "I'm not sure you're aware that we videotaped a large percentage of the company retreat."

"I wasn't." *Fuck.* I quickly run through my interactions with Madison, trying to think if there's anything inappropriate besides the fact that I probably look at her inappropriately every ten seconds.

"I thought it would be fun to put together a recap and show it to the staff. I watched it yesterday." Another pause. I don't normally sweat through my shirt, but this morning might be a first. "I couldn't help but notice you and Madison look very fond of each other."

"We are." There's no sense in arguing what he's seen with his own two eyes. "She's a great assistant and we work well together."

"I have to ask if I should be concerned?"

Shit. Shit. Shit. "What do you mean?" I know exactly what he means, but I'm not ready for this conversation.

"It means I know you're both attractive, single twentysomethings who spend a lot of hours together, which leaves little time for outside relationships."

"True." It's my turn to pause. I'm formulating how to continue when my phone chimes with another text. It sits closer to James than me and he glances down at it before I pick it up. It's Michaela again and she's texted in emoji only—eggplant, lips, and a wink.

A few months ago my dick would have stirred at the obvious innuendo, but not anymore. Only one girl has power over me below the belt now.

James grins. "Who's Michaela?"

And just like that my immediate problem is solved. "She's a girl I've seen a few times. She works in HR for Goldman and likes to get together whenever she's in town."

"I take it she's visiting soon?"

"This weekend, actually. Unrelated to work, though. She's got a friend's wedding to go to."

"You're her plus-one?" James has never inquired into my private life this much before, no doubt set off by the video from the retreat.

"No. We're meeting for drinks tomorrow night."

He rubs underneath his chin. "She's based in New York?"

"Yes."

"If it isn't too big an imposition, think I could join you? My younger sister recently moved to Manhattan and is looking for a new job. Maybe I can put the two of them in touch."

"Uh, yeah. That's fine."

"I won't stay too long. You'll have plenty of time to take her up on her offer."

I frown in confusion. "Her offer?"

"The text?"

"Oh, right. Thanks." I force a smile. I think I've just made my life even more difficult.

He stands. "I'll see you in the conference room for lunch."

"Okay. And about Madison…" I feel like I have to give him something, so I tell him we've known each other for years through mutual friends and that's probably why we look at each other differently. I apologize for keeping that fact to myself, but I didn't think it pertinent since it was a temp agency that sent Madison and we weren't close friends.

"Got it," he says and leaves my office.

I look through the glass wall toward Madison's desk. She turns her head, makes quick eye contact, then scoots her chair closer to her desk and gets back to work. I follow suit, clicking on my email.

For the rest of the day it's business as usual except for one stomach-aching fact. The tension between us is so thick, it's like we're strangers.

Chapter Twenty-Four

MADISON

"It's weird that he told me to take the day off, right?"

"What's weird is you not enjoying a paid Freebie Friday," Harper says. We're walking down a tree-lined street not far from the office to check out an apartment I saw for rent. Harper makes her own work schedule, so she was on board with accompanying me today.

"I mean I know he said his schedule changed and he'd be in an all-day meeting, but I can't shake the feeling he didn't want to see me."

Harper stops, her sunglasses meet mine. "Maddy, he didn't. And that's not a bad thing. After everything you told me, he needs time to process things and so do you."

"I guess you're right."

"I usually am." She links her arm with mine. "Now come on, let's find you a kick-ass place to live."

The second-floor apartment smells like someone puked in it. Harper actually tells the building manager that. The woman apologizes and says she can have it taken care of, but I'm not convinced. Plus, we've got more apartments to look at.

I'm excited to live on my own for the first time in my life and I have this idea in my head of what I want it to look like: Light, airy, and simple, so I can add my own touches. Besides my bed—which I'm bringing from home, much to my mom's chagrin because she's afraid I'll never come visit for the night, even though there are three other available beds in the house—I plan to buy a secondhand couch and dining chairs and reupholster them in this really pretty Prussian blue fabric. The chairs will go perfect with the small Pottery Barn dining table I've got my eye on as my one splurge. I'd also like to have a bathtub, but it's not a requirement. A small space to sew in is, though. And lastly, I envision fresh flowers sitting in a vase on the kitchen counter all the time.

Apartment number two is a bust, too. But the third one is really close to what I'm looking for. It's a newer building and there is more than one apartment available. I decide to think on it because it requires a one-year lease. It's not like I have to move out of my parents' house immediately, which is a nice luxury to have in this situation.

Finished apartment hunting for the day, we walk over to the nearby farmers market—another plus if I end up choosing this rental. There are three rows of sellers, each booth shaded by a giant blue or red umbrella or pop-up tent. The sun is high up in the sky. A light spring breeze carries the scent of fresh fruits and vegetables.

"Whoever decided to put sugar on popcorn is a genius," I say. "Kettle corn is the best." I pass the large clear bag to Harper.

She digs her hand in for a scoop. "Agreed, but I hate that it gets in your teeth."

"The one downside. Hey, can I ask you something?"

"Of course. Anything."

"Do you think I'm being naive about work?" We turn down the last aisle that I quickly dub Tomato Street.

"What do you mean?" Harp hands me back the kettle corn.

"Elliot pretty much called me out on being an amateur and not understanding how the business world works. It's true this is my first real job, and I'm still learning the dynamics of the company, but I do trust Auggie not to say anything."

"As long as you're confident about that, then I don't see how your inexperience matters. I think Elliot is just upset he doesn't have total control over the situation anymore."

"I get that."

"And he needs to get that women have a code. Auggie might not have his back, but she's got yours, and that means she won't say anything."

"I wish he'd at least made time to keep our lunch date today. I hate that things are weird between us."

"It won't last forever. And sometimes weird leads to really great things."

We walk around the white roadblocks sectioning off the farmers market and step onto the sidewalk to get to our car. "I knew you were sad, but I didn't know you felt weird about the time you and Levi were apart."

"Very weird. It sucked. But look at us now."

They're totally in love. Both of Elliot's roommates are, and it hits me how much I miss being a couple.

Harper taps the alarm to unlock her car. "Ready to go back to my house?"

"Yes. Thanks for helping me look at places."

For the rest of the afternoon we sit by the pool, read *Cosmo* and *People* and talk about which celebrity couples we love the most. Teague gets home from work and we hang out for a bit before heading to Donahue's for dinner.

We grab a booth and order food and drinks.

"We're doing a wedding for the cutest couple," Teague says. "Listen to how they got engaged. She's a marine biologist and they were at an aquarium. He takes her to stand in front of a giant tank where they do feedings. There's a tank keeper or whatever they're called, standing there, too, and he tells the group waiting to watch the feeding that they're going to play a trivia game. When he looks at our bride to ask her a question, he tells her instead of him asking the question the diver inside the tank is going to. She turns and sees the diver holding a sign that says, WILL YOU MARRY ME, and our groom is on one knee."

"That's so special," I say. Henry did the usual proposal. Fancy restaurant, champagne, diamond ring sitting on top of my crème brûlée, which was *his* favorite dessert. I'd much rather eat something chocolaty.

"If Levi proposes to me in public, he's in big trouble," Harper says.

"*What* did you just say?" Teague asks, her back going ramrod straight.

"Don't get your panties in a snit. He's maybe mentioned wanting to marry me *one day*. And I've told him one day is perfect."

"I can't wait for your one day," Teague says with sisterly love.

"I have a feeling yours will be here before mine."

"I have a feeling you're right."

Now my and Harper's backs straighten. "Why do you say that?" Harper inquires.

"Mateo's just been…he's been so amazing lately, not that he isn't always, but he's also been kind of secretive, which is not like him at all, so I think he's planning something."

"Like a proposal?" I say, making a mental note to casually question him about it.

"I hope so." Teague stares off into the distance, all dreamy-eyed.

I follow her gaze out into the restaurant. All the tables and booths are occupied. The bar is full, too. As I pull my attention back, I'm stopped midway. Sitting at a table are Elliot, James, and what was her name? The HR girl who definitely wanted in Elliot's pants the night he offered me a full-time position as his assistant. M-something. I blink repeatedly hoping to recall her name. *Michaela.*

Michaela wasn't scheduled on Elliot's calendar, and an uncomfortable lump takes shape in the back of my throat.

It does look like they're having a business meeting, though, albeit a cozy one. James is talking, engaging Michaela in conversation. There's smiling. Laughing. I need to chill. I have no claim on Elliot. He's free to do and see whomever he wants, whether it's work related or not.

But then James stands up and leaves, and it's just Elliot and her and it bothers me. Even more so when she puts her hand on his arm and laughs at something he says.

"Maddy? Are you okay?" Teague asks.

I tear my gaze away from Elliot. "No."

Harper's eyes track to where mine just were. "What the hell? I'm going to strangle him."

I'm not sure we need to go that far, so I quickly say, "She's a colleague from his old firm. And our boss was sitting with them until a minute ago, so I'm sure it's nothing."

"But it doesn't feel like nothing," Teague says with compassion, noticing the reason for my unease and Harper's anger.

"I'm surprised to see them together is all, and since I think they hooked up in the past, it doesn't feel that great, no. Especially given the way he and I left things." Is this his way of fixing our situation? By reconnecting with someone else? I sink down into the booth. I'm confused and want to disappear.

"Should we grab their attention?" Harper asks.

"No. I don't want to bother them."

"I'm sure they're just talking work stuff." Teague's reassurance does nothing to ease my growing anxiety.

Michaela looks way more sophisticated than me. More experienced. She's probably got tons more in common with Elliot than I do, work-wise *and* relationship-wise. I'm reminded of the strain between us in the office yesterday and how impossible it is for us to be together right now.

She smiles at him. Smiles are supposed to bring joy, but hers brings misery. I can't sit here and watch them enjoy each other's company. "I think I need to go."

"Don't let him run you off," Harper says.

Teague takes the cocktail napkin I'm shredding into tiny pieces out of my hands. "You should go talk to him."

I agree. I should. But rational or not, I'm hurt at simply seeing them together, and I can't get my feet to take me over there. I feel like an outsider from way over here, so I imagine it would be way worse up close. The last time the three of us talked at this restaurant didn't exactly go my way.

Michaela leans over, practically into his lap, and whispers something in his ear. I can't take it anymore. "I'm sorry. I have to get out of here and grab some air." I snatch up my purse and escape, head down, eyes on the floor. I have no choice but to walk close by their table on the way to the exit. When I stupidly strain to hear what they're talking about and Michaela says, "my hotel" I forget how to breathe.

I rush out the restaurant's front door. Immediately my hands are on my thighs as I try to catch my breath. Have I been made a fool a second time? I promised myself after Henry I would never let that happen again.

Someone bursts through the door. "Madison?"

It's Elliot. I don't move from my position. Maybe if I stay

like this he'll go back inside.

He bends over, too, hands on his thighs, putting us at eye level. "Is there a reason you're not answering me?"

Yes, you're a giant jerk and I hate you.

"All right. Let me take a guess. You saw me with Michaela and thought the worst."

I lift up. "Who?"

My question sparks a knowing grin. He crosses his arms, his dress shirt stretching across all the sinewy muscles I know are underneath.

"Okay, yes. I saw the two of you together."

"It's nothing you need to worry about."

"Really? So having girls fawn all over you is normal?"

He studies me. "Are you jealous?"

"No." I so am.

A couple steps out of the restaurant and almost bumps into us. Elliot puts his hand on my lower back and guides us away from the entrance—and the possibility of being seen by anyone. He positions us against the side of the building where it's dark and leans into me, one hand pressed to the wall just above my head. "I think you are." His warm breath fans my neck, making my skin warm.

"What brought the two of you together tonight?" I ask with a straight face.

"Exactly what you think, but I told her that wasn't happening," he says sincerely. "I was also hoping she could help me with our problem given she's an HR shark."

"You were?"

He drops his arm, creating some space between us. "Yeah, but I didn't get a chance to ask because some gorgeous blonde distracted me when she ran out of the restaurant."

"Oh."

"I smelled you."

My stomach flutters at that. He's memorized my scent.

"And then I saw the sexiest ass and this shiny long hair"—he rubs a few strands between his fingers—"and I jumped out of my chair to find you."

"Here I am."

"Yes, you are."

We quietly stare at each other until I utter, "What are we doing, Elliot?" It's the second time I've asked him this, but so much has changed since the first time.

He opens his mouth, then closes it, I suspect because he notices the seriousness in my eyes and whatever cheeky thing he was about to say isn't going to help my mood. He turns so his back is against the wall, our sides lightly touching. It worries me that he doesn't want to talk to my face.

"James has big plans for the company. And for me. He wants me to take more of a leadership role at the office, and he wants to send me overseas for a few meetings. Have me put my French to good use in person."

"That's great." It truly is. I've never once wished for anything but the best for Elliot work-wise.

"I'm halfway into my five-year plan and because of ZipMeds, I've surpassed where I thought I'd be."

I'm ashamed to admit I've never had a plan other than get married and have kids. My life was practically mapped out the second Henry and I got serious. But hearing Harper and Teague talk about marriage tonight, I realized I don't want to get married for a while. I do want to love one person with all my heart and soul. And I want to live life the same way. Being, doing, feeling, pushing myself out of my comfort zones, surprising myself and others, finding my limits and then surpassing them, that's what I want—what I *need*.

My heart tells me all of that is possible with the guy standing next to me, but that he doesn't feel the same.

Chapter Twenty-Five

"I've just started my plan and I've surpassed my expectations, too," Madison says with pride.

I let those words sink in. On the busy street beside us, cars continually zip by, the sounds and energy of city life swirling in blurred shades of red, orange, blue, and black. I stare unfocused, wondering how the fuck I can get out of this mess without hurting her.

The reality is I can't. I'm about to rip her first job out from under her and there's not a thing I can do about it short of never touching her again. Today's marathon meeting with James cemented my place with ZipMeds for the next two years. I'm completely dialed in—a promotion and raise not far off. I couldn't have scripted a better job scenario, and all of this before I'm twenty-five.

"I should add it's because I love working with you."

Fucking hell. Of course she does. I've been a better boss with her. I've treated her like my equal. Given her tasks to challenge and teach. Respected her suggestions and valued her input.

I love working with her, too, but after today, not enough to jeopardize my career. This makes me a total asshole, I know. I *knew* better. I knew better than to get involved with her and I chose to be stupid over smart anyway. It wasn't like I didn't try to be on my best behavior. I did. I just couldn't stop the magnetic pull to have her body on mine.

"Madison."

She turns her head and looks at me with guileless blue eyes that slay me. The depth of intelligence takes it up another notch. She knows my tone. What's in my head. She's waiting on me to say something she won't like.

"I don't think this is going to work," I say, the words bitter on my tongue. I hate myself right now.

She looks away. Painful seconds of silence tick by. "Five minutes ago you made it sound like you were trying to figure out a way."

"You're right. But—"

"Save it." She waves her hand in the air. "I don't need to hear the reasons why being together is a bad, not to mention an impossible, idea. You've made it perfectly clear your job is the most important thing to you, and I get it. My job is my top priority, too, so no worries. We had some fun and now it's over. We knew it was a mistake to begin with."

Wait. What? She's misunderstanding.

"Actually," she continues, "this is a huge relief. Now I can keep my focus on work. And lucky me. I've got a boss going places, which means I am, too. I see having my own assistant one day, you know."

No. I did not know. *What did you expect, your arrogant prick? Did you think she'd declare her love for you and say she'd happily find another job?* I know she loves it at ZipMeds. That she's made friends. Seamlessly become part of the team.

She steps forward, clearly ready to end our conversation with her shoulders squared, her chin lifted. Good thing, since I'm at a loss for words. "I guess I'll see you Monday morning. Have a good night."

"Madison." I reach for her hand but pull back before making contact. I've got my pride and no way am I letting her see how much it bothers me to be dismissed so easily. I can't believe how wrong I was about her feelings for me. "Never mind."

This is for the best. It's a win-win on the work front. Mostly. That I'll have to see her every day won't be easy, but I can't think of anyone better to make professional strides with. The stupid emotions making my throat thick will fade. I pray sooner than later.

She heads back inside the restaurant and joins Harper and Teague. I sit back down with Michaela. Five minutes later we get up to leave. I feel Madison's eyes on my back until I'm out of sight. Let her think the worst, my bruised ego says, when in reality I say good night to Michaela and go home alone.

• • •

I swing the bat and miss the fastball for the third damn time in a row.

"Dude, who taught you how to hit? Your grandma?" Levi jokes. "Remind me to send her half of the hundred bucks I'm about to win from you."

I push the stop button on the indoor batting cage so I can catch my breath and give Levi a, "Fuck you." It's Sunday afternoon and we're at the cages, our bet over who will get the most hits in the seventy-five-mile-an-hour cage almost ever.

"Aw, is Elliot sad he's about to lose to me again?"

No. Elliot is pissed he can't keep his head in the game, but that's about to change. I'm going to crush these last five pitches and beat my roommate's sorry ass. "Watch and learn, pretty boy."

I hit the start button and get in position with my back knee, hip and head in a straight line. Top arm bent, head in the middle of my feet. The pitch machine cranks up. I zone in on the mouth of the machine, focus, clear my head of all the other shit taking up space, see the ball release. I swing. Hit against a firm front side, back foot on its toe, and the sound of the bat cracking against the ball echoes in the warehouse.

One down, four more pitches to go.

Next pitch. *Smack.*

Three, two, one, go down the same. My grandmother didn't call me "Slugger" for nothing. I lift my batting helmet off, tuck the bat under my arm, and turn to gloat. "I'll take that Benjamin now."

Levi shakes his head as he pulls a hundred-dollar bill out of his wallet. "Way to come back. I knew you had it in you."

"What's that supposed to mean?" I exit the cage and we walk over to the vending machine. Loser also buys the winner a Gatorade.

"As soon as I pissed you off you forgot about your girl troubles and focused."

"I don't have girl troubles."

"Says the guy who just this morning asked me the age-old question, love or money."

"No, I said, I need to get me some honey. And I don't mean the kind from bees."

He laughs as we sit down on a bench near the slow-pitch cage where a couple of young kids are taking turns batting. "This is worse than I thought."

"Says the guy who moped around for a month over some pussy."

"Correction. I moped around over love and you know it. I suspect you might even feel it yourself."

"With who?" I've pushed the L-word out of my thoughts. I never should have toyed with it in the first place. Madison set me straight on that score.

"Quit the bullshit. We both know who." Why did I tell him about Friday night? Oh, that's right. I didn't. Harper did, and then I had to set the record straight by informing him she walked away from me because her job meant more.

It meant more to you, too, remember?

"Doesn't matter anymore."

Levi gives me a narrowed sidelong glance. I know he's got my back in all things, but I don't need him right now. I want to drop it.

"Excuse me?" a kid says, eyes on me, with a bat almost taller than he is in his hands.

"Hey, bud," I say.

"I saw you hitting and was wondering if you could show me how. My mom doesn't know anything about baseball."

I look beyond the kid to a woman standing near the cage fence. She's hot. Around thirty, I'd guess. A definite MILF.

"Sure." I stand up, notice the woman smile. My battered ego gets a boost. "Be back in a few," I tell Levi. The mom is grateful and flirty while I help her son, Cody. She's not wearing a wedding ring and when I get Cody set up inside the cage to bat, she asks if she can thank me with dinner tonight. It's a nice offer, and I should take her up on it, but fuck if I can't get a certain assistant out of my head.

Cody gets some hits and beams after each one. We fist-bump when he's finished, his grin still in place. I bend to his level to share a few top-secret pointers just between us men, then Levi and I take off.

I hit the sack early with Socks curled up near my head, eager for Monday morning to get here. Sleep is fitful, but I'm at the office early as usual. What isn't usual is the envelope on my desk. Not because I haven't received this particular type of note before. But because it's eight a.m. and there's no sign of Madison. She must have come in over the weekend to leave it for me.

Mr. Sax,

You are an excellent finance manager. That being said, your interpersonal skills could use some work. I believe there are classes at the local community college that may help you with this. Check them out online. I'd also like to inform you that I quit, effective immediately. I've contacted the temp agency and a new assistant will arrive this morning at nine sharp. I sincerely hope he or she meets with your approval, or at the very least is tolerable. We both know there will never be anyone else like me.

Best wishes,
Miss Hastings

I fall back against my chair. Madison quit? She didn't only quit me personally. She's left me professionally, too? What the hell? She couldn't give me fucking two-weeks' notice? Come in this morning to talk through whatever prompted this decision? Nope. Instead, she single-handedly dealt with our situation. Damn, but I drastically underestimated her.

I'm pretty sure she also damaged my heart if the pain in the middle of my chest is any indication.

James strides into my office. "Good morning."

There is nothing good about it. "Morning."

"I got an email from Madison. Did you know she was quitting?"

Great. She didn't even give me the courtesy of a heads-up. "No. I just found out, too." I tuck the note back inside the envelope.

"Is she okay? Any idea what happened?" He takes a seat across from me, concern creasing the corners of his eyes.

After the faith he's put in me, I owe him the truth. Not that I know precisely why she quit, but I'd bet money she'd still be here if we hadn't crossed the line. I give him an abbreviated version of what happened between us, adding my apology at the end. His quiet concentration is something I've grown used to over the past several months, but it's unnerving given the topic of our discussion. Finally he speaks up. One pass is all I get, he tells me, none too pleased about how I acted.

"She saved you your job, you know," he says as he gets to his feet. "She's not only smart, but generous. I'll see you for our exec meeting."

"Right."

Madison Hastings *is* smart and generous…

And she's the winner of our workplace strategy.

**"Sometimes things have to become completely undone,
before they can be mended."
—J. Iron Word**

*Sax/Hastings
Workplace Strategy
Scorecard*

*Sax – 3
Hastings – 7*

Chapter Twenty-Six

MADISON

Seattle looks very different when the sun is shining. Sitting in a comfortable leather chair and staring out the tenth-floor window in the reception area of the elegant executive building, I'm lost to the urban city landscape, blue water, and mountains in the distance. With this beautiful view to keep me company, apologies that I've been kept waiting are more than okay. Besides, it doesn't hurt to have a little more time to mentally prepare.

It's been a little over two weeks since I quit ZipMeds. I couldn't keep working there knowing Elliot chose his job over me without giving me any say. Leaving like I did may have been cowardly, but giving up the job was easy compared to the thought of seeing him every day.

I run my sweaty palms down the navy skirt of my power suit. I'm here. *Having a meeting.* My stomach roils, this time having nothing to do with the nauseating drive from the airport. This is either the worst or best idea I've ever had. I'll confirm which when my meeting is over.

Madison Michelle. It has a nice ring to it, don't you think?

The idea to start my own handbag company first occurred to me a couple of months ago, a little seed in the back of my mind that never really went away. With free time on my hands over the past two weeks, though, I've done nothing but cultivate it (my fingers hurt from all the sewing!) and put my finance knowledge to good use—spreadsheets, financial forecasts, market analysis, profitability, expansion.

For the thousandth time, my mind drifts to Elliot and the note I've memorized. I know our notes back and forth weren't based in truth and were meant to mask our mutual attraction, but I haven't been able to get this particular one out of my head. *I suspect the heart of a risk-taker beats underneath your whip-smart attitude. But in the competitive world of financial management, you also need to be fearless.*

Thank you, Mr. Sax, for making me mad enough to realize other options. I'll be forever grateful.

In truth, I never would have had the courage to start my own business if it weren't for him and the things he taught me. About business. And about myself.

"Madison? Joaquin is ready to see you now. Again, I'm so sorry for the delay," Joaquin's assistant says, interrupting my thoughts.

"No worries. I was enjoying the scenery." I pick up the large hard-case hatbox off the shiny marble floor. The deep, round box that I splurged on from Nordstrom is a great carrier for my handbags.

I follow Ms. Roy—I think she said that was her name—down the hallway toward Joaquin Santos's office. When he agreed to meet with me, I did a happy dance around my bedroom that may have included some twerking. After I reached out via email last week, he'd said he remembered me very well. He asked to see my business plan, I sent it, and the very next day he invited me to a sit down. The cost to fly here and meet with him personally is an investment I pray pays off.

"Hello, Mr. Santos," I say as I walk into his spectacular office. My legs are shaking, my stilettos a little wobbly. I ignore both, fake it till you make it and all that. *Deep breath, Madison. You've got this.* I hear the *click* of the office door behind me, Ms. Roy giving us privacy.

"Miss Hastings, it's nice to see you again." He strides around his desk and extends his hand. His handshake is warm, friendly, a nice compliment to his good looks. I hope he doesn't feel my anxiety through my palm. The last time we were together, Elliot did most of the talking.

"Thank you for meeting with me. And please call me Madison."

"I appreciate you considering me as an investor in your new company. Please have a seat." He gestures toward a couch. "And call me Joaquin."

"Okay," I say, taking a seat. He sits across from me in a high-back chair. There's a dark wood coffee table between us. And then because I'm nervous, I launch right into the pitch I've practiced over and over again since scheduling this get-together. It's nerve-racking, approaching a businessman instead of a businesswoman, given most men don't carry purses or bags so they might not understand my passion, but Joaquin has his hands in many different businesses, and we'd met before, so I figured it was my best place to start.

I open the hatbox, showing him several of my purse designs as I continue to speak. "The line includes shoulder bags, handbags, tote bags, lightweight travel bags, and special occasion bags. Each purse is a fabulous piece of unique and distinctive wearable art all handmade in California. And all of the bags are made from man-made upholstery fabric, not animal products."

"Nice," he says.

This is my biggest comfort zone, talking about my product, so I keep going. "Each bag features a decorative front panel with organza roses in a variety of reds, purples, and pinks with a splash of green. The insides are lined with satin and feature a phone pocket, as well as other pockets arranged at different heights and sizes, so contents can be organized rather than left in a jumbled mess at the bottom. All of the bags are surprisingly roomy and can hold loads of essentials. Or not. It's up to the owner. And with an adjustable strap, each bag is versatile in how it can be worn or held."

"May I?" He reaches for one of the bags.

"Please."

While he checks out my handiwork, I open my tote and pull out a hard copy of my business plan, referring to specific numbers as I take the time to personally provide and interpret the financial information I sent him. He listens attentively.

"I also want to make a difference," I add. "And would like to donate a percentage of sales to women's charities across the U.S."

Joaquin flashes his very nice white teeth. "This is all very impressive."

"I'm glad you think so," I say aloud. Inside I'm screaming, *Holy shit he thinks I'm impressive!* I'm also quite pleased I got through everything without throwing up on his Italian leather shoes.

He runs his hand across his strong clean-shaven jawline. "I'm in."

My heart flips over. "Really?" *Jeez, Madison. Could you sound any more like an amateur?*

"Yes, really. I'd be happy to invest in your company."

It takes all my willpower not to jump up and down on the couch like a ten-year-old. I'm an adult and need to act like one.

"Your plan is solid, but I do have a few thoughts."

"I'm happy to hear them."

He glances at his watch. "Unfortunately I have another meeting in a few minutes. Are you staying in town overnight? If so, we could grab dinner."

"Thank you, but I've got to fly back tonight." I gather my purses back into the hatbox.

"Phone call then." He stands and helps. "Do I have a number for you?"

I made a few business cards with my cell phone number on them for just such an occasion. I pull the card out of the top pocket inside my tote.

"Another thing those pockets are good for," Joaquin says around a smile.

"Yes."

He walks me to the door, my legs much steadier now that I've secured my first investor. I give him a firm handshake. "I think I forgot to say thank you for investing in Madison Michelle. You won't be disappointed."

"I've no doubt. Have a safe flight home."

The second I've got my seat belt on for the car ride back to the airport, I call my dad. He offered to finance my business for the first year, but I turned him down. This has to be all mine—my successes, my failures, my learning curves. All of it. He understood and told me there was only one other time he'd been prouder of me. And when I asked which time, he said the time I left my groom at the altar. It was the first time he'd intimated such a thing, let alone stated it out loud.

He apologized for waiting so long to tell me. I apologized for not calling off the wedding sooner. Then he hugged me close for a long time and said I had nothing to be sorry for, that I had the best heart of anyone he knew, and I should never apologize for it.

Dad doesn't answer the call. I dial my mom. She doesn't

pick up, either. Harper and Teague are AWOL, too. Where is everyone? I'm bursting to scream this news. I reluctantly send texts instead. While doing so, I notice I missed a text from Brooks. I call him back.

"Hey, Madison."

"Hi! Guess what?" I don't even give him a chance to answer "what" before I launch into what happened with my meeting.

"That's awesome. Congratulations. So where are you now? I think this calls for a celebratory drink."

"I'm in the back of an Uber on my way to the airport." I stare out the passenger window at the Seattle landscape.

"We'll celebrate when I help you move then. You still want me on Saturday?"

"Yes, please."

"So, how does it feel to officially be your own businesswoman?"

"Amazing."

"I'll be able to say I knew you when."

I like the sound of that. Brooks has turned into a good friend. Someone I can talk to and rely on. "'When' what exactly?"

He clears his throat. "When I had to thread a needle for you."

"I was drunk!" Brooks invited me over to his condo for dinner to cheer me up after I quit working at ZipMeds. He cooked a frozen vegetarian lasagna and made me cocktails from a bartender's recipe book his roommate has. We ate and drank on the couch and watched John Oliver. When he asked if I could sew a button back on his uniform for him, I said sure. Talk about hilarious. I couldn't focus on the needle and poked myself a gazillion times.

"I'll leave that part out."

"Brooks!" That makes it worse. I think.

He laughs. "You are so easy."

"You wish." I press my lips together. I have no idea why I said that.

"You flirting with me across state lines?" he teases.

"Not on purpose." There's only one person I want to flirt with and we haven't said a word to each other in weeks. It hurts, thinking about Elliot and how much I miss him.

"I know. I'll see you Saturday, Mad. Congrats again. I'm really proud of you."

"Thanks, Brookie."

He groans. He hates when I call him that, but it's his fault for plying me with enough drinks to come up with the nickname. A minute after I hang up with him, my dad calls. Then my mom. They're proud of me, too. Texts with Teague and Harper follow and go like this:

Yo the Boss Woman! So excited for you.

You're legit, girlfriend. So happy for you.

Drinks on us!

Will you name one of your handbags The Harper?

Congratulations! Love you.

XOXOXOXOXO

There's one more person I should text: Mateo. He'll hear the news from Teague, but I know he'd like to find out from me. The thing is, I've mostly avoided him the past two weeks through no fault of his. He's reached out. Called to make sure I was okay. I just need a little more time away from anything that reminds me too much of Elliot.

The flight back to L.A. is uneventful. When I land, I see a text from Auggie. Besides losing Elliot, I've kind of lost her, too. It's my fault. It's hard to talk to her and not ask about him. How's he doing? Is his new assistant nice? Does he ever mention me? But Auggie insists we keep in touch (I love her for it) and when I told her about my plans and that I was meeting with Joaquin, she was thrilled for me.

How did your meeting go?????

Great. He's in. This is really happening!

Oh my God. That is fantastic. Congrats! We're going to lunch to celebrate. I know you don't want to, but tough shit. We're going. I'll meet you somewhere one day next week, k?

Okay. Thank you. I include a kissy face emoji.

She sends a bunch of happy, congratulatory emojis back.

It's past nine o'clock by the time I get on the freeway, so traffic isn't bad on my way home. The house is quiet when I get there, the usual lights left on for me. Only two more nights, then I move to my own place. I did accept a small loan from my dad so I could rent an apartment. I'd told my parents about the place I found with Harper before I quit my job, and after I quit, Dad said he understood how much I wanted to live on my own, so why not let him help. I agreed as long as he understood that when I could, I was paying him back. I may be living on cereal for a while, but I'm cool with that.

I turn the light on in my bedroom and immediately latch on to a huge bouquet of yellow and pink roses on my desk. The arrangement is gorgeous. Their floral scent fills the room. My parents shouldn't have. There's even a note card. I slide the card out of the envelope.

My heart jumps to the back of my throat.

Congratulations, Madison. Your successes are just beginning, and I look forward to watching you soar. Best wishes with your new company, Elliot.

Shock barrels through me. My body shakes from a mix of happiness and bafflement. How did Elliot know about *Madison Michelle*? And does this mean he misses me? Is this his olive branch? He threw our relationship away so carelessly, if he thinks flowers are going to win me back, he has no idea who he's dealing with.

He promised me we'd figure things out. *We.* And then he broke that promise when he decided what was best for both of us. I'm still not over the hurt. Not even close.

I plop down on my bed. Nothing in the note indicates he wants me back. I'm delusional. Harper or Teague probably told Levi or Mateo, and one of them told Elliot and he felt the need to congratulate me, is all.

Pulling my phone out of my bag, I start to text him a thank-you. That's the polite thing to do. *Thank you. The flowers are beautiful.* Delete. *Thank you for thinking of me. I love the flowers.* Delete again. I try a third time. *Thank you.* I stare at those two little words. They're innocent enough. Simple. Meaningful without meaning too much by themselves. People say them all the time, even to strangers.

Still. I delete them.

Chapter Twenty-Seven

I don't want Madison taking up all of my thoughts, but fuck if I can't stop thinking about her. She's been in every single one of my dreams for the past three weeks. I picture her at her desk constantly. I imagine her naked and pressed against me a million times a day. I'm not exaggerating this. I'm a finance guy. I know about numbers.

I wonder what she's doing right now. I've been fucking wondering it for the past hour. It's Friday afternoon and I'm getting shit done because the only thing I want to do is be in the same room with her. I miss her to the point of pain. Seriously. My chest *hurts*. Maybe I should have reached out immediately after she quit.

Maybe I should have done a lot of things differently.

It's not too late.

Screw it. I shut down my computer and tidy my desk. I have to see her, if for no other reason than to find out if she received the flowers I sent. I'd hoped the gift would spark conversation between us again, but I didn't hear a word back. I'm so damn proud of her for starting her own business. I couldn't have timed a call to Joaquin better. He'd just finished a meeting with her and filled me in. If he knew my history with her, he probably wouldn't have.

"Rita, I'm leaving for the day," I tell my assistant on the way out. "Why don't you go home early, too. Have a good weekend and I'll see you Monday."

"Okay. Thanks. You, too."

Rita is the third assistant I've had since Madison, and I'm thinking she's a keeper. For thirty years she assisted a finance exec at Disney. She retired to spend more time with her family, only to find herself bored. She's no-nonsense, smart, and has no trouble putting me in my place in a motherly sort of way. I like her.

I'm out the door, in my car, and steering toward Madison's parents' house a couple minutes later. I've reached my breaking point, expecting a response from her about the roses for the past week. *You've been hoping for any word from her since she quit, you fool.*

Traffic sucks, so I've got time to think on the drive over. I've always enjoyed working, even on tough, nothing-goes-my-way days. It's more than a source of income. It's what gets me excited about waking up every morning. It's what gives me purpose and a sense of accomplishment. More so since I started at ZipMeds. But in the past couple of weeks, I've lost something. Something I didn't even know was missing—someone to share it with.

Going into work every day knowing Madison was there made it better. Being so familiar with someone, and counting on that someone, eliminated the shitty days I'd occasionally have.

The more I recall the weeks we worked together, the more I remember *all* the things we talked about. It was impossible not to get personal with her, our conversations during lunch or in the break room or over a chocolate croissant in the mornings slipped into friendly territory without us realizing it. Madison was more than my assistant, she was my...family.

It's fair to say that recognition has me almost continuing to drive past her house. I'm no chicken, though, so I park my car. I *am* nervous when I knock on the front door. I've no idea what to say to her, only that I need to say something. The door opens and a woman—I'm guessing Madison's mom—says, "Hello. Can I help you?"

"Mrs. Hastings?"

"Yes. And you are?"

"I'm Elliot. It's nice to meet you." I extend my hand. Her expression remains friendly, but neutral, which leads me to believe Madison hasn't said much about me. "I'm a friend of your daughter's and was hoping I could talk to her."

Her expression turns skeptical. "A friend?"

Maybe Madison did mention me more than in passing. "We also worked together at ZipMeds. Is she home?"

Mrs. Hastings crosses her arms. "You were her boss."

"Yes." I give Mrs. Hastings my Boy Scout smile—it's sincere and sweet and usually gets me what I want. Right now I want entry into the house. The woman is an exceptional door block.

"And the one who sent her flowers."

"She got them?" Great. One question answered, a few more to go.

"Yes." She drops her arms to take a more relaxed stance, but her eyes narrow, like she's contemplating turning the tables and asking me a bunch of questions.

I tug at my shirt collar. I wasn't expecting a discussion with her mom and don't want to screw it up. When she doesn't immediately say anything else, I jump in with, "Would it be okay if I come in?"

"She's not here."

"Oh. Will she be back soon?"

"She doesn't live here anymore."

For a second I'm sucker punched. How come I didn't know this? She's wanted to move out of her parents' house for a while and this is big news I should have known about. Who helped her into her new place? Is she living alone? Where is she?

"She moved last weekend," Mrs. Hastings supplies, picking up my slack. It's taking me a minute to find my voice.

"Can I get her new address?"

"Of course. Give her a call and she can share it with you."

Smart answer, I suppose, given Mrs. Hastings has only just met me. The thing is, if I call her I lose the element of surprise and risk her turning me down. Wait a second. I bet my dumbass roommates know about this and their girlfriends probably asked them to keep their mouths shut.

"I'll do that. Thanks." I turn to go, then pause. "Your daughter is an exceptional human being and I hope I see you again."

She smiles. It's warm, appreciative. "Thank you. We think so, too."

My grip is tight on the steering wheel as I drive home. I've hated myself for how things ended with Madison, but it seems our parting of ways was the best thing to happen to her. She's unstoppable—new career, new place to live. Is it selfish of me to reach out to her now? I don't want to complicate her life again.

Fuck it. Yes I do. I want to be her must-have, the essential part of her day. Because that's what she is to me, and if she gives me a second chance, I'll never let her down again.

As luck would have it, Mateo is at the house when I get there. Perfect.

"Hey, you're home early," he says from the couch. As

usual, my mind takes a detour to Madison and all the places I had her naked. Since spending the weekend with her, the house isn't the same. Her essence fills every room, sparking memories and a desire for more.

I sit down next to him. He's got his laptop in his lap. "Yeah, I thought I'd go see Madison only to find she doesn't live there anymore."

He stops typing, looks at me. "Go ahead and say it."

"You're an asshole."

"Feel better?"

"No."

"Look, she asked me not to tell you." He quickly types something, then his attention bounces back to me.

"I'm your best friend."

"She's my oldest friend and like a sister to me."

"Fine." I settle back into the couch. We're both quiet. Mateo is loyal to a fault, and I don't want to come between his and Madison's friendship, but this is a special circumstance. "I understand."

"Do you? This is why I warned you to stay away from her. I didn't want to be put in the middle when she was hurting."

"I'm hurting, too," I admit aloud for the first time. "I can't sleep. I lose focus at work and can't remember details I never used to forget. I…I love her."

"What?"

"You heard me." God, I feel like a weight has been lifted. I love Madison. I love every single thing about her.

Mateo takes a minute to study me. "If this is for real, then there's nothing I'd like more than for you guys to be together. But are you sure?"

I glare at him. "What do you mean am I sure?"

"Let me clarify that. Let's say you had to choose between her and your job. Which would you choose?"

"Is this a trick question? I already chose both."

"How'd that work out for you?"

He's got a point. "Things are different now. The job is irrelevant."

"True, but Madison's been hurt enough, and the person who gets her has to be willing to give up everything for her. So. Door A is Madison. Door B is ZipMeds. Which one do you walk through?"

I take my time to think about this. I love my job. I've said it all along. It sets me apart. From my siblings, my friends, the coworkers I left behind at my old job. Yet things are different. The drive is there, always will be, no matter the company I'm working for. It's that further realization—*no matter the company*—that makes my answer easy. That and the fact there is no other girl like Madison. She's what matters most. She's what makes love worth having and keeping. She makes me feel like I'm enough just as I am.

"A."

"That's what I wanted to hear."

"So you'll tell me where she's at?"

"I will, but..." He sighs like he's still indecisive. "Shit, man. She's got a date tonight and I set it up."

"What the fuck?" I say, all indignant as I turn my body toward him like I'm gearing up for a fight.

"Chill, dude. It isn't like I knew you were going to come to your senses."

I take a deep breath, hold it, let it out slowly. "You should have asked me first."

He grunts. "I hate to tell you this, but you're not the keeper of her social calendar. Plus, it just sort of happened. There was no premeditation. I was at her apartment when I got a call from a guy who coaches summer soccer with me. Madison was laughing at something and he heard, asked who it was, and a minute later I had them set up."

She does have a great laugh.

"I don't want her to go out with him," I say. This makes me a childish and possessive prick, I know, but the thought of any other guy near her is agonizing. "Can you cancel?"

Mateo laughs. "I'm not going on the date, so no."

"How well do you know this guy?"

"Not well, but enough to think he'll be nice to Maddy. She deserves a good night out."

There's not a chance in hell she's having a good night with anyone but me. I run my hand down my neck, thinking. I've crashed her other dates, why not this one? "You know where they're meeting?"

"Yes, but—"

"You've got to tell me."

"Elliot."

"I love her, remember? If our roles were reversed and we were talking about you and Teague, you'd demand the same thing."

I've got him now. He spills the time and place. "Don't mess it up," he says.

I promise him I won't. Then, "I forgot to ask you, did you get the ring?"

My roommate smiles bigger than I've ever seen. "I did. I can't fucking wait to make Teague my wife."

"What's the plan?"

"I don't know yet, but I'm thinking about asking her when we're in Vegas next month and then actually doing the deed there, too."

"Bro, she'll never go for that."

"I know, but like I said, I can't wait. I'm hoping she'll agree to get married there, then come home to plan a big wedding and we'll do it again, this time in front of all our family and friends."

"That could work."

"Odds would probably be higher if I had some backup."

"Meaning?"

"Go get your girl, and then you and Madison and Levi and Harper can join us. Having our best friends there will make my plan much more doable, not to mention more special for Teague."

"The six of us. I like the sound of that."

"Me, too."

I can't help it—I hug my best friend. He hugs me back.

Love found me by accident. I wasn't looking for it when Madison showed up at my office, eager, innocent, and so beautiful. I think back on all the times I saw her before that morning but never really looked at her. She belonged to someone else, so I never ventured beyond a brief "hello."

Now she belongs with me.

I hope I'm not too late.

Chapter Twenty-Eight

MADISON

The best way to get over a broken heart is to go on a date, right? That's what I told myself when Mateo played matchmaker and set me up with his coaching colleague, Kyler. The guy sounded nice enough when Mateo put him on speakerphone, so I figured why not? I've moved on with my professional life. It's time to move on with my personal life, too, even if it's difficult.

I get to the restaurant first and the host seats me at a table for two near the back. He pulls out the chair facing the wall and a row of tables. Normally, I like to sit looking at the restaurant so I can people-watch, but I don't want to be rude, so I take the seat. A funny feeling fills my chest as I notice a huge bouquet of red roses on the middle of the table across from me. There's someone sitting behind the flowers, but I can't make the person out. It's a man by the looks of the long jean-clad legs underneath the table.

The person shifts slightly, and a strange sense of

recognition prickles my skin. Weird, since I can't see him.

A waiter jolts my attention to hand me a menu and asks if I'd like anything to drink while I wait for my companion. Just a glass of water, I tell him. I open the menu to keep busy, reading through the selections while also peeking over at the roses. The man's date is late, too.

"Hello, Madison?"

I look up to find a good-looking guy with light-brown hair and hazel eyes. "Yes. Hi."

"Wow, you're gorgeous. Thanks for agreeing to meet me." He takes the seat across the table, blocking the roses. His eyes dip to my chest.

I'm wearing a simple pale-pink sundress with a scoop neckline and cutaway shoulders. It's not revealing but does accentuate my curves. "Thanks for asking," I say, slightly uncomfortable for some reason. He's staring a little too intently, like he's never seen a girl in a dress before.

"How does the menu look? I'm starving. I haven't eaten in three days."

"You haven't eaten?" I ask, alarmed.

"Not solid food. I've been on a juice cleanse." He opens his menu. "Ever done one?"

"No, I can barely make it between meals," I say, relaxing now that I know the common reason for his hunger. "I've read it's smart to eat several small meals a day, so I do that a lot."

"I've read that, too, but my girl—nutritionist says it's good to fast, too."

Alarm bells sound in my head and my body grows immediately tense at his blunder. "Do you have a girlfriend?"

"Sorry, that slipped out by mistake. My ex-girlfriend is a nutritionist."

"Ex?" I ask to be sure because there is no way in hell I'll ever be the other woman, even if it's just a casual dinner.

"We broke up eight days ago."

"That's not very long. Are you sure you want to be out with me?" I'm not sure I want to be out with him. The more time that ticks by, the more weird vibes I get.

"You are really beautiful," he chooses to say rather than answer my question.

"Thanks." Okay, buddy, pick a different topic before I pretend I have to go to the hospital to visit my sick aunt.

"Ready to order?" the waiter asks.

If Kyler wasn't starving, I'd say I needed a minute, just in case I decide to bolt.

"Yeah. I'll have a double bacon cheeseburger with fries, please," Kyler says. "And whatever you have on tap."

I laugh out loud. I can't help it. "That's what you're eating?"

"I said I was hungry."

So much for keeping his system clean. "I'll have a Caesar salad with shrimp, please," I tell the waiter. He nods and gathers our menus, leaving me under the watchful eye of my date.

"So yeah, April—that's my ex—thought we should see other people. Or more specifically, she thought I should."

That's strange. "Why?"

Kyler looks around the restaurant, to make sure no one is eavesdropping, I guess. I take a moment to look over his shoulder at the table with the roses. The man sitting there is still waiting for his date.

"I'm a virgin," he whispers.

Oh.

"And April isn't," he adds like that explains the situation. At my frown he continues. "She wants me to lose my virginity to someone else. Maybe have a few one-night stands. She suggested I hook up with experienced women and that way when we get back together, I'll have the skills to keep her satisfied."

I choke on my water. I really didn't need to know all that. We could have had a nice dinner, some normal conversation, then said goodbye. But noooo. I'm stuck with another lunatic. Do I look like someone experienced? Or like someone who puts out on the first date?

"I choked, too, when she suggested we go on a break. Do you think…" For the rest of the meal he goes on and on about April because, he says, "you're easy to talk to." I have no idea why he thinks that. Probably because I'm speechless as he recounts their relationship *while on a date with me.* I also shovel my salad into my mouth so fast I don't have time to talk.

This date cannot be over soon enough. And if he thinks for even a second this is leading anywhere, he's delusional.

Boldly delusional because I cringe when he tells me he can "flex his penis and make it wiggle" and would I be interested in seeing a demonstration later? That would be a hard no. (I silently crack myself up at the pun.) I prayed all my bad dates were behind me, but apparently not.

"What do you think about shaved balls?" he asks next, barely taking a breath in between inappropriate questions. "Better for intercourse or does it not matter?"

Oh my God, this guy is way too comfortable with me. "Kyler."

"Yes?" His eyebrows shoot up as he finally stops talking.

"Thanks for dinner, but I need to get going."

"No problem." He waves the waiter over and hands him his credit card. At least he has good manners when it comes to paying for dinner.

"If you'll excuse me a minute, I'm going to use the restroom," I say.

"I'll be right here waiting."

Swell. I should give him some pointers when I get back. Not that I'm an expert, but I think most girls would be turned off by his forwardness. When I return to my seat, though, he's no longer sitting there. The table is completely cleared except for a piece of chocolate cake at my place. I sit down thinking Kyler must have ordered it and gotten up to use the restroom, too.

"Madison?" the host who seated me says. "Your friend had to leave. He wanted me to tell you good night."

"Oh, okay." Strange, but okay.

He hands me a small white envelope. "This, along with the dessert, is from the gentleman." He nods his head in the direction of the roses.

"The guy with the flowers?" I ask with surprise.

"Yes," he says, then walks away like this sort of thing happens all the time.

I have no idea what to make of this. Is "the gentleman" worried about me seeing his face? Is he embarrassed his date never showed and figures he'll try with me? Am I supposed to pick up my cake and join him?

I look down at the envelope and suddenly the air in the room changes. A hot, one-of-a-kind current of awareness raises goose bumps on my skin. My heart skips a beat. The wings of a million butterflies flutter deep in my belly.

And I know. I don't have to see his face to know who's been sitting in this restaurant with me the whole time.

My hands tremble as I pull the note out of the envelope.

Madison,
Je t'aime
Always,
Elliot

I look up and there he is, standing beside the table looking beyond handsome in jeans and a royal blue button-down, the sleeves rolled up to his elbows.

"Mind if I sit?" God, I've missed his voice.

"No."

"'No' you don't mind or 'no' I can't sit?"

"I don't mind." I've dreamed about being this close to him again a gazillion times.

"You look beautiful tonight."

"Thank you. So do you." He smiles at that. "How did you know I was here?"

"I got the intel from Mateo."

Traitor. Although I'm really not upset about Mateo telling him anything about me. I think I secretly hoped he would. "I didn't realize you two talked about me like I'm a secret project."

"Forget about Mateo. Would you like to know what the note says?"

"I'd like to know what you said to my date. What if I wanted to leave with him?" I fire back as I run my finger along the edge of the note card.

Elliot's heart-stopping blue eyes stay glued to mine. "I made sure that wouldn't happen. From the minute you got here, I had a plan."

"Kind of presumptuous of you. Not to mention rude and—"

"Would you like to know what it says?" he repeats, knowing my limited understanding, but love of, French. He leans forward, elbows on the table. His yummy scent hits my nose and I can't help but lean in myself.

I really, really want to know, but I kind of like making Elliot squirm a little. He's yet to apologize for how we left things. "Will that get you to leave me alone?"

"I'm never leaving you alone again."

Be still my heart.

He reaches across the table, moves the chocolate cake aside, and takes my hand in his, rubbing his thumb over my knuckles. "I've missed you so damn much, Mads. I was an idiot, and I'm sorry for not saying or doing the right things when I should have."

I swallow nervously. This is a good start to whatever he came here for. "I'm sorry I didn't have the guts to quit to your face."

"I'm not. If you had, I probably would have tried to convince you to stay and you wouldn't be where you are now. I'm in awe of what you've accomplished in such a short time. Someone must have been a good influence."

"It's not like you to fish for compliments."

"It's safe to say I'm a little out of my element here."

"What do you mean?"

He takes my hand in both of his now. "I guess I need some reassurance. For the first time in my life I feel at home with someone, and that someone is you. You're the thing that matters most to me. Need a CFO for your new company? I'm your man."

"You quit ZipMeds?" I'm shocked.

"Not yet, but you're more important to me than any job. You're the reason my heart beats faster and the reason my mind goes blank. My head's in the clouds in the best possible way when I'm with you, and wherever you go is where I want to be. I love you, Madison. *Je t'aime.*"

I shake with adoration for this man. He loves me. In English and French! After weeks of missing him and trying to talk myself out of loving him, this moment is everything. He came after me.

"We do work well together," I say, purposely drawing this out a little longer.

"Amazingly well."

"But I'm not hiring you."

"No?" Worry lines crease his forehead and between his brows.

He's so cute and sexy and I've tortured him long enough.

"No. ZipMeds is where you belong. And I belong with you outside of it. I love you, too."

His mouth locks on mine a second later, hungry, devouring, greedy, and I love it. Elliot's kisses are always powerful, but this one carries more purpose than any before it. Like he's staking his claim not for a weekend but for the future. "Take me home with you," he whispers against my lips.

"Mmm...'kay."

He grabs the roses and my hand. "Do you want the cake to go?"

I shake my head. "I just want you."

He kisses me again. "You've got me."

"Did you have the host put me at that table?" I ask on our way out of the restaurant.

"I did."

"So I could stare at the roses and wonder about the mysterious man behind them?"

His eyes flit to mine. "Did you?"

"Maybe."

"It killed me seeing you on a date with another guy. The second you got up from the table he was out of here."

"Elliot!"

"What? Dude was somewhere he didn't belong. Now should I list all the places *you* belong?" He pushes the restaurant's front door open with his shoulder.

"Okay," I say, all breathy.

"My house, my bed, my shower, my car, my porch, my backyard, my couch, on top of me, underneath me, riding me, at baseball games, dinner dates, movie nights, in coffee shops, art galleries, Paris." He lets go of my hand to brush my hair behind my ear. "I want you next to me always."

I blink back tears of happiness.

He kisses one eyelid, then the other. "I love you."

I cup his face in my hands. "I love you back."

"You'd better get your car before I show you how much right here on the sidewalk." He slides a finger down the middle of my chest, causing zings of pleasure to fan out. "And I don't care who sees."

"Where's your car?" I squeak out.

"I Ubered." I give him a look. "Mads, you weren't leaving here without me."

His determination and possessiveness fan the flames growing hotter inside me. I break every traffic law to get us quickly to my new apartment. We stumble inside, hands all over each other, bodies straining, mouths devouring.

Elliot pulls back to take a peek at our surroundings. "Nice place."

It's small, but my very own, and I love it. I love it even more with Elliot taking up space. "Thanks. You've been the only missing piece."

He pins me in place with so much tenderness in his blue eyes, my legs nearly give out. Then he scoops me up and carries me to bed. We slowly undress each other, stroking, kissing, and worshipping every exposed body part. His touch is unbearably sweet and sexy and fierce all at the same time.

I'm desperate to have him inside me, and he knows it. Braced on his elbows, he smiles down at me. He holds my gaze as he enters me. He holds it while he moves his hips. He holds it as we rock against each other. It's intense.

It's everything.

It's the kind of intimacy I've always wanted.

He murmurs sexy things. Makes me come once. Flips me over onto my knees and makes me come again. His release follows, powerful, insatiable, committed. He collapses onto his back beside me.

I fold my arms underneath my head and rest my cheek on my hands to stare at him.

He rolls his head to the side to meet my regard.

"So," he says, "since you're now a CEO, does that mean I'll have to make an appointment to see you?"

"Probably." I try to say this with a straight face.

"Okay," he says, nodding, going along with me. "Do you do standing appointments?"

"I suppose for certain people that could be arranged."

He rolls over and props his head in his hand. "How about boyfriends?"

I grin. I can't help it. "Boyfriends do rank pretty high up."

"Especially yours." He gives me that sexy, cocky, yet charming grin of his that makes me want to climb inside him.

"Especially mine," I say amiably.

"Because he's the lucky guy who gets to brag about his gorgeous, amazing, smart, warmhearted girlfriend."

"I'd say they're both lucky."

Acknowledgments

Huge hugs and thanks to my awesome editor, Stacy Abrams, who partnered with me on this series and whom I appreciate more than I can say.

Thank you Liz, Melanie, Holly, Riki, Curtis, Katie, Heather, Laura, and everyone behind the scenes at Entangled. I'm so grateful for all you do!

Samanthe, Charlene, and Hayson, love and thanks for the talks, the coffee dates and meals, the laughs, and the unwavering support. I'm so lucky to have you in my life.

Thank you Amber, Vania, Leslie, and Marina for listening to me talk about my writing life and being so supportive. Extra thanks to Vania for sharing dating stories that made me laugh out loud and helped with the dating scenes in this book. And extra thanks to Amber, too, for sharing my stories with your friends, writing reviews, and talking furiously about our love of books.

Thank you to my lifelong friend, Suzie, who came to my rescue when I was stuck near the end of this book and needed a fresh perspective. Suz, you rock!

Nicola, thanks so much for your unwavering support, your emails, and understanding exactly what's in my head. I appreciate your friendship more than I can say.

Thank you, Rachel, for giving me a great title, and for being a wonderful friend.

There is no better man than my husband, and I'm so thankful for his support, love, and patience. Thanks, honey, for everything! I love you and our boys more than anything in the world.

And lastly, thank you so much to all the readers and bloggers whose support comes in many forms and all are gifts I treasure from the bottom of my heart.

xoxo
Robin

About the Author

When not attached to her laptop, *USA Today* Bestselling Author Robin Bielman can almost always be found with her nose in a book. A California girl, the beach is her favorite place for fun and inspiration. Her fondness for swoon-worthy heroes who flirt and stumble upon the girl they can't live without jumpstarts most of her story ideas.

She loves to frequent coffee shops, take hikes with her hubby, and play sock tug of war with her cute, but sometimes naughty, dog Harry. She dreams of traveling to faraway places and loves to connect with readers. To keep in touch sign up for her newsletter on her website at http://robinbielman.com.

Discover more New Adult titles from Entangled Embrace...

MAYBE SOMEONE LIKE YOU
a novel by Stacy Wise

Their paths never should have crossed. The bright, accomplished new attorney and the tattooed and laid-back kickboxing trainer. But when Katie opens the door to the gym instead of the yoga studio next door, everything she ever imagined was about to change. Everything.

UNDER A STORM-SWEPT SKY
a novel by Beth Anne Miller

An eighty-mile trek across the stunning beauty of Scotland's Isle of Skye isn't something I imagined myself doing. Ever. This isn't a trail for beginners. Rory Sutherland, my guide on this adventure, is not happy. We clash with every mile, but we recognize a shared pain. The tension between us is taut with unsaid words. And hope. He's broken. I'm damaged. Together, we're about to make the perfect storm.

Until You're Mine
a *Fighting for Her* novel by Cindi Madsen

You might've heard of me, Shane Knox, the guy who rose quickly through the MMA fighter ranks, only to crash just as fast. I've finally convinced the owner of Team Domination to take a chance and get me back in fighting—and winning—shape. What I didn't bargain for is the guy's spitfire of a daughter. The closer we get, the more I want Brooklyn, but she's the *last* girl I should be fantasizing about.

Cinderella and the Geek
a *British Bad Boys* novel by Christina Phillips

I'm not looking for love or a Happily-Ever-After because I know how that ends. I just need to concentrate on my degree and look after myself. But there's something about my boss, Harry, I can't resist. It's crazy since he's so hot and smart it should be illegal. But I'm off to pursue my dreams, and he's taking his business to the next level. There's no way this fairytale has a happy ending, but that doesn't keep me from wishing for it.